Praise for *How to Kill Men and Get Away With It*

'Cracking … it's funny, outrageous, gruesome,
and thoroughly entertaining!'
Charlotte Levin, author of *If I Can't Have You*

'You won't ever want to eat a sausage roll again,
MAY vomit every time you go near milk, but it'll
be worth it. This is such an awesome debut'
Caroline Corcoran, author of *Through the Wall*

'A wickedly brilliant read'
Julia Crouch, author of *The New Mother*

'Dark, twisted, clever, funny, original, heartfelt.
I could go on … Absolutely brilliant'
Sarah Clarke, author of *A Mother Never Lies*

'Just a few chapters into this and I am S.M.I.T.T.E.N'
Pernille Hughes, author of *Ten Years*

'BRILLIANT'
Kerry Barrett, author of *The Girl in the Picture*

'A properly addictive, cutting original'
Robert Dinsdale, author of *Paris by Starlight*

'Razor-sharp and immensely funny'
Jessica Moor, author of *K̶e̶e̶p̶*

KATY BRENT is a freelance journalist and has been in the industry for over fifteen years. She started work in magazines back in 2005. In 2006, Katy won a PTA award for New Journalist of the Year. More recently she has focused on television journalism. Writing a book has always been her dream and lockdown finally gave the time she kept using as an excuse for not doing it.

HOW TO KILL MEN AND GET AWAY WITH IT

KATY BRENT

ONE PLACE. MANY STORIES

HQ
An imprint of HarperCollins*Publishers* Ltd
1 London Bridge Street
London SE1 9GF

www.harpercollins.co.uk

HarperCollins*Publishers*
Macken House, 39/40 Mayor Street Upper,
Dublin 1 D01 C9W8, Ireland

This edition 2023

3
First published in Great Britain by
HQ, an imprint of HarperCollins*Publishers* Ltd 2022

ISBN: 9780008536695

This is for every woman who has ever walked home with her keys between her fingers.

And for my mum, who has always shown me what it means to be a strong woman.

'When we are struck at without a reason, we should strike
back again very hard; I am sure we should – so hard as
to teach the person who struck us never to do it again.'

—JANE EYRE

'It seems I could do anything when I'm in a passion.
I get so savage, I could hurt anyone and enjoy it.'

—LITTLE WOMEN

Prologue

Before all this started, I'd thought that squeezing the life out of someone would be easy. The right amount of pressure on their windpipe and they'd just go limp, like when a kitten suddenly falls asleep.

It's actually nothing like that.

When someone who doesn't *want* to die, realises they're *going* to die, they fight.

Holy fuck, do they fight. It's astonishing how even the world's worst monsters are desperate to keep living. Are they worried about what comes next? Can they feel those fires of hell warming their faces already?

Take the monster I'm with now, for example. He's not worked out that struggling is pointless. He's cuffed to the bed. The easiest thing for him would be to let it happen. Instead, he's squirming, bucking and just hurting himself.

I give the nylon stocking I've wrapped around his neck an extra hard tug and watch as his eyes bulge and contort, like they're trying to escape from his head. I like these particular stockings, they've got crystals on the back seam, which really give you some excellent grip. Then his eyes burst – and the whites turn completely red.

I like it when they do that.

Red eyes, blue lips, a pale yellowing skin. Oh, and some gorgeous shades of purple later as the blood pools in the lowest parts of the body. The colour palette of death is really rather pretty.

'How does that feel?' I say. 'Nice and tight? That's how you like it, isn't it?'

He's trying to say something, but it's coming out guttural and muffled. I lean over and pull the other stocking out of his mouth, holding my knife – a £350 Shun, beautiful Japanese steel and newly sharpened – to his throat. I want to hear his last words.

'Please, the kids.'

'I think you know *exactly* how they feel about you right now.'

'You're a fucking bitch.'

'I didn't fuck you though, did I?' And with that I give the stocking around his throat one last tug to cut off his air supply for good.

The other thing about asphyxiation is that it takes *so much* longer than you'd think. I've been straddled here, crushing his windpipe for a good six or seven minutes and he's *only just* dropping into unconsciousness. I think about the chilled glass of Montrachet waiting for me in the other room.

Then he becomes still.

I lean forward and peer at him. He finally looks like he's

shuffled off his miserable mortal coil. I press my chest up against his, letting my ear drop to his lips.

Silence.

I ease his eyelids down over his eyes and sit back to admire my work. This is my favourite part. He looks childlike and peaceful, lying against the crisp white linen.

Almost innocent.

Almost.

I have to admit, she's right. It *does* look authentic this way.

Also, there's no blood. Blood is a shocking stain to get rid of. Even Mrs Hinch has nothing helpful on that. I once had to burn a beautiful pair of cream Max Mara slim-leg trousers because it just doesn't come out.

And nothing is worth that.

1

GREENSPEARES, CHELSEA, JUNE

I'm treating myself to a breakfast out. 'Treat' is a bit of a fib to be honest as I come out for a walk and a smoothie as part of my breakfast routine most days. But this time I'm actually *eating* something. It's only mushrooms on toast. And I've left most of the toast.

I'm tucked away in my favourite seat: a bright-pink loveseat right at the back. It's the best place to people-watch, pretend – for fifteen to twenty minutes – that I'm just like they are. It's been my long-term go-to for soul soothing.

I'm about to take a long slug from the caffeine-heavy (come on, even angels like me deserve a vice), non-dairy but ethically sourced beverage. I'm breathing those freshly ground beans right into my solar plexus, my anxieties getting ready to hide away in a corner of my mind, when I hear—

'Kitty! Kitty Collins? OMG. IT IS.'

There's a squeal that seizes up every muscle in my body. I see two skinny teenage girls – with excellent brows – saunter towards me before I can take even the tiniest of sips.

'Oh my God. This is un*real*. Can we get a selfie with you? Please? Like two seconds, tops.'

Oh God, please not right now. Pretty please not right now. I look up and see them watching me as I try to take a sip of my coffee. But it's no good. I have a thing about eating and drinking in front of other people.

My internal annoyance system is flashing dangerously close to amber. I just want a peaceful morning drink without an audience. Instead, I close the magazine I was (not) reading and smile at them. Big smile, with teeth, and extra twinkles of joy in my eyes. Just for them.

'Of course you can!' I say, beaming the smile that my millions (yes, millions) of followers know from Instagram-me. But the smile *does* seem to squash down the furious banging of irritation that's started inside my head.

The girls squeeze in tight next to me – on the seat for two – waving their iPhones in our faces, swiping through filters with the sleight of hand of a magician. I can tell without even looking that they're both posing and pouting trying to make themselves look sexy. Those 'likes' *do* provide an intense dopamine hit. I get it.

But I want to shake them.

Violently.

They're probably no older than fourteen but, with make-up learned from YouTube, easily look ten years older. Do teenagers not go through an awkward phase any more? I feel

5

a mix of pity and envy creep over me, prickling my flesh like a thousand tiny microblades. Their skin is so dewy and smooth, it's ethereal. I have to stop myself from reaching out and stroking it.

Because that would be weird.

'I totally ordered some of that skinny tea stuff you endorsed last month,' Girl One says.

It takes a moment to realise she's talking to me. What tea? She clearly reads the confusion on my face, which is something of a triumph considering how much Botox I've had pumped into it. And no, Botox *isn't* completely vegan friendly, but something has to give.

And it's not going to be my face.

'You did a detox. With *tea*!' she gushes, blonde hair with brown eyes almost weighed down by fake lashes. 'You said it felt like a physical and spiritual cleanse. And you lost like five pounds in a week.' She sighs, like she's found nirvana.

Her eyes are shining like patent Louboutins, staring at me in the same way I stare at the New Arrivals page on Net-a-Porter.

I feel sick.

'Oh God, no. Don't do that,' I say. 'It's not for girls as young as you. And OMG, where have you even got anywhere you could lose five pounds from?' Possibly, eyelashes. But no. I don't care how much the skinny teadox morons are paying. I will *not* kick-start eating disorders in girls. No. 'You know, just bottled water with a squeeze of lemon is better for a colon cleanse.'

They stare at me a bit longer and I am wondering if I'm going to have to explain 'colon cleanse' while some of the finest SW3 residents eat their avocado toast around us. But they're more interested in their content for social media than me. Girl Two, cheekbones I'd pay someone with a syringe for, snaps a few more selfies. Then she asks me to take a couple of 'candids'. Jesus Christ. Then suddenly One shrieks and grabs Two by the arm.

'We need to go, or we'll miss the best stalls on Portobello,' she says. 'You know what Jynx is like if we're late. Thanks *soo* much for the photos, Kitty. It was great to meet you.'

They smile their goodbyes and bustle out. Two holding her phone high, recording their journey to meet whoever Jynx is for her Insta/TikTok/Snap. I watch as they sashay down the road, oblivious to the men turning towards them as they pass, watching their slinky hips as they walk.

I sigh, deeply. I've helped create an unstoppable monster.

An older lady sat nearby gives me a look. It's probably time I went home, away from people.

My drink is cold and miserable now so I order another coffee to take away and start the short walk back to my apartment block on Chelsea Embankment. My phone pings with a notification from Instagram telling me I've been tagged in a post.

'Ran into this absolute stunner in #greenspears. What a babe. #KittyCollins #Chelsea #SuchASweetie.'

Several more notifications come through as followers of the girls – whose names are Eden and Persia, of *course* they are – respond.

'OM-ACTUAL-GOD'.

'Squeal! You're so luuuuuuucky!!!!!!'

'Was she super nice????'

'What does she smell like?'

I turn my phone off.

This is beyond tedious.

2

KITTY'S APARTMENT, CHELSEA

By the time I reach my building, I've walked myself into a ferocious mood. It pains every bone, as my heels click-clack over the expensive marble floor, and I muster a smile for the on-duty concierge. I have to, though, it's part of my 'brand'. No one wants to follow a surly, spoiled bitch on Instagram. Luckily, it's Rehan on today, one of my favourites. He stands to greet me.

'Sit down, Rehan,' I say, mock-scolding him. 'I'm not the bloody queen.'

He does a big grin. 'Maybe not, but you the princess in my tower for me to protect.'

I give a little giggle and an eyeroll. Not feminist at all, but he likes it. And I need him to like me.

'It's looking to be a beautiful day already.' He peers past my shoulder and squints into the sun, which is already beating down an uncomfortable heat despite it not even being 10am. I don't share his enthusiasm about the current heatwave, which is making me irritable and sweaty. My T-shirt is already

9

clinging to my underarms and I wish I'd ordered something iced from the coffee shop.

I nod in agreement. 'Glorious.'

Rehan summons the lift for me and I step inside.

'Of course, *you* are the brightest sunshine around here, Miss Kitty.'

Then the door closes, shutting him out. I let the fake smile slip from my face and massage my cheeks with relief. Why is just going out for coffee so much *effort*?

The elevator takes me up to my penthouse apartment. Yes, it sounds spoiled and entitled but it was actually a leaving gift from my mother before she fled to the South of France with her toy boy after my dad went missing.

It's not a bad little sweetener for being abandoned, I guess.

Like all the other promising young women who live around here, I have money. Or rather my family has money. Lots of it. My great-grandfather was Christopher Collins – better known as Captain Collins – founder of Collins' Cuts, the reconstructed meat products you see in every freezer and supermarket in the country. Dead animals aren't exactly the most glamorous way to make money but thanks to the turkeys, cows and pigs of the UK, my family is stupidly rich. Although there's only really myself and my mother left now.

So aside from the social media stuff, I don't have a lot to do, and that existential void has been insidiously expanding into my life wanting more and more of my attention. I try to fill it with activities like 'normal' people. Two hours of yoga and one hour of either weights or cardio with my personal trainer each day. I travel and stay in exclusive resorts. Sometimes for free if I plug them enough on my stories or whatever. I go to parties and launches and drink Champagne and watch other people do drugs in the loos. I leave the parties with eligible men and have drunken, soulless sex. I post stories on social media giving make-up tips, trying diet and workout routines, showing how to pull your knickers just the right way to make your legs look long and your butt thick, and praising products I've never even tried. That is my existence.

And I hate myself for it.

I mean, *truly loathe*.

So why don't I stop?

Who knows? A combination of daddy issues and the instant dopamine hits from those likes and comments. I've never been one to be able to wait for gratification. Even my £250-an-hour therapist couldn't get to the bottom of that.

I spent last weekend in Marbella with my friend Maisie (607k followers), where I'd tried out the new La Perla swimwear they'd sent from their upcoming collection. I uploaded the pics last night. My favourite photo is of me in a sunset-orange bikini, staring out to sea. The colour of the two-piece makes my tan pop, my hair is the right amount of beachy and the pose makes my breasts (natural, thank you) look about as perfect as non-surgically constructed boobs can.

Perfect boobs. Perfect life. I guess that's my 'brand'.

I open Insta on my MacBook and start scrolling through the new comments, taking a long sip of my coffee. But it feels strange and wrong in my mouth, and I gag on it.

Dairy.

I take the lid off and look inside the paper cup. The liquid is thick and disgusting, riddled with fat and cow hormones. I take some slow, deep breaths as I resist the urge to throw it against the wall and ruin the expensive Janine Stone paint job that was finished only last month.

When I'm calm, I turn my attention back to Insta and my followers. They'll make me feel better.

'Wow. You are so beautiful Kitty. Inside and out.'

'Such a gorgeous view 😍 😉'

'Eres simplemente impresionante.'

'LOVING the beachwear, Kits! When's it in shops?'

'Wish I could've rubbed the sunscreen on your back babe. Lol.'

'Perfection.'

'Just beautiful babes. Enjoy!'

'Hi Kitty! We'd love to send you some of our weight loss coffee to trial. Could you check your DMs please? Lots of love!' etc.

I scroll through several pages of comments, picking my way through the 'LOLs' and tsunami of emojis, before I catch sight of something that turns my bones to raw ice.

'I'd love to watch the pattern you'd make as you bleed out over that white sand. After I cut your throat.'

He's back.

He's calling himself something different this time but it's undoubtedly him. The creep who spent most of the last year sliding into my DMs. His profile picture gives him away. It's the one he used before: a warped image of a naked female torso, string wrapped around her like she's a topside of beef. Headless, no limbs.

I sigh.

Having a stalker is a classic sign you've reached peak influencer status, but why can't I have a nice one who sends things? Nice things. Why do I have to have one of the weirdos who fantasise about using my blood as lube while masturbating?

I slam my laptop shut and pace around the kitchen, wondering if I should call the police and tell them. They were useless last time though and I don't want to spend hours in a grotty police station going over it all again. Again.

Instead, I call my go-to crisis-friend Tor (850k followers). 'Brunch?' I ask when she picks up. 'The Creep's back.'

'Ouch. Okay. Bluebird in an hour?'

3

BLUEBIRD CAFÉ, CHELSEA

'The thing here,' Tor says as she sinks her (third?) mimosa. Her voice is getting high and loud as it always does when she's en route to Drunk City. 'Is that I think you handled it perfectly last time. Don't stop doing you, babe. Don't let him see you're scared.'

'I'm *not* scared,' I say.

'Well you should be,' she tells me pointedly. 'He could be dangerous. Definitely report him.'

'What's the point? They'll only tell me to block him. Then he'll set up *another* account and do the exact same thing again. And honestly? He's probably just a very sad man, living in his mum's box room. In Croydon.'

Tor shrugs and attacks her eggs Benedict with surprising savagery. Pre-noon booze and righteousness have clearly built an appetite. I wince as she jabs her knife into the yellow jelly-ish domes, popping them and letting the yolk ooze out like pus.

'That reminds me, have you been watching *Dr. Pimple Popper*? She's squeezed out some mindblowers this series.'

Tor rolls her eyes at me. 'Oh look, there's Ben. Shall I wave him over?' But she's already doing it, so I don't know why she bothered asking me.

'Ladies.' Ben (3,100k followers) is our friend Hen's brother. Yes, Ben and Hen.

He oozes like Tor's eggs as he pulls out a chair without being asked and sits between Tor and me. He thinks he's a total supermodel after getting a gig collaborating with a second-rate men's fashion line. I mean, he's not *bad* looking if you're into really, *really* pretty boys who preen themselves and eye up women all day. He's recently had a sleeve tattoo done and it reminds me of a mug I saw on Etsy saying, 'It doesn't matter how much ink you get, you'll always be a mainstream cunt.' He makes me shudder. Mostly because he looks like Hen in a wig.

'You're both looking very lovely this morning.'

He's speaking directly to my boobs then brays like a posh donkey as he looks up at Tor and me. 'You pair look all right too!'

Tor hoots with laughter that I pray isn't real.

I smile sweetly but what I really want to do is take my spoon and scoop his eyes out, then use the back of it to smash them like the avocado on my sourdough.

'Poor Kits is being hounded by that maniac again,' Tor says to Ben, who isn't listening. He's busy trying to see down the waitresses' tops when they lean over tables. 'I'm telling her she should just carry on as normal, so he knows he's not getting to her.'

'He's *not* getting to me,' I attempt to interject.

'Totes,' Ben agrees, reclining back into his chair, with the arrogance only a rich, white man can possess, spreading his arms out wide. 'Wait. What?'

'Kitty's stalker's stalking her again.' Tor frowns at him. 'Have you always been this irritating?'

Ben nods, grabbing a roll from the breadbasket on the table. I won't be touching that now. I don't even want to think about where his hands have been. 'Yeah, babe, it's why none of you lot will go out with me.' He laughs and Tor rolls her eyes again. She'll end up with vertigo if this continues. 'What you need is a night out, and some hot photos. Show the sicko you don't care. It will make him so crazy,' he says, nodding at me. Ben clearly has some nefarious anecdote about why this works but I'm not in the mood for his particular brand of misogyny right now.

'We should go out tonight!' Tor says, because she loves any excuse to go out and get annihilated. Even me being stalked by a maniac. 'Get Maisie and Hen involved too. We haven't had a proper Girls' Night Out in aaaages.'

By 'aaaages' she means about a week and a half. Before Maisie and I went to Marbella. She's doing the puppy-dog eye thing too. And her eyes are just so huge and brown and pleading that even I find her impossible to resist.

Ben stretches his arm out and around the back of my chair. 'You know, I could tag along and pretend to be your boyfriend if you like, Kits? Scare him off with my extreme manliness.'

Ben has professional blow-dries and tints his lashes.

'I think I'll be all right, thanks.'

And so, it is decided. A Girls' Night Out is 'exactly what

I need' along with posting some 'seriously hot pictures to the Gram' to prove that I'm not going to be intimidated by mind games. It's the last thing I want to do tonight but my friends can be very persuasive.

There's a reason we're called Influencers.

I'm not the biggest fan of girls' nights out at all to be honest – in fact they're something I detest with the full coldness of my heart – but I've quickly learned they're something I have to tolerate. Aside from the whole clichéd female bonding experience, the worst thing about these nights is that they inevitably end up revolving around men. Either Maisie will be found sobbing in the loos about some prick who's dumped her. Or Hen and Tor will be on the prowl for anything with a pulse and a penis. These 'girls' are educated, well-travelled women yet put them in spitting distance of anyone with a Y chromosome and a bit of chest hair and it's like being on a hen party in Magaluf.

I'd imagine.

I can barely contain my unexcitement.

4

CALLOOH CALLAY, CHELSEA

We start the night off in Callooh Callay, which is one of the few places I can tolerate without wanting to stab someone in the eye with a cocktail stirrer.

It's moderately busy when we arrive. Most people are outside enjoying the hot summer evening. We order cocktails and check out who's around. Tor gives a half-wave to a group of other girls – we call them The Extras. We're not really friends, but they seem to be omnipresent on nights out – and in our comments sections. I've looked them up on Insta, obviously, and their follower numbers aren't particularly impressive. A couple of them could learn a thing or two from watching my make-up lives.

After the cocktails, another round of cocktails appears, then a bottle or two of Veuve, which I think Maisie buys, more cocktails and someone – possibly me – suggests we all have Blow Jobs because alcohol brings out my inner basic bitch.

Things get a bit blurry after that. We take a lot of photos with our drinks. Then we move on. Our next stop is another bar where we have even more cocktails and seem to pick up three extra people – a trio of random men who, actually now I think about it, *may* have paid for the Blow Jobs. So obviously they think they've earned the real deal later. I whisper something to Tor about shaking them off but she just laughs.

'Why, Kits? They're funny!'

She *must* be drunk. I turn to Maisie but *she's* draped over one of them and is laughing as he talks, all teeth and big hand gestures. I'm confused. I'd been stuck next to him at the bar and he'd bored my ears off talking about his job 'in property'. He referred to himself as an 'entrepreneur'.

Which everyone knows is shorthand for twat.

Bored, I look around for Hen but she's nowhere. I'm stuck with the rowdiest and pushiest of the threesome. He's leering over me, complaining about his girlfriend, and has been plying me with drinks, which *I've* been plying into the pot plant next to me. I hope alcohol doesn't hurt plants. I don't usually drink very much alcohol on nights out, to be honest. I like to stay in control. Drunk lips sink ships etc, and I don't want anything ruining the life I've built. There are some secrets even my very best friends don't know. So, when I *do* get drunk, it's because I want oblivion.

And I do it alone.

Anyway, back to now and the pig sweating away next to me. He's had his hand on my thigh since we sat down and every time I slide away from him, he slides closer. So I'm now backed into the corner of the booth we're in, both his arms blocking any chance of escape. Unease prods at my stomach and my headache is back. All this horrible stuff with the stalker must be bothering me more than I realised. I quickly stamp the feelings down and head to the loos to get a grip.

And check my make-up.

Hen's already at the mirror when I get there, reapplying highlighter to her already perfect face.

'Looks like you've pulled,' she says. 'He's quite hot.'

'He's also got an extreme case of Friendly Hand Syndrome. And a girlfriend,' I say as she admires her reflection.

'Urgh! What's *wrong* with them?' She gives my shoulder a sympathetic squeeze before making her way back out to the bar. I splash water over my face and try to focus on my breathing, fighting the banging in my brain and the anxiety everywhere else.

At around 12.30am I've had enough. Everyone is talking about moving on to a club but just the thought makes me feel queasy. Too many bodies and not enough antiperspirant. Anyway, I need some head space to think about what to do re the stalker situation.

I see Tor sitting alone at another table. She seems to be the only one of my friends sober enough to talk to.

'Hey, I'm heading home,' I say, perching opposite her.

She sticks her bottom lip out, pretending to sulk. 'Oh, come to a club with us, Kits? It'll be super fun, I promise.'

I shake my head. 'I just want my bed and a cup of green tea. But thanks for forcing me out tonight. I got some good photos for Insta.' I slide my phone to her and she scrolls through the pics I've posted – posing with a tray of shots, a cocktail served in half a watermelon, pulling standard Instagram poses to show off our incredibly expensive outfits.

Jesus, it's all so desperate.

'Great job. You look amazing. Slip off now and I'll let the others know you've gone. You don't want a drunken Maisie trying to force you to stay out. You know how relentless she can be.'

I laugh. Drunk Maisie thinks 'no' means 'convince me'.

'Will you be okay?' Tor asks. 'Text me when you're home okay? So I know you're safe.'

'I will,' I promise and give her a hug before I grab my bag and head for the door, blowing her a kiss on the way out.

My apartment is within walking distance of most of our favourite spots, but I usually get a car back anyway. Especially when – somewhere out there – someone wants to use my blood as a K-Y Jelly sub.

But tonight, I need the fresh air – well, thick, humid air but air nonetheless – to clear my head of thoughts about The Creep and the general stress of spending a night being cornered and groped by someone I had made it quite clear I wasn't interested in. This is exactly why I don't enjoy going out.

It's not long before I regret my decision to walk though. My feet hurt in my heels, and I wonder if they were designed by men specifically to make women easier to catch.

The streets are dark and imaginary would-be assailants are lurking everywhere. I hear at least two wolf-whistles and cross my arms over my chest, trying to hide myself, to make myself small. I pick up my pace, which really isn't easy in these heels. I try to relax my breathing, holding my keys between my fingers as a makeshift knuckle-duster. I fumble in my bag for my phone but can't find its reassuring weight.

Fuck.

I didn't pick it up from the table before I left. Should I go back for it?

I'm nearer home now than the bar so I'll deal with it in the morning.

But, fuck.

Kicking myself for making such a rookie mistake, I don't realise there is a man so close behind me, he's almost in my skin with me, until he grabs my upper arm. Hard.

The shock makes me gasp and as I spin around, I see the handsy sleaze from earlier, holding a bottle of wine like a weapon.

He's pissed.

And pissed off.

'You didn't say goodbye or finish your drink,' he says. 'That was a bit rude. Considering I paid for it.' He holds the bottle out to me. 'Go on. Drink it now. Show a bit of gratitude, you stuck-up bitch.'

I pull away from his grip and step backwards.

'Listen, I'm really grateful that you paid for a drink, but it doesn't mean I owe you anything. And it's very not okay to follow me like this. I'm going home. Stop following me.' I turn my back and continue walking, trying to remember how to stay calm.

'Prick tease,' he shouts after me. Then I hear the smash of glass hitting concrete, wetness splashing up my bare legs. I spin back around to face him and he's smirking at me. The broken bottle is centimetres away from my feet.

'Did you just throw that at me?'

He stalks over. 'I *know* who you are. You're that Instagram bird. No wonder you've been acting like you've got a pole up your hole all night. You think you're too good for me.'

I stand my ground even though I'm now very aware of his

thick, muscled arms and the five or so inches he's got on me. Something inside me begins to stir, stretching out after a long sleep, batting my fear away with a paw.

The sleaze – I don't even know his name – moves closer to me. Until he's right up in my face. Close enough I can smell his booze and gingivitis breath. He grabs my arms pushing me backwards until I'm right up against the low wall that separates the embankment from the murky water of the Thames.

'I could do you right now. That would teach you a lesson for being such an ungrateful slag.'

My knees buckle as he leans closer into me. He's right – he could easily 'do me' if he wanted.

He could rape me.

He could strangle me.

He could throw my weak female body into the water and watch on the news as I'm eventually dredged up. Another woman killed because she didn't do what a man wanted.

Not me.

Not tonight.

I bring my right knee up between his legs with as much force as I can. Which is quite a lot thanks to all the yoga and whatnot. He makes a low moan of pain and lets go of me, his hands reaching down to his crotch. He wobbles, drunk and stunned. I put my hands on his chest and shove him away from me. Hard. The movement sends him even more off kilter. He staggers backwards, unable to balance himself, and spins round, falling onto the pavement, his hands still cupping his groin as he lands facedown. He didn't even put his hands out to break his fall. His face is going to be a mess.

Oops.

I wait for him to get back up, bracing myself.

But he doesn't.

I gingerly take a few half-steps towards him, expecting an arm to lash out and grab my ankle.

But nothing happens and this is not a horror movie.

It's worse.

There's a rivulet of dark, thick liquid oozing its way across the concrete towards my feet.

Blood.

I lean in closer, still scared he's about to jump up.

A large shard of glass sticks like an icicle through his neck. He's fallen right onto the broken wine bottle. It's embedded into one of the big carotid veins and torn off half his face.

He makes a gargling sound so loud in the darkness that I startle.

Then silence.

Silence.

Silence.

Where is everyone? Where are the revellers? The party people? The people I need to help me? The streets are dark and empty. Eerily so, for a not-that-late London night.

The blood continues to pump from his body. It flows towards my shoes for a moment, transfixing me.

Then I step around it and continue my walk home.

Well.

It's not like I can call an ambulance, is it?

5

KITTY'S APARTMENT, CHELSEA

The door buzzer wakes me up from a sleep so deep and beautiful, I almost forget about the previous night. I wrap my robe – a magnolia silk kimono, from Wolf & Badger – around me and pad down the hall to the entry buzzer.

Hen is there looking like a phantom as I buzz her in. It's early, my smartwatch says 8.34am. It's not like Hen to be up before midday after a night out.

'What's the emergency?' I ask.

'Just passing. I'm out for a run,' she says as I hand her a glass of water from the built-in purifier. 'Which is just as well because you left *this* in the bar last night.' She pulls my phone from the hidden pocket in her Lululemons.

I'd totally forgotten about it. You know, with the dead man and stuff.

'Oh God, thank you, Hen. I didn't even realise until I was home.'

She peers at me. 'Are you okay, Kits? You're normally surgically attached to that thing.'

'What? Oh. Yeah, I'm fine. Must've been drunker than I thought!'

'Well, you need to be more careful,' she says after a long glug of water. 'You could've had an emergency. You could have been kidnapped and murdered and how would you contact us?'

'Probably not on the WhatsApp chat, if I'm dead.'

Hen laughs. 'Don't make me have to microchip you, like a dog.' She gulps down the rest of the water. 'Ooh, maybe you should get a dog. Or a man?'

'Your brother actually volunteered his bodyguard services,' I say and Hen makes a face.

'Not that type of dog.' She laughs. 'Right, I need to finish this run before it gets any hotter. Can I fill my water bottle up quickly?'

'Of course, no problem.'

'Thanks, Kits,' she says when she's done, standing at the door. 'See you later.' She gives me a peck on the cheek and a tinkly little wave from the elevator before we're separated by the steel doors.

Jokes with Hen aside, *I* can't believe I forgot my phone. And then forgot about forgetting it. It's dead, of course, so I amble into the living area and plug it in. I curl up on one of the sofas – the Jonathan Adler Claridge in Belfast Stone – and wait the few seconds for it to come to life.

I open the news app but it takes a lot of scrolling to find what I'm looking for. The body was found by a 'reveller' walking home after a night out. The reveller is being treated for shock but the death of Matthew Berry-Johnson (thirty-four and 'in property') isn't being treated as suspicious. A Met spokesperson said: 'We can confirm we aren't looking for anyone in connection with the tragic death of Matthew Berry-Johnson. An autopsy will be carried out, but it appears he was heavily intoxicated and died as the result of an unfortunate accident. We are appealing for any witnesses who may have seen Mr Berry-Johnson last night.'

A quick Facebook – yuck – search tells me he's left behind a sad girlfriend, Hayley. I scroll through her photos. Lots of nights out with friends. Lots of holidays too. She's young and pretty. She'll love again no doubt. The idiot. They also seem to have a daughter. She looks about two or three. Chubby cheeks and blonde hair, always smiling. She's called Lucy. I zoom in on some of the photos of her. She's so happy.

I'm glad I killed her dad.

Now she has the freedom to grow up unblemished by his toxicity. He can be whoever she wants him to be. She won't have to deal with the truth about him.

That he was a cheat. A liar. A danger.

He can live on, forever perfect, in her memories.

I wish I had that unsullied version of my own father.

God, I loved my dad so much when I was that age. He was my hero and I absolutely worshipped him. He knew everyone and everything. He always had a hilarious story for me or a fascinating snippet of information. Did you know, for example, that pigs have a similar anatomy to humans? They have the same thoracic and abdominal organs as us.

Not like cows with their four stomachs, the freaks.

Honestly, his mind would be blown now if he knew pigs' hearts and kidneys are being successfully transplanted into humans.

One of my favourite 'dad memories' was when I was about seven or eight. I was sad because I'd missed the summer fair at school. It was something I always loved going to because it was a proper fair with a Ferris wheel and rides and toffee apples, not soggy cakes on a sad trestle table in the school hall.

I'd been ill with tonsillitis. But my dad *actually* put on a fair in our garden, complete with clowns and trapeze artists, everything, when I was better. He invited my friends without telling me. There was even a candy floss machine. It was the best day of my life. Everyone at school talked about it for months. It still comes up in conversations now occasionally. Before people remember Dad's now a 'missing person' and it gets all awkward. I wish they wouldn't do that. Sometimes I'd like to talk about him. To let everything I need to say come bursting out.

Of course, I can't though.

My mum, on the other hand, has always been distant. I never doubted her love, and still don't, but she'd spend days in bed or would disappear off to some retreat or another for weeks. She seemed to get exhausted by life very easily and suffered from terrible and frequent migraines. Funnily, these symptoms have all cleared up now she's living her best life in the Côte d'Azur with oodles of cash and a man fifteen years younger. But I can't deny her any happiness.

Not after everything.

When I was really little, I used to beg her to take me on her trips, but she'd just kiss me on the head before swishing out of the door with her oversized Chanel sunglasses perched on her nose.

I gave up asking in the end.

Things changed between my dad and me when I hit my teens. I became incredibly aware of where our money came from and increasingly annoyed that it wasn't something more glamorous.

Ben and Hen's dad, James Pemberton, is a big deal in the music industry and they were constantly hanging out with pop stars and getting to go backstage at all the best gigs. I mean, I got to go with them too, but it wasn't the same.

Maisie's dad used to be an F1 driver and is still involved in it – don't ask me what he does though. Or how. He must be about a thousand years old. Her mum was a famous model in the Eighties and Maisie and her sister, Savannah, spent most of their teen years in places like Monaco, hanging out on superyachts with supermodels.

Tor's mum adopted her from Sierra Leone when she was a baby. Her birth parents had been murdered and Sylvie Sunshine-Blake – a singer, sometimes actress and UN ambassador – took home the beautiful baby girl she'd fallen in love with during a televised visit to an orphanage.

That's the official story.

Tor isn't quite so convinced and thinks her adoption was nothing but a PR stunt, forced upon a bemused Sylvie because everyone else was doing it at the time. There are so many pictures online of a young and startled-looking Sylvie – part eco-warrior, part earth-mother – posing with her new baby. And it's surely no coincidence that baby Tor was the Most Beautiful Child in the World. She's often mused to me what her life would be like if she'd been born with a cleft palate or something. Tor gets on well with Sylvie though – they're genuinely close – but the bond isn't *quite* maternal. Sylvie's like this mad, adoring older sister. And she idolises Tor. We all do. Anyway, my point is, it's all a lot more interesting than meat.

Dad tried to get me excited about murdering animals by dragging me along to his abattoirs and meat processing plants, where he barely knew the names of the people working for him. Nothing like a nice day out at a slaughterhouse on Take Your Kid to Work Day.

'It's your heritage, Kits,' he told me one particularly miserable morning after watching two absolute thugs laugh while shooting a cow with a bolt gun that didn't even kill her. Then they heaved her into something they called the Bleed Area, hung her up by her back legs and cut her throat.

I cried.

Dad wrapped his arm around my shoulders and guided me away from the Bleed Area. 'Don't cry,' he whispered. For the tiniest of split seconds, I thought he cared about me, or the cow. But he didn't want his staff seeing his kid sobbing over a dead animal. That was the first time I'd seen blood spill from something that had been jumping and kicking just moments before.

'It's called "sticking",' Dad told me as I vomited into a feed

30

trough, the metallic smell of cow blood so potent, it filled my mouth as well as my nose. It's a good name. It certainly stuck with me.

I haven't eaten meat since that day.

6

I don't know why I decide that going to Matthew Berry-Johnson's funeral is a good idea. It's in SE4, for a start. And should I really be linking myself to what happened that night? Obviously the answer is no, but there's part of me that just can't stay away. The FB videos of that gorgeous little girl singing 'Let It Go' without a care in her world.

I need to know I did the right thing.

I need to know walking away while he bled to death hasn't made me a monster.

The funeral is ten days after his body was found. It was all over Facebook so it didn't take much brain power to find out where he was being buried. I'm still not sure what I'm hoping to gain from going. Maybe I want to make sure he was truly as horrendous as he seemed and not just a lairy lad after too many drinks.

But as I slick my lipstick on, I shake the thought from my head.

It's not an excuse.

32

Humans have been able to at least *act* civilised for thousands of years now. If boozy nights out turn us into animals, we'd all be shitting in the streets, killing each other and chowing down on the body parts, instead of waiting (mostly) patiently in queues for kebabs and cabs.

I shakily pull on my classic Chanel funeral dress and over-sized vintage sunglasses. I've got my cover story ready in case anyone asks who I am. It's simple – he helped me buy some commercial property and I want to pay my respects.

I take an Uber to the crem and as we do the usual stop-start-stop journey through London, I hope that the funeral guys did a good job on his face after the laceration from the bottle. I've tried not to think about the way the side of his face looked like raw beef.

When we finally arrive, there's quite a few people here, which momentarily stuns me. But then they all get in their own cars and cabs and I realise they're not here for Matthew Berry-Johnson.

The crematorium is what you'd imagine. Bland brickwork, covered in flowers and crucifixes, trying to look like it's something spiritual and not just a massive oven and chimney. There are still a few people milling around outside the door; I can see the girlfriend, Hayley, but not the little girl. A surprise tear leaks from my left eye. I'm thankful Hayley's decided the funeral of her daughter's father isn't a social media event. I'd been concerned about videos of a distraught Lucy plastered over Hayley's Insta, TikTok, FB, etc., purely for 'likes' and sympathy validation.

Once most people have gone inside, I slink in and sit in one of the back rows, next to a middle-aged lady who's holding a giant box of Kleenex. One of those huge cardboard ones, usually found in relatives' rooms in hospitals. Clearly planning on doing a lot of crying then. She sees me, gives me a watery smile and offers the box. I shake my head.

'I worked with him,' she sniffle-whispers to me. 'Such a lovely guy.'

I try to marry this up with the man who threatened to rape me and it makes zero sense. I nod, offering my own watery smile.

The celebrant – or whatever they're called – starts talking about the life of Matthew Berry-Johnson. She's clearly never met him, but regales us with that fake joy only funeral comperes can nail, about how much he loved life, cricket, his family, Lucy, along with violence towards women and girls.

I made the last one up.

Then we all stand and sing some hymn I know neither the words or tune of, but nor does the woman next to me, so I'm in good company at least.

The master of ceremonies is back after that and warbles through a pre-prepared eulogy that paints Matthew as a loving partner, devoted father and much-adored son, brother and colleague. Hayley and an older woman are crying Biblical-level tears now and a part of my limbic brain wants me to stand up and shout that he threw a glass bottle at me when I refused to give him what he wanted.

I don't, of course. Whoever made Matthew Berry-Johnson the entitled gobshite he was, wasn't any of these people. Not individually anyway. And they are grieving a man they love.

Christ, I bet even fucking Hitler had one or two people who mourned him.

Then Hayley stands up, flanked by a woman of a similar age – a sister or friend, I'm guessing. She wipes her eyes. There's no mascara dripping down her face so I assume she's had lash extensions done for it.

'*Going for the Russian lashes, babe? Special occasion?*'

'*Cremating the body of the father of my child who no one knows was a violent, lecherous dickhead.*'

'*Ah, that'll be nice. I'll make sure you look super gorge, hun. Show him what he's missing.*'

Hayley shuffles a few papers in front of her and a photo montage of Matthew's life appears on two screens at the front of the chapel.

'There's a void now, which you once filled,

'An empty chair, I'd often willed,

'A silence I prayed for, before you were gone,

'But I have your child, she'll carry you on.'

There's a hushed silence, before she continues.

'I know it's not the done thing to say at times like this.' Hayley juts her chin up a tiny bit, an imperceptible move that no one else seems to notice. Nor do they see the flicker of steel in her eyes. 'But Matthew wasn't a saint. Yes, he worked hard. Yes, he loved his mum and brothers. And yes, he adored Lucy. But he was often appalling to me. I'm sorry, but I can't stand here and lie. I can't stand here and say we are saying goodbye to a great man. He *could* be great. He could be the best. But he could also be cruel, angry, violent.' She turns to a woman in the front row who is howling out sobs from the darkest place inside her. She's got mother-of-the-dead written all over her, she may as well be wearing a placard. 'Gillian.'

Then Hayley is on her knees, holding Gillian's gnarled old-lady hands. 'Gillian. I loved him so much. You know I did. And there was so much to celebrate.' She softly touches Gillian's powdery cheek and guides her face towards the screens where a glowing Matthew is holding his baby daughter for the first time. Hayley's almost whispering when she adds: 'He wasn't a saint, Gill. He was a man.'

Gillian crumbles into Hayley's arms. She knew exactly what her son was.

I can't take any more.

'Could I borrow one of those, actually?' I fake sniff to the lady next to me, who's been watching the whole thing like we're in an immersive theatre production.

'Yes, sure.' She hands the box to me, her eyes barely leaving the commotion at the front. I pick up my bag – Gucci, vegan obvs – and slip out, as unnoticed as a social media account with under 100 followers.

7

MAISIE'S APARTMENT, FULHAM

Matthew Berry-Johnson is still on my mind a couple of weeks later when we're all summoned to Maisie's to help her with an 'emergency situation'. That's what she said in the WhatsApp group chat. I'm immediately dubious as Maisie's idea of an 'emergency' doesn't always tally with the rest of mankind's. There was the time she got stuck in a dress in Comptoir des Cotonniers, for example, and refused to call a sales girl in. Not to mention the time she pulled out of being her cousin's bridesmaid *on the day* because of an eczema flare-up *under the dress*. But she's promised to provide sake and sushi. So essentially an emergency situation, but make it Japanese.

'We should have like a special name for our meetings,' she says, looking perkier than I was anticipating when I arrive and sit beside Tor at the giant marble dining table. Hen's here too, picking through the sushi selection that's already been delivered and laid out. 'You know like the government have the Viper Room.'

'What?' I say.

Tor hoots with laughter.

'You mean COBRA,' Hen says.

'Do I?'

'Yes. Cabinet Office Briefing Room A. The Viper Room was a Hollywood nightclub.'

'Nothing to do with the government?'

'Nothing to do with the government.'

'Well, live and learn,' she says, pouring sake into glasses for us. 'Anyway, I didn't ask you over to talk about snakes. Although, it's potentially quite a fitting theme'. She takes a dramatic gulp of her drink. 'I've had my heart broken.'

Now I notice her eyes are rimmed with bags Balenciaga would be jealous of. Her nose is pink and I suddenly panic that she's contagious.

'Are you sick?'

'Love sick,' she says, sinking her sake. 'I've been dumped.'

'That's awful, darling,' Tor says, slowly, carefully. 'But I'm not sure we're all on the same page here. Who's dumped you, sweetie?'

Maisie stares back at her, face wild with disbelief.

'Joel,' she says, sharply. 'My *boyfriend*, Joel. Joel. The guy I met in Callooh? *Callooh guy*?'

'You haven't mentioned him to me,' Hen says, twirling her hair around her fingers as she shakes her head. 'In fact, a few weeks ago you went home with that thing you picked up in Callooh.'

I shudder. Nobody notices.

'That was *Joel*,' Maisie says, her mouth turning into a puckered little hole. 'We've been seeing each other for like *three* weeks. There's *no way* I haven't told you.' She looks around at all of us again, her face turning from white to puce.

She's mad.

'You're all so obsessed with your own lives that you don't even remember me WhatsApping you. The ticks were *blue*! There are messages literally *still* on our group chat.'

My brain niggles with a vague recollection of Maisie messaging us something about a man she was talking to. But, in my defence, I *was* sort of dealing with the fallout of accidentally killing someone. A friend of his. Okay. This is concerning. Interesting, but concerning.

'Maze, we're sorry,' I say. 'Why don't I pour us all drinks and you can tell us everything from the beginning? And this time you've got us right here, so you know we're paying attention. And we'll try to make up for being the worst friends ever.'

Maisie takes a shuddery breath but thaws at the prospect of being the centre of attention for the next few hours. I pour the drinks while she settles down, ready to tell her tale like she's doing the *CBeebies* fucking bedtime story. PS – I only know this because Tom Hardy reads them sometimes and it is prime masturbation material.

'Okay,' she says. 'But don't think I won't remember this next time one of you need my help.'

We listen as she tells us about her failed relationship with this Joel person. They went home together after the horrendous GNO and had drunken sex. Maisie had assumed it was a one-night stand but then they matched on Tinder the next day and 'omg, synchronicity or what?'

Imagine our collective awe to hear how they had *absolutely loads* in common. Joel is every bit as obsessed with golden lab puppies as Maisie and had even worked as a guide dog puppy trainer once. He does something in IT now, but Maisie doesn't find this Olympian career vault even slightly concerning. He likes the same music as she does and even the same films. Would you believe it? It's *almost* like she posts every single personal thing on her social media accounts. And he's read them.

'We had such a connection,' she says. 'I really thought he could be my person.'

'You know he could find out all that stuff by just looking at your Insta, right?' Hen says.

'And you told him a *lot* on the night out. You only stopped talking to eat his face,' Tor adds.

Maisie looks crushed. I feel bad for her. It's not her fault life hasn't dealt her enough duff hands to be bitter and cynical.

Tor rushes over and gives her a little cuddle as she finishes up her tale of woe. After three weeks – she tries to round it up to a month – of chatting, dating and having 'the most incredible sex', Maisie messaged him five days ago.

And hasn't heard a thing back since.

Shocker.

'His phone just rings out. There's not even voicemail.' She tops her glass up with more vodka and knocks it back in one. Having known Maisie for as long as I have, I'm painfully aware her drinking at this rate will not end well.

'So, you've had nothing from him at all?' Hen asks. 'He's not even watched your stories?'

Maisie shakes her head. 'No. I don't understand. It was amazing. Do you think something's happened to him?

Something awful? He was friends with that guy who impaled himself on a bottle near the embankment. Maybe he's depressed? Maybe I should go and see him?'

'Did he invite you to the funeral?' Tor says. Then in a gentler voice, 'Honey, you've been ghosted.'

Maisie looks gutted. 'I'm such a dick.'

'No,' I say. 'You're not. You're kind and open and you trusted someone. Those are *not* dick moves. His actions are *not* a reflection on you. *He*'s the dick here, babes.'

'I've been conned. I'm like one of those sad women on Channel 5 who end up having their life savings tricked off them by a stranger off the net. Only I've been robbed of sex,' she wails.

She folds into herself and looks so fragile, like she'd fall apart if you touched her. My heart aches for her.

I've never believed heartbreak is taken seriously enough.

It can destroy you.

'Show us his Tinder,' Hen says. 'Has he been active on there?'

Maisie shakes her head. 'Yes. And I tried to message him but he unmatched me. And his photo is gone from WhatsApp so I know he blocked me. What did I do wrong?'

'Nothing,' I say. 'You've done nothing wrong and you deserve better than someone who makes you feel like you have.'

'I just want to know what happened. One conversation. How can someone I was falling in love with suddenly turn so cold?'

'It's dick behaviour,' Tor says, through a mouthful of salmon sashimi. 'Urgh. I could kill men sometimes.'

Me too.

8

Later that night I pour myself a glass of wine and settle down on my favourite sofa – blush pink, Sweetpea & Willow – with my phone. I'm setting up my own Tinder account to find this Joel. Maisie's right – she *does* deserve an explanation. Even if it's painful, it's closure. She'll be able to move on. Being left in limbo hurts more than anything because there's always this part of you that clings on to the false hope that they'll come back.

And false hope is worse than no hope. That's what I read on Refinery29 anyway.

I can't lie, I get a kick out of making Fantasy Kitty.

Is this how men feel when they're scattering their breadcrumbs? I use one of my sexiest photos as my main image.

It's a black-and-white shot. I'm wearing a low-cut black bustier from Victoria's Secret. I'm looking over my left shoulder, smiling at someone off camera. It's a secret smile, a hint of something only I know, my face barely visible. It's a few years old now, taken by my last boyfriend, Adam.

Technically, Adam was my first boyfriend too. He took this photo while we were in one of the guest rooms of a private members' club in Soho. Adam had been doing a reading from his novel – he was a 'dazzling' author, 'one to watch', etc. – to a crowd of red-faced, enthusiastic ticket-holders, mostly female, mostly literature students.

He was bubbling with exuberance when he came offstage. He whizzed around talking to everyone, more of a social missile than a butterfly. When he eventually wore himself out, he found me upstairs in the room we'd been given, sulking, holding back tears I'd refused to cry.

'Babe,' he tried. Brushing the tiniest wisps of kisses on my neck, my shoulders, down my back until my skin betrayed me and shivered with the pleasure.

'You ignored me all night,' I'd said.

'Kitty, my angel, I was *working*. You know I hate all that shit.' He ran a finger along my bare shoulder and collarbone. 'Obviously I would have much preferred to be up here with you. Is that the underwear I bought you? You look incredible.'

'Adam, I'm angry. You knew I wouldn't know anyone there. I felt such an idiot.'

'Well, can you put your anger on hold for a few minutes while I photograph you? You're more exquisite than I've ever seen you. I want to keep this moment. I want to know this moment, when you were perfect, when I'm old and everything is chaos.'

I was putty. I was ridiculous.

He took five photographs on his expensive camera before we drank Champagne and fucked for hours.

This one was the best one by far. I'd clearly forgiven him at that point.

It was a great night in the end. But back to now. I take a few deep breaths to ground myself.

I choose words that a man like Joel would fall for. He cannot know that I'm the hunter here. He needs to believe he's in control. There's also a chance he'll remember me from the night out, so it'll be interesting to see how that plays out.

Kitty, 29, London

<occupation> Influencer

<location> SW3

<about me> Hi I'm Kitty and I'm new to online dating so please handle me gently. Freshly single after discovering I like my men how I like my coffee – able to keep its dick out of other women.

Apparently, I have daddy issues.

But I don't even know my dad.

Humour, but also enough to suggest my extreme vulnerability. Because nothing attracts hideous fuckboys quite like a woman with low self-esteem.

I should know.

It doesn't take me long to find him. I've barely even hit publish and scrolled through some very questionable profiles when I see him.

Joel.

Six-foot-two, according to his profile, but memory tells me five-foot-ten in real life. That stylised beard that says 'cock' rather than 'cool'. His hobbies – aside from ghosting – are golf, cricket and rugby. 'More watching than playing these days. Lol.' I can't understand what Maisie sees in him. His profile pic – which is actually of him, so at least he hasn't got a secret wife or girlfriend or both – is clearly supposed to be a candid shot of him laughing at something off camera.

It screams staged.

'Hey, look at me. Look how happy and fun I am. Look how much better your life could be if you date me.'

Maisie's red-rimmed eyes and complete distress all caused by this *ordinary* man fill my brain, and I swipe right.

9

JOEL'S HOUSE, GREENWICH

As predicted, it took less than a nanosecond for Joel to match with me. And initiate a conversation that made me wish I'd never been born. But I played along like a nice girl. Which is why I'm here now, pulling into a driveway in Greenwich, about to meet the man who broke my best friend's heart.

I check myself in the rear-view mirror – I'm not sure why, it's not like I'm here to impress this tool – and climb out.

I ring the bell and the door opens within a second or two. He's keen. No letting me stand on the doorstep, with time to get anxious. In fact, he's probably been keeping watch behind the net curtains. Jesus, Maisie, there's your first screaming red flag. He greets me with a smile and arms wide open, like we're old friends having a long overdue catch-up.

'Kitty!' he says. 'It's a pleasure to see you again.'

Ha.

'Hey, Joel,' I say, dodging him as he tries to move in for a 'friendly' hug. 'Can I come in? I'm bursting for a wee.'

He grins like a simp and stands aside to let me in.

'If you take the first left, that's the lounge. Or you can go straight down to the kitchen so I can pour us a drink? There's a loo on the right before the kitchen.'

'Okay great,' I say. 'Just something soft for me though as I'm driving.'

He grins again and leads me through the hallway. I'm looking around the house and notice there are lots of pics of Joel and people who must be siblings or cousins on the walls. I pop into the tiny toilet, which has been built into the understairs cupboard, and run the taps while I have a quick reccy. Nothing special in here apart from hand soap. At least he takes hygiene seriously.

I join him in the kitchen, which is not what I expected a single thirtysomething man's to look like. It's like Cath Kidston simultaneously exploded and threw up.

'This is nice,' I say.

Joel smiles inanely at me again. 'Well, it's not really my style to be honest with you, Kitty. It's actually my parents' house.'

Lives with his parents. Of *course* he does.

'They're away at the moment,' he adds. 'Spain. We've got a villa in the south of Spain.'

'Ah okay, so you're house-sitting?'

Another sheepish smile, a quick glance to the left – I wish I could remember what that's supposed to mean – eyes back to me.

'Alexa, play new music. Not exactly. I still live here. Well, not still, I mean I moved out for uni and lived with my ex, but . . .'

What did Maisie see in this loser? I mean, I get that not

everyone can buy their own house easily but, Jesus, surely he could rent somewhere? That couldn't be that expensive. I mean, what does he even do?

'Right. So . . . what do you do?'

'Oh, I'm a computer programmer, but I went freelance after my company let me go last year and things haven't really picked up since then.'

At least, I think that's what he's saying – in all honesty, whenever someone starts talking about their job I just switch off. Joel, I notice, is quickly refilling his wineglass after gulping the last one down. Is he an alcoholic?

'So, your main thing is Instagram then?' he asks me, several swallows into glass number two. 'What does that involve?'

'Not much actually,' I admit. 'Just posting a few photos and keeping my followers up to date on what I'm doing. It's really not very interesting. Are you on there?'

He shrugs. 'Yeah, but only for work really. I don't have that many followers!' I make a mental note to check his page out later.

'Are you sure you don't want a glass?' He waves the bottle of wine in my face. 'I mean, one is fine, isn't it?'

A high-tempo dance track suddenly blares out of Alexa, making us both jump.

'Urgh. Alexa, skip.'

'I really shouldn't,' I say, because I shouldn't. 'But go on then. Just one.'

He pours me a glass of something no doubt purchased from the corner shop. I imagine him going in and browsing the chilled wine section, examining the choices, hovering

48

briefly between the cheap Pinot he usually picks up for dates and the ones costing over ten pounds, before settling on the more expensive one. Because, surely for that price, it's more likely to get him laid. I take a sip and repress a shudder as the liquid burns its way down my throat.

'So, how have you found Tinder? Have you had many dates?' I ask.

He shrugs. 'A few. But not anyone I've really clicked with. It's weird, isn't it? You can never tell if you're gonna have proper banter with someone in real life or not. I'm really surprised that you matched with me though.'

Proper banter. Vomit.

'Oh? Why's that?'

'Just thought it might be a bit awkward with the whole Maisie thing.'

'Well, I've not exactly told her. So, can we keep it to ourselves for a bit please? I don't think she'd be very happy to be honest.'

He nods. 'Yeah. Bit of a psycho, that one.'

Which reminds me. 'Gosh, I saw about your friend on the news. Matthew, wasn't it? The one who fell on a broken bottle. You must be gutted?'

Joel shrugs a little. 'I didn't really know him that well, he's more a pal of a pal. Nathan, who we were with that night too. But yeah. Awful thing. He had a little girl. The funeral was heartbreaking. She went up and put a little teddy on his coffin and asked Daddy to take it to heaven with him. Pure broke my heart to watch that.'

Hmm. I don't remember that bit.

'So sad,' I agree. 'Shall we talk about something else? How's Tinder working out for you? Apart from Maisie, obvs.'

'Oh, you know, met a few girls, liked a few of them. Realised they were mental. Same old story. What about you?' he asks.

'I've met a couple of men,' I lie. 'But like you say, it's hard to work out if there's any chemistry without meeting in person. I don't think I actually know anyone who's met their soulmate on a dating app.'

Joel nods in agreement. 'They're more a place to get hook-ups than meet proper girlfriend material. I mean . . . not you, obviously. Ah, shit, sorry.' He hangs his head in mock shame. 'My mum says I only open my mouth to change feet.'

I laugh. 'Don't worry. I forgive you. At least you're honest.'

'Girls do the same thing though,' he says. 'I've messaged loads of girls who've made it clear they're not looking for a relationship. It goes both ways.'

'It's probably good to get that conversation out of the way quite quickly,' I say. 'So there's no awkward moment down the line when someone wants more than the other.' I watch Joel for a moment, trying to spot any flinch in his face. There's nothing.

'Okay. So, what are you looking for, Kitty? Relationship? Bit of fun?' He nudges me in what I suspect is meant to be a playful and flirty manner. Proper banter in physical form.

I do not like it.

'I'm not sure. I think I'll know when I find it. What about you?'

'Same as you really. Looking for someone I click with who doesn't end up being too clingy.'

'Was Maisie too clingy?'

'A bit. Gotta be careful what I say here, ain't I? Is this a trap? You wired up or something?' He laughs. 'She got clingy. No lie, she was texting me all day, every day and would get really upset if I didn't reply within minutes. It did my head in in the end.'

I'll give him his credit, he actually looks a bit regretful.

'I couldn't take it in the end. I mean, she was a nice girl and decent in bed but . . .' he trails off. 'Sorry. I forgot who I was talking to for a minute. It must mean I feel comfortable with you already.' He smiles in a way he probably thinks is charming. Twat.

'How did you break it off? It seems she took it quite badly.'

Joel looks surprised. 'Is she okay?'

'Yeah, she's not about to top herself or anything, she's a bit confused and sad.'

'Well, we were never really a thing, so I wouldn't say we needed to break up.'

'I don't think that's how Maisie saw it.'

'Yeah, but it wasn't like we were exclusive or anything. I mean, she was pretty much someone to hook up with.'

'So, she was just a shag basically?'

'Well, yeah.'

'And did Maisie know that?' My skin begins to prickle.

He at least has the decency to look uncomfortable. 'We never said we weren't seeing anyone else. I assumed she knew that it wasn't serious. Well, not from my point of view anyway.'

Alexa is now playing something by Coldplay. '*Alexa. Fucking. Skip.*'

'So, what? You just stopped calling her?'

'Kitty, I don't really want to keep talking about it if I'm being honest. What's the point?'

'Sorry. I'm baffled by how men think it's easier to just ignore someone than have a conversation with them. It fascinates me.'

It's hideous.

He takes another huge gulp of wine and lets out a long breath. 'Why don't we move into the lounge? It's much more comfortable in there. Or we could go out?'

'Lounge would be lovely,' I say as he moves to top up my wine.

'Have another one. You can always get an Uber home and pick up your car tomorrow. Unless you're just here to grill me about your mate?'

I let him pour me more then he guides me through to the lounge, which is as twee as the kitchen, floral fucking everything, and some dodgy-looking shabby-chic furniture. Joel spots me looking at a particularly offensive bookcase and misreads my horror as interest.

'Mum made that,' he says. 'Well, she didn't make it, she upcycled it. She's got her own online business and everything.' He's so proud I could vomit.

Seriously, you can give anyone a broken-down cabinet and a tin of Farrow & Ball and they think they're the next big thing in interior design.

'It's lovely.' I smile, checking out the titles on the shelves. I spot the Fifty Shades series tucked in among some other predictable bestsellers and learn all I need to know about Joel's background.

The shelves are dripping with holiday souvenirs buried among the books. There's a rather cross-looking brass cat holding its paw up in what looks like a Nazi salute, a wooden elephant, a tribal drum and – in pride of place – a metal sculpture of the Burj Khalifa. I turn my grimace into a smile when Joel catches me staring, wide-eyed.

'The 'rents' – he shrugs – 'they love a bit of travel tat.'

He sits down on one of the floral horror-show sofas and pats the space next to him for me to join him. I sit but make sure I'm at least an arm's length away.

'It's funny, isn't it? The difference between men and women on dating apps,' I say. 'Maisie was really into you. She felt you had a connection.'

He sighs. 'Kitty, if you're here to get me to go back out with Maisie, you're wasting your time. She's a sweet girl. She really is, but she's not for me.'

'So why couldn't you just tell her that? Why would you leave her thinking she'd done something wrong, or that something awful had happened to you?'

Joel jolts a little and looks at me.

'Isn't that disgusting and disrespectful?'

'Yeah, it's not a great way of ending things,' he says. 'I'll do better next time. Promise.'

'I think you should call her,' I say. 'And explain.'

He pulls an expression somewhere between exasperation and annoyance. 'Kitty, this is getting a bit weird now to be honest. Maybe you should go.'

'Not until you call her and tell her the truth. She was devastated. Don't you care?'

'No. To be honest. Why are you so stuck on that? Men and women meet on apps, they fuck, they move on. It's not a big deal.' His phone is on the side of the sofa and I make a grab for it.

'Call her,' I tell him.

'Don't be mental, Kitty. Go home.'

'CALL. HER.' I'm serious now. I open the contacts on his phone, surprised it's not locked, and swipe through names like Anal Daphne, Big Tits Kayley, Smelly Muff Erin, Mental Maisie. I'm thrown for a moment as Joel lunges at me to get his phone back. He knocks me to the ground and I bang my head on the fucking Farrow & Ball monstrosity.

'Give me my fucking phone back, you mad bitch.' Joel's sitting on my legs now, pinning me to the floor. I can't move. Apart from behind me. I make a grab for something from the bookcase of horror, which happens to be the metal Burj Khalifa, and – closing my eyes – I swing it in Joel's direction. The force of the thrust stuns me and I'm surprised by the noise it makes as it connects with his head. I was expecting a thud, but it was actually much wetter – like dropping a watermelon. I know then that it's bad. Joel hits the floor with a short howl of pain.

And then silence.

I force my eyes open and see that I've managed to hit him straight in the face, the long spiny tip of the tower totally impaling his left eye. Surprisingly, there isn't much blood, just a sort of fluid leaking down the side of his face. But he's dead. There's no doubt about that.

Fuck.

10

JOEL'S PARENTS' HOUSE, GREENWICH, WITH A DEAD BODY

Fuckfuckfuckfuckfuck.

Don't panic, don't panic. This can be sorted.

I think.

I drink the wine, which isn't the best idea but I need to calm myself down. I take some deep breaths too. Centre myself. In a front room. In fucking Greenwich. With a dead man.

I drink Joel's wine too. Breathing alone won't cut it here.

I need to get him out of here.

I need to get *me* out of here.

I run into the kitchen and rummage through some drawers before I manage to find some bin liners. I take them back through to the lounge and struggle to put one over Joel's head to stop any gunk leaking onto the carpet. But I almost scream with frustration as it takes me about a hundred years to get one open.

Then I empty the bottle of wine and shove it in my bag, before washing the wineglasses up and, making sure my hands are covered with a tea towel, hanging them back on the rack with the others.

I tentatively attempt to pull the Burj out of Joel's eye, but it's stuck in a lot harder than I realise. In the end I have to give it a proper knee-on-his-chest yank to get it out. Having grown up around gore, I find it usually takes quite a lot to gross me out but even I recoil at the bits of brain and eye on the top of the tower. I dry heave as I wipe it on my dress (Ganni, annoyingly) and shove it in my bag, glad I had the foresight to bring the Chanel bucket instead of a clutch.

I have to get him into my car somehow. House to car with no one seeing. A grown man. And the phrase 'dead weight' is not a fucking exaggeration by the way.

Then I have a brainwave. I do so love it when my brain kicks into gear like this. Joel's parents are on holiday, but *he's* not. So, there *should* be at least one suitcase upstairs. I pull the sleeves of my cardigan (Lulu Guinness, ethically sourced wool) over my hands as I make my way upstairs with trepidation.

The front bedroom is Joel's parents', so I stay out of there. The first room is the main bathroom, and it is unsurprisingly suitcase-less. But the second bedroom proves more fruitful. I spot a large-ish case squashed into a space next to a stand-alone wardrobe and grab it, noting a hopeful condom on his bedside table as I leave.

Oh, to have the confidence of a very average white male.

Getting a body into a suitcase isn't much fun as bones have to be snapped and I have to sit-bounce on it quite a bit to get it to do up, even then. But finally he is packed and all I have to do is get the suitcase into the boot of my car. Still not easy.

Particularly when it's full of some of my weirder purchases like a diamanté sombrero, a pair of roller-skates and some sort of dismembered mannequin, from when I was going through my 1920s Paris décor stage.

I get into the driver's seat and gingerly reverse off the drive, unsure where I'm going.

Fuck, fuck, fuck. What the hell am I supposed to do with him? I only wanted to get some answers for Maisie and now I have a corpse in my boot and a murder weapon – a tacky one at that – in my bag.

I drive around for bit, clutching the steering wheel for dear life, desperately trying to think of something to do with the body. What do people do with bodies? Burn them? Throw them into the Thames? Feed them to pigs?

The solution comes to me so suddenly that I laugh. I do an actual LOL.

It's so obvious.

11

KITTY'S RANGE ROVER EVOQUE, 70MPH, A3

So, it turns out that the simplest way to get rid of Joel is to go back to my roots. I quickly tap my sat nav and phone off and soon am heading out of London, along backstreets and windy lanes. As the buildings and streetlamps turn into fields and trees, I have a weird sensation pumping in my veins. I travelled these very roads hundreds of times as a child, my dad desperate to get me interested in the family business and where our fortune comes from.

I feel like I'm coming home.

12

COLLINS' CUTS SLAUGHTERHOUSE, NORTH HAMPSHIRE

After about an hour or so, I see it, as imposing and dark as it always was, even though it's nothing more than a large building on an industrial site. As a child, the sight of it looming towards us would make me shudder, but it's surprising just how quickly you can become desensitised.

It's almost 11pm now, so none of the abattoir workers are here. I pull up to the entrance and dig around in the glove compartment for the keys. My mother used to look after everything to do with Collins' Cuts, before she swanned off to the South of France. She has a general manager – Tom? Tim? Something like that – but she says she feels comforted having a member of the family on hand for any emergencies.

Even if it's me.

I make my way into the building I've not set foot in for over twelve years, turning my iPhone back on and using the torch app to light the way. The first thing that strikes me is that smell, still stomach-churningly recognisable after all this time. I hold my sleeve over my nose as I wave my torch around enough to notice that everything is pretty much the same as it was back then. I wander over to the small office and click off the CCTV.

Then I head back out to the car, pop the boot and begin heaving the suitcase into the factory. The thing my dad told me all those years ago about pigs and humans is on my mind as I drag Joel out by the feet, along to what was called – and still probably is – Pig Alley. This is where the pigs are hung by their ankles, gutted and blow-torched to get rid of any hair, after bleeding to death. After this they're either moved to a freezer where they can chill before being sent back to farms or to butchers. Or they're sent to the slicing area, where they're crushed, minced, sliced, smushed up or whatever, before being reformed and eventually sent to supermarkets as sausages or ham. The bits and pieces not fit for human consumption get ground down into animal feed. I look at dead Joel. He's definitely animal feed.

The whole process takes me almost all night, especially as waiting for him to bleed out seems to take hours and I keep having to hose the blood down the drain. But eventually, as the sun begins to peep out over the Hampshire countryside, it's done. Joel is gone.

Exhausted, I let myself out, remembering the suitcase, and head back to London, feeling . . . well, as if I'd been up all night disposing of a dead body in a meat factory, to be honest. When I finally make it back to my apartment building, I park my car, pull a coat over my blood-spattered clothes and spot Rehan at the front desk. He gives me a knowing wink as he taps his watch.

'Five am, Miss Kitty.' He chuckles. 'I hope you've not been getting up to no good?'

I give him a contrite smile and he continues chuckling to himself as the elevator doors close me into the metal box. Claustrophobia hits me like a stun gun and I have to remind myself to breathe.

Slow, Kitty. Calm, Kitty.

I'm surprised how, after I shower the smell of Pig Alley off me, I feel almost revitalised. I hadn't meant to kill Joel. Truly. But I can't feel any remorse. In fact, it's the opposite. Because of me, one fewer woman will lie awake at night wondering what she did wrong. Wondering why she wasn't enough.

I watch my reflection in the mirror as I finish my hair. Is it just the light or does it look a tiny bit shinier? And my skin is absolutely glowing, you'd never know I'd been up all night. Actually, I look incredible. I grab my phone and take a mirror selfie as golden rays from the sun through my window illuminate me like I'm under a spotlight. No point in missing such an Insta-worthy photo op.

I upload it and tag it: #KillingIt and am bowled over by the amount of comments and likes I get. I mean, I always get a lot, but my Insta just goes crazy.

'Natural beauty, Kitty.'

'How are you so pretty this early in the morning? I wake up looking like I had a fight in my sleep. Lol.'

'You woke up like this? I woke up like *this* 🐷'

And then one that makes me feel like my own blood has been hosed down a drain in a slaughterhouse.

'I know what you did last night 🐷'

I already know who it's from before I see the grotesque image of his avi.

The Creep. My stalker.

Okay, this could be an issue.

13

MAISIE'S APARTMENT, FULHAM

It's about a week since I fed Joel through the mincers at the abattoir. His parents must've returned from holiday not long after our date as he's now officially a missing person. Not in a particularly big way, he's only earned a few lines on Metro. co.uk.

But it's enough to make Maisie's face look pretty with hope again when I show her as we sunbathe on her balcony.

Local man reported missing by parents

Joel Gidding, a 32-year-old man from Greenwich, has been reported missing. Joel, who lives with his mum, Moira, and dad, Geoff, hasn't been seen since the couple returned from their holiday home in Spain last week.

'We spoke to him two days before we were due to fly home,' Moira, 63, told us. 'He was meant to pick us up from the airport, but didn't turn up. We had to get a cab instead and it cost an arm and a leg. We're really worried.'

Joel was last seen leaving a pub in Greenwich and heading in the direction of his parents' home.

His mum suspects he might have been kidnapped after an attempted burglary. 'It's very strange but a sculpture of the Burj Khalifa in Dubai has also gone missing,' she told us.

Anyone with any information about Joel is urged to call Thames Valley Police.

Maisie's cheeks flush with what seems to be excitement.

'Should I call them?' she asks while we sun our legs and sip espresso martinis.

'And tell them what exactly?' I ask her, mopping away my creamy moustache. 'That you've literally not heard a thing from him in weeks? That you thought he'd ghosted you?'

Something approaching a smirk of satisfaction passes over Maisie's face.

'I *told* you something terrible must've happened to him,' she says, eyebrows raised over her cocktail. 'I knew there was no way he'd just gone cold on me like that.'

I stare at her open-mouthed for a moment as she sips her drink and stretches her lithe body out under the sun. Is she seriously happier that he's missing, presumed who-the-fuck-knows-what, than just ghosting her? A little smile plays on her lips as she wriggles herself into a comfier position on her lounger.

'It's fine anyway,' she says with a sly smile. 'I've met some-one else.'

Are you fucking kidding me?

Some people are so ungrateful.

14

KITTY'S APARTMENT, CHELSEA

Tinder has now become my hunting ground and I'm absolutely loving it. Opening the app and swiping through the 'honest, easy-going' men with great senses of humour, desperately looking to find someone they can connect with on the most basic of human levels, is *soul* destroying. I pity the women who actually use apps like these to find love.

But.

Those photo-less profiles, the hazy pics where you can't make out the face, the ones shrouded in dirty, deceitful mystery get my pulse racing like nothing else ever has. No drug or sex has even come close. For these are the men who need wiping from our society. These are the men who leave women crying into their pillows at 3am or wondering why they haven't come home. These are the men who destroy families, whose children grow up with more issues than they can ever work their way through, even with the help of the most expensive therapists.

The world is better without these men, these cheaters, liars and predators. I'm just helping out really, cleansing a society that's almost too grubby to bear. I know what it's like to be that woman. At home, trying to untie the sick knot in my stomach, the inner alarm system telling me something isn't right. I've sat in bed, crying my eyes raw, wondering why I wasn't enough. There is no pain quite like that of a broken heart. No matter what anyone says. Time doesn't heal and nothing can prepare you for it.

Even worse, nothing can fix it for you either.

It was Adam who broke my heart, of course. Adam Edwards. Older, successful and the toast of London at the time thanks to his first published book, 'a hugely experimental work of fiction that will make you not only question your place in the world, but whether you deserve it'.

Yeah, I know.

But I was very young.

And Adam was very beautiful, well, he still is, I suppose. I didn't kill him, that's not where this is going. He's dark-haired and dark-eyed with skin that tans like toast. His face, perfect. The kind of defined jawline that goes missing somewhere around the age of forty. But it wasn't his looks that got me, it was his brain. He knew everything and could make anything sound interesting. When Hen introduced us at one of her dad's soirees, he kissed my hand and said, 'There are darknesses in life and there are lights, and you are one of the lights, the light of all lights.'

Bram Stoker.

I was hooked right away. But, even back then I was wise enough to realise that Adam absolutely did not need to know this.

'It's very nice to meet you,' I said. 'Congratulations on your book. I hear it's made quite the impact.'

I ignored him for the rest of the night.

Predictably, it wasn't long before he managed to wrangle my number from one of my friends. He began his seduction with a tsunami of iMessages a few days after our first meeting.

Adam: Beautiful Kitty. I was so charmed by you at Hen's party. I'm very sad we didn't get time to talk again. You're a very popular lady.

Adam: Oh, I got your number from Ben btw. Hope you don't mind. I get it's a bit stalker-ish. But I can confirm 100% that I'm not a murderer.

Adam: Which I now realise is exactly what a murderer would say.

Adam: Anyway, what I'm trying, badly, to say is that I'd like to see you again when I'm back in London. Things are a bit crazy at the moment with the novel but I should be around in a couple of weeks. Can I text you?

Looking back, there were obviously so many red flags. The barrage of messages, the reminder of how important he was, the fact he'd obviously asked for my number without my permission. But as I said, I was young. Hindsight is a bastard. And I was really fucking flattered. It was the days before Instagram had fully taken off and, while I was obviously living a wealthy and healthy life in Chelsea, the only people who paid much attention to me were the people I already knew. And now there was this successful, young, gorgeous writer who wanted to see me again. So yes, I was flattered. Flattered and stupid.

I texted back a day or so later.

Hey Adam. Sure it would be great to meet you properly when you're not tied up being so busy and important. Please feel free to text when you're around next xx

Urgh. The fucking kisses. I'd slap twenty-two-year-old me if I could.

Our first date was to see a play written by a friend of his. Somehow it had got a run at the Old Vic, which baffled me because it was absolute toss. Afterwards, he trotted me around the bar, introducing me to various horrible friends like a trophy wife. All women. All literary types. All desperate to prove, in front of Adam, how uneducated I must be by asking me questions about books, hoping to trip me up.

'So, who are you reading right now, Kitty?' asked one blonde with features too small for her moon face, a sneer making her look even less attractive. She asked it in the same kind of way I'd ask Maisie who she was *wearing*. She was very clearly a smug bitch.

'Actually, I can't read. Not a word. Totally illiterate.' I smiled and exited stage left.

I absolutely refuse to be around anyone who thinks they're better than me because a) who has the time to waste hanging out with anyone you just will never get along with and b) no one *is* better than me. Storming out of places is not really my style though, but Adam was clearly into the sass and as I walked down Waterloo Road, I heard him call my name. I stopped, not turning around, waiting for him to catch up with me.

'I'm so sorry,' he said, eyes dripping with concern, which seemed genuine. 'Saskia can be a bit of a twat. Well, a lot of a twat actually. Expensive education and yet not one solitary manner, I'm afraid. Are you okay?' He gently brushed my cheek with the tips of his fingers. The same fingers I'd later stare at, mesmerised, watching them dance across his keyboard as he wrote. The same fingers that would pull orgasm after orgasm out of me.

'I'm fine,' I'd said, curtly. 'I'm just above hanging out with people who act like pretentious dickheads.'

Adam caught my face in his hands. 'They *are* pretentious dickheads.' He laughed and then kissed me. Hard and purposeful. I was caught off guard as his lips crushed against mine. Intoxicated by the taste of whisky and the smell of cigarettes, which at the time seemed dark and necessary rather than just grim. With my face cupped in his hands, under the shadow of Waterloo station, I melted into him.

When we finally broke apart and flagged down a black cab, we couldn't get to mine fast enough. Even in the lift, we were clawing at each other's clothes, his shirt half unbuttoned and my dress around my waist by the time we fell through the door. We bit and pulled and tore all the way to my living room where he pushed me hard down onto my sofa. I was writing with my need for him as his mouth made its way down my body. He fucked me with his tongue first, making me gasp, before pulling out and pushing my thighs apart and kneeling in front of me, totally exposed to him. And these were the days before I made expensive monthly appointments to have painful lasers destroy my pubic hair.

'You have the most beautiful cunt,' he said and instead of recoiling at the word, I felt that, from his lips, it made me wetter. Then his mouth was on mine and I could taste myself on his tongue as it pushed into me, while his cock pushed into me too. 'Keep your eyes open. I want to watch you come.'

I remember thinking it was very bold of him to assume he could make me come with just his dick, but as he pushed my knees up against my chest and started moving inside me at an angle I'd never felt, I soon discovered I was *very* wrong. I could feel every inch of him as he moved in and out, hitting that spot buried inside me with each thrust. Soon I felt my entire body begin to clench around him.

'Keep your eyes open,' he said again as I came, with a shuddering climax that felt even more intense because of our locked gaze. He stroked my hair, kissed me deeply and let himself release inside me, before falling on top of me, sweaty, spent. 'Don't let a drop spill out,' he whispered as we lay there. I didn't want to. From that moment I wanted to keep every bit of him inside me.

Our relationship was a heady mix of sex, alcohol, parties and drugs. We spent weeks, months, in our own world where nothing existed except each other and our pleasure. My friends began to annoy me, whining over text that they didn't see me anymore. I didn't care. All I wanted was Adam. Anyway, even when I *did* see them while he was away doing book tours and book talks and meetings about his 'difficult second book', they just complained that I only saw them when Adam was busy. Which was true. But I couldn't help myself. He was addictive. He'd burst into my apartment, which he'd semi-moved into after about three months, and tell me to pack a bag. And then we'd suddenly be in Cannes or Paris or Barcelona, drinking Champagne, chopping lines of coke and having that urgent, intense sex.

'I love you, Kitty Collins,' he'd breathe into my mouth as our bodies, orgasms now perfectly synchronised, heaved in post-passion bliss. 'I fucking love you.'

But almost as suddenly as he hurricaned into my life, a manic whirlwind of pleasure, he began to withdraw. While the highs were up there in the cosmos, the lows brought me hurtling back down to earth with all the power and speed of a meteor.

And the fallout was extinction level.

He stopped doing coke, preferring instead to smoke himself into catatonic states. The parties stopped and he'd brush me off, blaming work and the pressure he was under to get that 'difficult second novel' nailed. Meetings became more frequent and when I visited his Primrose Hill house – he'd stopped coming to mine by this point – he barely raised an eyebrow to me, let alone anything else.

It was at this point I learned a lesson that would serve me well for the future, but tortured me at the time. The more I felt Adam recoil from me, the harder I tried to cling to him and the harder I clung, the further he would retreat. I'd send him absolute essays of text messages, declaring my love for him. He'd reply with one word. If at all. I'd call, frequently. He cancelled the calls almost every time. When we did speak, all he did was talk about himself and his pain.

'I'm fucking depressed, Kitty,' he'd snap if I suggested we went for dinner or drinks.

Then I'd cry and he'd roll his eyes, mumble a half-hearted apology and tell me that he loved me, I just needed to be patient.

'You don't understand the pressure I'm under from my publisher. I'll make it up to you, I promise.'

Eventually he agreed to see a GP, who in turn agreed that yes, Adam was indeed suffering from clinical depression and anxiety. He was given pills, which made him even more withdrawn, while I sat by him, reading everything I possibly could on how to support a partner with depression. I read him stories by writers I knew he loved. I took him to Charing Cross Road and led him into bookshop after bookshop, trying to get the light back into his dark eyes with first editions and 'Look! This one's signed!' I cooked for him and watched as the food went cold and stale in front of us. I kissed him and straddled him and tried to suck his cock, but it was as if it had died.

Adam was broken and my heart was breaking.

The pills began to properly kick in after a couple of months and – bit by bit – he came back to me. A smile when I handed him a plate of home-cooked food. A kiss when I presented him with another 'rare find' from a bookshop. Actual sex after an enforced walk in Hyde Park, where I encouraged him to feed ducks like a toddler. Because I'd missed these most basic of relationship needs so hugely during his crash, I treated every single one like he was handing me the keys to a magical kingdom of love.

I was pathetic.

As Adam began to shine again, his meetings became more frequent. He'd come back, to mine again now, talking excitedly about his plans for the second novel, how his publisher was certain he could repeat his success, even better it. He kept me up late talking about Bookers and Pulitzers and possible movie deals and moving to LA.

'You have made of me a madman,' he said one night, after sex, and I fell for him all over again. The lows of the depression were forgotten.

'Have you considered Adam's bipolar?' Tor had asked me over lunch.

'Have you considered Adam's a fucking dick?' Hen asked me over dinner and, even though I glared at her, still desperately loyal to my lover, I'd already begun to wonder this myself.

'Mental illness can make you selfish,' I attempted in a weak argument.

'Yes, but it doesn't make you an absolute cunt.' She had a point. A very painful point. But I was still so much in Adam's thrall that bringing it up with him didn't even occur to me. Well, not very often.

As the hype about the second novel – which I wasn't completely sure he'd written a word of – began to build, the invites and social whirl started up again. Adam loved showing me off to paps at any event he was invited to. We were constantly in the society pages of *Hello!* and *Tatler* and we had several calls from various production companies asking if we'd consider a reality show.

'I couldn't,' Adam said. 'I'd rather remain mysterious.'

The breaking point for Adam and me came in summer. He was in his bedroom, preening for another night out. I was in the lounge watching some reality rubbish on his laptop. He'd smashed his TV during one of his rages and had not replaced it. It was still there, months later, not working, glaring at the room with an angry crack across the screen, like a scowl.

As I was watching some spoiled, rich Americans argue with each other, a message popped up on the screen. He'd obviously linked his iPhone to his laptop and I registered vague surprise to see Saskia's name.

Saskia: Hi baby. Missing you. Have you ditched the bitch yet?

Adam: She's here now. Sorry baby, I'm trying. But I can't just bin her off.

Saskia: Why? I'm going to start thinking you actually like her if you leave it any longer.

Adam: Kitty's fragile. She's still suffering with the whole dad missing thing. I don't want to be responsible for her doing anything silly.

Saskia: Well just hurry up and get it sorted. I'm sick of feeling like your side chick.

Adam: LOL! You know that isn't how it is. I love you. Just remember all the publicity I'm getting from her. It's not for much longer.

Saskia: Okaaaaaaaaaay. I love you too. Just. Hurry up.

I wasn't sure what I was reading at first. I mean, I *was*, but it was as if the words were about someone else, like I was reading a story, some fiction he'd written because how could this be true? Saskia and Adam? Adam and fucking *Saskia*? This couldn't be right. But after the tenth time reading it, I realised exactly what was going on. And, if Adam thought he had rages, he'd seen nothing. But while his anger was white-hot exploding stars, which involved smashing things up and screaming at everyone in earshot, mine was quieter. A simmering pressure cooker of fury – volcanic and destructive.

So, when he skipped downstairs ten minutes later, ready for our night out, I was waiting. From the kitchen I asked him if he wanted a drink.

'Please baby, let's get pre-gaming. What are you watching?'

I didn't answer, instead letting him sit on the sofa with his back to me. The laptop screen untouched in front of him. The messages between him and Saskia there for him to clearly see. I headed back into the living room and watched the back of his head as he realised his secret was out. He jerked around to face me, his mouth already open, ready to deliver the killer blow. He'd either lie to me or break my heart.

I didn't give him the chance to do either.

I left him there and walked home, where I curled up in a ball for a week.

15

KITTY'S APARTMENT, CHELSEA

After putting Joel through the mincers and making sure that Matthew Berry-Johnson hadn't been a beacon of virtue, I realised that not only had I killed two men, two *horrible* men, okay, technically by accident, but I'd got away with it. And not only had I got away with it, I'd even enjoyed it. In a weird way. Not like in a psychotic way; snapping people's arms and cutting them up isn't exactly fun. But it's like I'm finally doing something more meaningful than just posting photos of myself online.

Even the presence of the stalker hasn't brought me down from my high. And the photos I *have* been posting have been my most popular yet.

'Kitty! You are absolutely glowing.'

'Are you using a new face cream or is this lasers or something?'

'That's the face of a woman in love. Spill it, Kitty.'

'Vegan glow, that's all I'm saying.'

My followers have grown by like 20k in a week, which

hasn't happened in ages, and everyone wants to know what I'm using on my face or hair or who I'm shagging. You know what 'look' this is, people? This is purpose.

Anyway, it's got me wondering if it's something I should be doing a bit more of. I mean, I'm only talking about the absolute scum of scum, right? I'll only be taking out men who are a very clear and present danger.

Anyway, in a sort of Dexter-esque way I've decided that there are people who really deserve to die. And those who don't. So, I've made my own list of rules. It makes me feel like I'm doing something good in the world.

KITTY'S CODE

1. First up, no women. None. And don't even bother coming at me with trans arguments or whatever. This is Chelsea. Tor still gets eyeballed because she's black. Women are *not* predators. Not in the same way as men. There's always an exception that proves the rule. Which is the most stupid saying in the fucking world. Good old English. I'm not saying that I've never *wanted* to kill a woman. Several of the Extras annoy me so much I have to bite my tongue 'til I taste blood. The way they hang around footballers and Z-list celebrities makes me want to tear their insides out and redo their make-up with their own innards. Their main aim is to get knocked up by one of these guys. Not even a wedding, just a baby.

    'It's a permanent meal ticket,' someone called Tiffany told me one night.

'But, you've got money, T,' I said. Her dad's some hotel giant.

'Money doesn't last, Kitty,' she'd said with a thin-lipped pout. 'Nothing is forever.'

2. Leave the innocent. Now, innocence is a bit of a tricky one as it's subjective most of the time. Did that sleaze from the bar innocently follow me home with the hope of a hook-up? Or was he out to get me for having the audacity to reject him? That's a no-brainer for me, but beyond reasonable doubt? Who only fucking knows. And that's why the bastards get away with doing it again and again. (Side note: Why the fuck the British public play such a big role in the justice system is mental to me. These are the people who apply for *Love Island* and *Tipping Point*. Jon Ronson really should write a book about it.) But I mean the real innocents – kids, animals, the mentally disabled. Anyone who doesn't have a voice.

3. Also off limits, the homeless or people who have fallen on hard times. The killings of vagabonds and prostitutes date back as far as records go and no doubt before this too. The vulnerable are too easy. They need help. Not murdering. And don't even get me started on the fucking Rippers and Bundys of the world. What I would give for half an hour alone in a room with them and a freshly sharpened Shun.

4. No doormen. They come in extremely useful.

5. And no police officers. Because likewise.

6. Don't get caught. I mean, this is so obvious it barely needs explaining. Being caught would mean prison.

For a long time. It would also mean grey tracksuits and flat shoes. And I'll bet none of the gym equipment gets sterilised.

7. Killing must serve a purpose or it's just plain murder. Okay, I stole this one directly from *Dexter*, but it's pertinent. I don't want to go around London hacking people to death because I'm *just* an angry woman. The men I kill deserve it. Every last little bit of it. So, it's not actually murder when you look at it that way.

I want to live in a world where I don't have to keep my keys between my fingers in case I'm attacked walking home. Not that I do that. I find a serrated hunting knife and a syringe of GHB much more reassuring. I want Hen or Maisie or Tor to be able to make the journey from wherever we are back to their homes without having to ping the WhatsApp chat that they're safe. I want to be able to walk around my beautiful London – this pocket of it at least – with earbuds in.

I remember this Influencer Party from a while back – however many rings of hell there are supposed to be, this place was an added extra. Everyone who attended was given a sparkly wristband with the influencer's particular branding on it. I can't even remember what the fuck it was about, some interiors shit. I arrived – with Hen – and the PR girl ticked our names off the list.

'Here you go.' She smiled and handed us two wristbands – one gold and one blue. Hen made a grab for the gold one like the magpie she is. 'Oh no, sorry, no.' The PR grabbed the bands back. 'The gold one is Kitty's and yours is the blue.'

Hen gave her dagger eyes as she slipped on the blue band. 'What the fuck was all that about?' she stage-whispered to me as we followed the red carpet into the venue, me squeezing the gold band onto my wrist. At the end of the red carpet there was another identical PR girl, guarding the entrance to the event like Cerberus guarding the gates of hell.

'Can I just check your bands please?' she almost sang at us. 'Okay, blue guests are slightly further down the hall. Gold guests, through here and up the stairs to the SO VIP area.'

'Excuse me. The *what*?' I'd asked as Hen stared, jaw almost hitting the peep toes of her Jimmy Choos.

'It's the super VIP room. Where anyone with over a million followers on Instagram goes. It's incredible. There's even a hot tub,' she whispered, like we would be impressed by a blow-up pond of STI soup.

'But my friend can't come up?'

The PR shook her blonde bob. 'No. But there are loads of great people in the Blue Room who can talk to you about how to build up your followers.' She smiled at Hen. 'Isn't that really useful? Great for networking.' She raised her microbladed eyebrows and nodded encouragingly at Hen.

Hen opened her mouth to say something, but I knew whatever words were on their way out were not to be said out loud.

'Actually, we've got another event we've said we'd pop in to and I don't have a swimming costume with me, so I think we're just going to go.'

Hen remained rooted to the red carpet, staring at Cerberus.

'Come on, Henrietta.' I slipped my arm around her shoulders and guided her back the way we'd come.

'What the fuck was that?'

'Clearly some stupid dick decided it would be a good idea to split guests by how "influential" they are as an Influencer.' I made a puke face.

'That's a really shitty thing to do,' Hen said. Her face looked like a balloon when the air starts to come out of it. She wasn't wrong. It was gross and what a way to make people feel super terrible about themselves.

'Come on,' I say. 'Fuck this shit anyway. Let's go and get drunk at mine and watch True Crime.'

She stared at me for a beat, then smiled, ripping her wristband off and handing it back to the other gatekeeper of hell at the first door.

'Thanks, but no thanks,' I'd said, giving mine back too.

'Wait, wait!' she'd called after us. 'Did you get a picture for Insta with the wings? Did you get your SO VIP goodie bag, Kitty?'

I turned back round.

'Ram it, Cerberus.' I linked my arm through Hen's as we went laughing into the night.

Anyway, the purpose of this little anecdote is, yes, I *know* it's not all men. But unfortunately, they don't come with coloured wristbands so we can tell the difference between the good guys and the bad ones. So there needs to be a system. It's my calling. I hear you. And I'm coming.

16

THE BOTANIST, SLOANE SQUARE

Urgh. Dearly beloved, we are gathered here today, at one of my favourite eateries in SW1, to meet Maisie's new boyfriend, Rupert. Joel is dead and long forgotten. By Maisie, at least. I asked her about him earlier and her eyes glazed over.

'Oh, *him*,' she'd said, laughing. 'He lived with his parents, Kits. What was I even *thinking*? Wait 'til you meet Roo. You'll adore him.'

I take a deep breath as I walk in and spot Tor and Hen already seated. Hen's eating bread, which is never a good sign, and Tor's looking around helplessly, knowing any moment, Hen will head to the loos and throw it all up. Is she nervous? Why would she be nervous? We're only meeting Maisie's new boyfriend.

I love the Botanist. The flowers outside make it seem like that gorgeous time of year where April bleeds into May and the cold, dark nights are such a distant memory it feels like they might never return. Considering the blistering heat we are still having, with no rain for weeks now, someone must be out there almost constantly watering the beautiful garlands that stretch round the awnings.

'Hiyeee,' Maisie says, as she ushers me into a seat next to Hen, while Tor's smile is so glaringly fake, it could be seized by border control. 'I'm so excited for you to meet Roo. He's just over there, getting drinks in.'

I look over at the bar and instantly spot what can only be described as a Blow-Dry in Red Trousers. I can feel Hen's eyes on me, waiting for my reaction. I can't even look at her, I'm already having to bite my tongue until I taste blood. Rupert is Maisie's classic type. Her string of exes all look exactly like this. It's partly why I found her attraction to totally-against-type Joel so weird.

'He's *so nice*,' she stage-whispers in my ear.

Rupert heads back to the table, precariously carrying a tray loaded with drinks. Maisie stands up to help him. He gives me a smile that is nothing but gums.

'Kitty, this is Rupert Hollingworth – my boyfriend. Roo – this is Kitty Collins, Instagram star and one of my very best friends.'

He puts the tray down on the table and holds out a hand and – as I move mine to shake it – he lifts it to his lips and kisses my fingers. My mind wanders to the hand sanitiser in my bag.

'A pleasure. I've heard a lot about you, Kitty.' He holds my gaze in a way he probably thinks is charming, but is actually just creepy.

'It's lovely to meet you, Rupert.' I smile at him and quickly pull my hand away before we all sit down and Maisie squeezes up to me gasping about how amazing and handsome Rupert is. I nod in agreement, pleased how happy she is, even though I have a feeling this will end in the same way as every other Hooray Henry she's dated. With her heart in bits.

'He was at Eugene and Jack's wedding,' she says and I think I have to be impressed by this, so I pretend I am.

Rupert can clearly hear Maisie's ridiculous fawning over him and doesn't even have the courtesy to look embarrassed. He pours me a glass of Veuve.

'So, how exactly did you guys meet?' I ask. Hen rolls her eyes. She's obviously heard this story several times. Tor stifles a giggle into her glass.

'Fate,' Maisie sighs.

'He's Maria's brother,' Hen says. 'He's been in various institutions for the majority of his life.'

'Maria? Institutions?'

'Extra with the bad tit job. Boarding school then Harvard, via Oxford.'

Ah, of course.

'We probably met when we were kids,' Rupert says to me. 'You see it on social media all the time, don't you? Naked toddlers in a paddling pool meeting up years later and recreating the photo.'

'Do you?'

'Kitty's childhood was a bit more *Carrie* than *Little House on the Prairie*,' Hen says.

'Of course, our very own Pork Princess. How's the dead animal business?'

'I wouldn't know. I don't have anything to do with it.'

Rupert looks dubious.

'I'm serious. Apart from the apartment, which my mother paid for, I live from my Instagram money. I have no interest in literal blood money.'

'But you must be worth millions?' Rupert's highly educated brain is struggling. 'What's going to happen to all that money?'

'Well, my mother is doing a jolly good job of spending a lot of it in the South of France.' I smile. I turn to Hen, not wanting to keep this conversation going in this direction. Talking about money like this is tacky, Rupert and his expensive education should know this.

'Where's Grut tonight?' Hen's been fucking the frontman of one of her dad's signings on and off for about six months. They either seem to be engaged in weeklong shagathons or she's screaming about what a cheating dick he is and drinking herself into a coma.

'I think Sweden.' She shrugs. 'Some shitty showcase thing. Dad's over there with them. They've taken the yacht so you can imagine the kind of trip.'

'I've got a yacht,' Rupert says. 'Probably not quite in league with your dad's though.'

Hen's dad has a ridiculous superyacht as well as a fleet of slightly smaller boats in various moorings around the world. We usually take one of them out several times a year. James was happy to teach me to sail, seeing as Tor was far more interested in lying on the deck and working on her tan.

'I've given in and joined Tinder,' Tor says.

'And how's that working out for you?' I ask.

She takes a big gulp of her drink. 'Well, I'm not going to be finding the love of my life on there, but I've had three pretty decent fucks this week. One thing I will say about dating apps is that they've normalised casual sex so much, men now don't need their map app to find my clit.'

A few people look around in horror and Rupert stares at her. His jaw on the floor, until Maisie nudges him in the ribs.

'I don't care,' Tor continues, just as loudly. She's addressing the table of slightly older women next to ours. 'I have a clitoris, I am a woman and I enjoy getting my brains fucked out. Anyway, aren't your gen supposed to be all *Sex and the City* and sexual empowerment?'

They ignore her.

'They're all married,' she says. 'Probably haven't seen a cock in months.'

Christ. How much has she had to drink?

'That leaves you then, Kits. Anything going on for you action-wise?' Maisie is desperate to make Rupert feel comfortable. But putting this on me is a terrible idea.

'Tons of action. Just a few weeks ago I killed a man by stabbing him through the eye. Then I chopped him into pieces and fed him into the mincers at one of my meat factories. There are probably a few sausage-roll fans chowing down on him as we speak. Before that I killed a creep who followed me home and threatened to rape me because I didn't fuck him for buying me a few glasses of shitty wine. And have I mentioned my dad?'

Obviously, that's *not* what I say.

'I'm not looking,' I say. 'I'm happy being single. Less drama.' And no one asking awkward questions like 'where have you been? Why aren't you answering your phone? Is that a human finger in your purse?'

Hen looks at me with something like pity on her face.

I don't like it.

'Babe,' she says. A lecture is coming. 'You've not had a proper relationship since Adam.'

'Yes, I am aware of that, Henrietta. Maybe it's because I don't want one.'

'I know he hurt you, but you can't live your life like Miss Havisham just because of one douchebag.'

'He *was* an uberdouche to be fair,' Tor says.

'Miss Havisham is a terrible analogy in this situation,' I say. 'We were stupid young. It wouldn't have lasted anyway.'

'It might've without that bitch Saskia always hanging around him like some book groupie,' Maisie says.

'Do you not think you should put yourself out there now though?' Hen asks. 'We know how much you loved him but, well, you're not getting any younger.'

'I'm on Tinder actually,' I say, hoping it will shut them the fuck up. Honestly, I love these women with what I imagine sisterly love feels like, but there are occasions when I picture cutting their fingers off one by one.

Maisie's and Tor's faces light up.

'Why didn't you tell us?'

'Because your preoccupation with my sex life is extremely unhealthy. And weird.'

'You need to get laid,' Hen says. 'There's already rumours going round that you were born with no vagina.'

The women at the next table ask for their bill.

17

CHELSEA EMBANKMENT, SW3

I don't usually let their words get to me but, as I'm walking home, sweating my tits off, I start thinking about boyfriends. Would it really be that bad to have one? Are there any good points? There's the sex and, as much as I love my Womanizer, it isn't great at hugging after coming. Also, it's quite a normal thing to have, isn't it? A boyfriend, I mean, not a state-of-the-art sex toy. Like Louis Vuitton luggage. Or veneers. And having something as normal as a boyfriend would be a useful cover for my hobby. It might even stop The Creep creeping if he thinks there is someone on the scene. The more I let the idea sink in, the less awful it seems. But who? I think about the men in my inner social circle and immediately dismiss each of them. Too conceited to actually spend any amount of time with without wanting to slice their throats open and watch them bleed out. Plus everyone has pretty much slept with everyone else so whomever I pick would piss off one of my friends.

Adam *did* break my heart, that's no secret. He did a really good job of it too. But what I did to him was so much worse. It wasn't even intentional. And it *would* be nice to have someone to snuggle under a blanket on the sofa with in the evenings. Someone to watch the True Crime channel with me. Actually, that could be a bit triggering. Maybe I could get into box sets like a normal human? That's what it comes back to really, the need for some kind of normality.

But, I need someone different. Someone new. Someone kind and normal who doesn't tell sexist jokes and make me want to peel my own skin off. Oh, and cheat for months with a little bitch. But where would I find someone like this out of a bad romcom? Definitely not an app. Even the thought of going on an actual real date from Tinder makes me want to hide in bed with a bottle of wine. But where else do people my age find love if it's not through dating apps or people they know? It's like looking for a unicorn on a council estate.

It's dark now and I pick up my pace, grateful for the Shun in my bag. I look around and spot a girl – well, a woman – over the other side of the street, next to the river. She's sort of level with me and is walking even faster than I am. I can just about make out that she's got her heels in her hand and is scuttling along barefoot. I look a bit further down the road, and imagine my shock (none) when I see a man skulking after her. It's like I'm watching footage of the night *I* was (almost) attacked.

'Hey,' I call out to the woman as I cross the road towards her. 'I've been trying to find you.'

She looks confused as I start walking alongside her, slipping my own shoes off to keep pace.

'You know there's a guy following you, right?' I whisper.

She nods. 'Yeah, he was trying to chat me up in a bar and I kept telling him no, but he wouldn't leave me alone.' There are dried tears that have left stripes in her foundation.

'Okay, cross the road with me. I literally live in that block there. I'll call you an Uber and wait with you 'til it comes. All right?'

She looks at me gratefully and I try to take her hand to cross the road, like we're old buddies. But something stabs me in the palm.

'Ouch.' The brief flicker of pain makes me wince.

'Keys. Sorry.' She shows me her hand, keys between her fingers, the standard weapon for a woman walking alone at night. I link my arm through hers instead.

'Fucking arseholes,' I hiss as I open the Uber app and book a car. 'What's your name? For the booking?'

'Claire,' she says.

'It's nice to meet you, Claire. Shame it has to be like this. I'm Kitty.'

She gives me a small smile. 'I know. I follow you on Insta. We come out in Chelsea quite a lot because you always make it look so fun. And safe.'

I look over the road again. The guy has carried on walking, but he's slowed right down now. Almost to a loiter.

'Same shit, different postcode,' I say.

Her car is with us in three minutes – gotta love Uber – and I'm relieved to see a female driver.

'Thank you,' Claire says as she gives my arm a squeeze. And accidentally stabs me with her keys again. 'God. Shit. Sorry.'

'You should probably put them back in your bag now,' I say, rubbing my arm.

She blows me a kiss as the car pulls away and becomes another set of lights in the dark. I narrow my eyes as I slip my feet back into my shoes and look again at the other side of the embankment. The guy is still there as I knew he would be. I take my Shun out of my bag and cross over to him, heart pounding, but it's not fear. It's more like excitement. Delicious anticipation. I slip the blade up the sleeve of my blazer.

'Sorry about that. Looks like I ruined your evening.'

He eyeballs me. There's no emotion in them as he looks me up and down. He's older than I thought. Now I'm closer I can see the lines around his eyes and mouth. Laughter lines, they're called, aren't they? Guess there's a lot more to laugh about when you're white and male.

'Dunno,' he says, eventually. 'You look quite fun. How do you know I wasn't following her to make sure she got home all right? Why am I automatically the bad guy?'

'Were you?'

'No. She's a fucking whore.'

'She was terrified. Do you not care?'

He shrugs. 'Shouldn't be such a prick tease then.'

I frown. 'I thought she was a whore. She can't be both.'

'Why don't you fuck off back to your Samaritan call centre or wherever the fuck you came from? You know nothing about the situation.'

'The *situation* is that you were following a woman and she was frightened. How can you not see that? Or rather, how can you see that and not care?'

'You really need to get the fuck out of my face,' he says, missing the irony as he takes a step towards me.

My reaction is animalistic. Before I even know what I'm doing, I've slid the Shun down my sleeve, into my hand and slashed it across his neck. It takes less than a second.

I step aside to avoid getting spatter on my clothes as his hands grab at his neck and he stumbles. It takes another split second to push him, already unsteady and woozy from alcohol, over the small wall that separates the road from the dark folds of the Thames. I watch, fascinated, as he falls backwards into the river. His face contorts as his expression passes from shock into fear, his mouth forming a perfectly round 'o' shape, blood still spurting from his neck.

I keep watching until he hits the water with a slap.

I wait for about three minutes until the water settles.

I let out a breath, wipe the knife clean on my thigh. And then I cross the road and head into my building, slipping the knife back up my sleeve on my way.

I give Rehan a little wave as I wait for the lift.

18

KITTY'S APARTMENT, CHELSEA

His body washes up a few days later in Woolwich. The news report is a bit more exciting this time, mainly due to the massive slash in his neck. I scroll through the articles on Apple News as I drink a revolting spinach and avocado smoothie, meant to replenish something I have plenished.

Body of half-decapitated man found in Thames

There is a large presence of emergency vehicles around the river Thames near Woolwich, Southeast London after a body – believed to be that of a male in his 30s – was spotted by a jogger early this morning.

Police and paramedics arrived at the scene but the man was confirmed dead, with locals on social media speculating his throat had been cut before his body was dumped in the river.

A spokesperson for London's Metropolitan Police said: 'Members of the emergency services are dealing with the discovery of a dead body which was spotted by a member of the public at 6.30am.

'As no identification has yet been made, we cannot confirm anything else at this stage. Locals are advised that the area remains safe and to go about their business as usual and to avoid discussing the matter on social media. Instead, if anyone has any information please call us on our local number.'

Police say they are treating the death as suspicious due to the nature of the man's injuries, although no one fitting the victim's description has been reported missing as yet.

As I gulp down the dregs of the smoothie, I wonder how long it would take before someone reported me if I went missing. It would probably be only a few hours before someone – probably The Creep – raised the alarm on Insta. I guess having an obsessed stalker has its uses at times.

I open my phone and see that Claire – the almost-victim from that night – has tagged me in a post.

'Tired of having to watch my every step while walking the streets at night after a scary experience at the weekend. Men should have an 8pm curfew. @KittyCollins #reclaimthenight #reclaimthestreets #letwomenlive'

She has got over 200 likes so far. I really hope it doesn't end up going viral, but she's tagged a load of other semi-famous Instagrammers too. I'm just pleased she's left out the details about being followed. At the moment there's no connection between her post and the dead man.

And I'd like it to stay that way.

Just as I'm about to close the app, a message notification pops up. I don't even need to see the twisted avatar to know it's from *him*.

'Feeling the heat about the body in the Thames yet? Remember, I'm watching you.'

There's the eyes emoji too, which I'm sure is meant to be scary, but it actually looks like a child has written it. I delete the message and close the app. Not today, freaky obsessed man-child, useful or not. Not today. I am very much not in the mood.

19

KITTY'S APARTMENT, CHELSEA

A few days later Hen and Tor are at mine for dinner. Maisie has bailed *again* because she's on a date with Rupert, whom she amazingly seems to be going strong with. It's not been very long admittedly, and one thing Joel *did* get right about Maisie is that she can be very intense. But this doesn't seem to bother Roo at all.

'He seems nice.' Hen shrugs as she pushes her food around her plate pretending to eat it. You can take the girl out of the eating disorder clinic.

'*Too* nice.' Tor eyes Hen's plate. 'Treats Maisie like she's made of glass or something.'

'Isn't that exactly the kind of man she wants though? She's always had a princess complex,' Hen muses.

'It's what she *thinks* she wants,' says Tor. 'What she really *needs* is someone with a backbone who will stand up to her now and again. That girl has some serious daddy issues.'

'Don't we all?' Hen mumbles. 'Anyway, you can see them both Wednesday if you like. Daddy's being awarded some gong or other for his charity work. There's a huge banquet in his honour and then a party afterwards. You should come. Grut and the rest of the band will be there.' She gives me a surreptitious wink. This means she's going to try to hook me up with one of his hairy friends. Grim. And no thank you.

But, it might be nice to have conversations with people who aren't obsessed with themselves and whoever they're sleeping with for a change.

'Will people from the charities be there?'

She nods. 'Oh, yes. It's at the V&A. It'll be teeming with do-gooders, doing good and trying to get people to hand over money. It's something to with orphan war-zones. Daddy's chucked a wad of money at it.' Her eyes widen to almost comic effect when she realises what she's just said.

'Hen,' Tor says. 'You're such a dick.' But she's laughing. 'And it's good that he's doing something about it.'

'Yes. But I wish he'd do it without all the bloody pomp and ceremony. It's vanity and virtue signalling and I wish he'd just write a cheque and shut up sometimes.'

Tor pats her shoulder. 'Well, there will be lots of other very rich virtue signallers there too whose purse strings will loosen the drunker they are,' she says. 'See it as a good thing. Obviously Sylvie and I won't be there.' She grimaces.

'Count me in though.' I clink my glass against Hen's.

20

By Wednesday night I'm convinced this party could be the sort of fulfilment I need to stop my blood lust. Maybe I can volunteer for a charity that helps with violence against women and girls or something.

I'm in a Ganni dress I bought a few weeks ago. Short enough to showcase my legs but high-necked enough that I don't look like an OnlyFans poster girl. I've had my hair blow-dried into perfect waves and Hen's make-up girl – Suki – has given me the most on-point natural-yet-sexy face. I'm just the right amount of serious charity chick and understated glam. A triumph. I take a quick snap and post it to Insta. Hashtag slaying.

The awards do is in the amazing grounds of the Victoria and Albert Museum. Hen's already here, hopping from one foot to the other by the velvet rope, when I arrive. She's gone full boho charity chic, long swooping skirt and loads of necklaces. I even catch a glimpse of a henna tattoo on her midriff.

She looks like she is *trying* to look like she's been volunteering with orangutans in Borneo for the last two years.

'Kits! You look beautiful!' She holds her arms open, inviting me in for a hug, which is a bit awkward as I'm still on the wrong side of the rope, begrudgingly smiling for the scattering of paps on the street.

'So do you, Henrietta. Very Sienna Miller circa 2004.'

She puffs her hair with faux self-consciousness. 'Thank you.'

We head inside and I am immediately overwhelmed. It's the typical combination of money, money and more money. The irony of how much this 'charity bash' is costing isn't lost on me and I grimace inside.

'Not a penny spared,' Hen says, raising an eyebrow.

We head towards the garden and a beautiful hostess guides us to a table where Maisie, Ben, Antoinette (Hen and Ben's sister), Grut, Hen's parents and Rupert – in his red chinos again – are already sitting. Maisie leaps out of her seat and envelops me in the second awkward hug of the night.

'Hello,' I say to the table. 'Nice to see you and your trousers again, Rupert.'

'Play nicely, Kits,' Maisie hisses in my ear.

I let my lips graze her cheek slightly. 'Always.' I flash her a winning smile before being pulled into another hug by Ben, who squeezes himself a little bit too tightly against me for it to be okay.

'Looking stunning as ever, Kitty,' he says, and I just about hold myself back from grabbing a butter knife and disembowelling him there and then.

Smiling prettily, I shake hands with James, Hen's dad – nice to see you again, blah, blah, blah, and kiss her mum, Laurelle, on her cheek, way too much perfume.

Everyone is already a few glasses of champers deep and are having vapid conversations about vapid people and things. My attention begins to wander and, while Maisie and the rest of the table chat, I scan the other tables and the rest of the grounds. Desperately seeking . . . someone.

I'm no believer in fate or sky fairies or any of that bollocks, but a lot of spiritual people believe that there is no such thing as coincidence. And that's something I'm coming round to more and more. Because while everyone else continues their inane small talk, I see him for the first time. Sitting on a temporary low-wall structure – which I'm guessing is to stop drunken rich people from jumping into the fountain later. He's fiddling with a piece of paper while chewing the skin around his thumbnail. I can see that the dark-blue-but-not-quite-navy suit he's wearing is expensive, but not bespoke like every other man's here. He's wearing black-framed glasses, which between thumb nibbles, he pushes back up his nose. His hair is sort of messy – but styled to look that way – too dark to be blond, but too light to be brown. His face is stubbly and he keeps rubbing it furiously between the thumb and glasses ritual. I'm concerned the friction might start a fire.

There's a good few metres between us but I can tell he's hot. *Really* hot. And there's something about his fidgety energy, the way he's constantly moving, that makes me unable to take my eyes off him.

Suddenly he looks up and catches me staring.

Embarrassed, I quickly move my eyes away but when I glance back, seconds later, he's still watching me. He gives me an awkward little wave and I can't decide if he's mocking me or not. I decide to brave it and wave back.

Maisie notices. Of *course* she does. Now she's all loved-up, she wants everyone else to be as well. This girl has a heart the size of the fucking moon. I really hope Rupert Red-Pants makes her happy.

'Go and talk to him,' she says.

'I'm terrible at that stuff.'

'No. You *think* you're terrible at that stuff. Just think of it like you're writing an Insta caption. What would you say?'

'Someone hose me down because my fanny-flutters have started a fire?'

'Yeah. Don't say that. Just say hi. Ask him what he's doing here.'

'Are you sure?'

'Kits. What's the worst that can happen?'

A billion thoughts whizz through my head at once, from my falling face-first into his lap, to his asking me to grab him a glass of Champagne because the other waitress is taking too long. I give Maisie The Look. The one that means I don't want to do something.

'I've not seen that face since you wouldn't go down that water slide in Dubai. And that was fine, wasn't it?'

'Maze, my bikini top came off, everyone saw my tits and I very narrowly avoided getting my own episode of *Banged Up Abroad*. But yeah, apart from that, it was great.'

She gives me a kiss on the cheek. 'I love you. Now go and

talk to him before he vanishes and you spend the rest of your life regretting it.'

Urgh. So dramatic, but I adore her. I take a deep breath, stand up and begin walking towards him.

'And keep your tits in this time!' she shouts after me.

I take it all back. She's an arse.

Still, I make my way over to him, my heels sinking into the mud where sprinklers have clearly been doing overtime to keep the grass green and luscious. Of course I have to look like a toddler taking its first steps when I *finally* see a man I fancy. I think I style it out though.

'Is this seat taken?' I indicate the wall next to him.

He looks momentarily baffled, like he can't quite work out why I'm talking to him. But then he smiles and I feel my insides go liquidy, but in a good way, as he pats the wall.

'Haha, no, sit down, please.'

I perch there, feeling the pressure to say something that's flirty but not cheesy and not overtly sexual. It's really not as easy as you'd think.

'Are you here for the awards?' I ask in the end, my tongue feeling like a thick slab of meat in my mouth.

His eyes meet mine. Dazzling green. I remember something about green eyes being the rarest of colours. 'Yes. Did you think I was one of the waitstaff?' he asks. 'Were you going to ask me to get you a drink?'

I must look horrified and he lets me suffer for the tiniest of moments before he lets out a laugh. 'I'm teasing you. Sorry. Yes, I'm here for the awards.' There's a beat of silence as we look at each other. 'I'm meant to be doing a speech actually.'

He suddenly stares down at the sheet of paper in his hands like it's a snake. A bad one. 'Public speaking isn't really my thing. Don't tell anyone, but I'm nervous as fuck.'

'You know the secret is to picture the audience naked?'

'Yeah, I've heard that.' He looks around the gardens, at the hordes of white middle-aged men and their middle-aged spreads. 'Can't say that's a particularly appealing thought though.'

He looks back at me and I hold his gaze.

'I don't know, I'm sure there are some men in this place worth seeing without their suits on.' I let the unsaid words hang in the air for a minute before I break the spell. 'So how come you're giving a speech?'

'I work for The Refugee Charity. It's, uh, one of the charities supporting the awards. We want to thank everyone who has helped us this year. It's been a really tough one. Especially for charities.'

I nod. 'You guys helped loads of women and children get homes over here, didn't you? That's some pretty heroic stuff.'

His eyes light up, surprised that I know anything about what he does.

'Don't look so stunned,' I say. 'Do I look like a total rattle-head?'

'Honestly?'

I nod. 'Apparently it's the best policy.'

He runs his eyes – and they are very green indeed – over my designer dress and styled hair. 'You just look like everyone else here. I mean, you look very lovely and everything. But I wouldn't have you down as an avid news reader.'

If only he knew.

'Were you never told not to judge a book by its cover? I'm Kitty by the way. Kitty Collins.' I hold my hand out to him.

'A pleasure to meet you, Kitty-by-the-way. I'm Charlie. Charlie Chambers.' He shakes my hand, strong, no rings. 'So, what brings you to our humble gathering?'

I laugh, looking round the elaborate garden venue, complete with stage, sound system and several outdoor bars. It's more like a festival than a 'humble' anything.

'I'm here to watch my friend's very rich dad collect an award for his generous and philanthropic nature, while we drink Champagne and tell him how brilliant he is before we all head back to our oversized homes to sleep in our oversized beds, grateful we've won the genetic lottery.'

Charlie laughs again before offering me a reluctant smile. 'Well, Kitty, as lovely as it's been talking to you, though very brief, I really need to try to memorise this speech. Dying on stage in front of the world's wealthiest people and a load of press isn't really on my bucket list.'

'Oh. Yes. Of course. Good luck.' I smile at him again, but he's already turned away from me and back to his notes. I'm more than slightly taken aback.

I stumble back to my table through the mud and slip into my seat as the starters begin to arrive.

I'm a little perturbed over what just happened. I mean, Charlie was perfectly polite, but he didn't act like most men do around me. I take a long slug of wine to douse the feeling.

'Nice chat?' Maisie asks as small plates of something beige and gooey arrive in front of us.

'Foie gras?' I look at my plate in horror.

'Oh gosh, Kits, I totally forgot about the vegan thing!' Hen says.

James looks over at me with a wide smile on his face. 'Are you *still* doing that vegan thing, Kitty?' he asks. For some reason James has always found it hilarious that I don't eat animals or their by-products. 'Your father would be turning in his grave.'

A chilly silence creeps over the table. Hen glares at her dad, her face murderous.

'He's *missing*,' she hisses. 'Not dead.'

'It's okay,' I say, trying to pour water on the awkward vibes. 'And, with all respect, if you'd grown up visiting abattoirs and meat production plants on your family days out, I guarantee you wouldn't touch this stuff either.'

I push my plate of swollen goose livers away.

The dinner passes in a blur of things I don't eat and conversations I don't listen to. Finally, as the sun begins to dip down behind the London skyline, an ear-piercing noise shatters the buzz of small talk, and feedback from the sound system fills the sticky summer air. An amplified, nervous cough echoes around the grounds and Charlie – gorgeous, gorgeous Charlie – appears on the makeshift stage in the centre of the garden.

There are little fairy lights wound around the trellises and waitresses who look like Victoria's Secret models dancing among the tables and lighting candles. The whole venue has a magical feel, like we've stumbled onto a film set. And I have to admit, up on stage, Charlie looks even more handsome. It's probably the lighting.

And the three glasses of Krug I've chugged on a virtually empty stomach. *Why* am I drinking?

'Ladies and *gentlemen*,' he says. 'I hear there are still some of us around.'

A ripple of laughter from the crowd.

'Thank you, each of you, for taking the time out of your busy social lives and schedules to attend our little soiree.'

The audience laugh again. This is anything but a 'little soiree'.

'As you know, we're gathered here— Sorry, I sound like I'm doing a funeral.' He pauses and his cheeks flush a little. He pulls the crumpled sheet of paper from earlier out of his jacket pocket. 'As you know, we're here tonight to pay tribute to one man whose generosity has kept The Refugee Charity going over a very tough year. So, ladies and gents, please raise your glasses and toast our wonderful patron and all-round saviour James Pemberton.'

Hen, Ben and Antoinette all gaze lovingly over at their father as he soaks up the glory of two hundred people applauding his philanthropy. He smiles his trademark dazzling smile – dazzling because of the unnaturally white shade of his teeth – and hops up to the stage beside Charlie. He's surprisingly agile for a man of his age. And size. Laurelle – a former model now nipped and tucked and barely recognisable as human, let alone herself – fizzes with pride-by-proxy as her husband delivers a speech about the importance of helping those less fortunate than oneself. He tells us all about the special feelings donating money to good causes like The Refugee Charity gives him, before encouraging everyone to reach into their pockets and make a donation.

'You'll find next to your seats buttons that allow you to donate to this wonderful charity right now,' James says as he pulls on a golden cord unveiling a huge screen behind him.

It currently displays nothing apart from £0.00 along with some images of women and children from various trouble spots around the world. 'We can even watch the amount we raise tonight as it updates. So, go ahead, ladies, press your buttons!'

There's another ripple of mirth as James uses his sexist catchphrase from a now-defunct TV talent show he used to be a judge on. 'I'm watching you, Ally Thomas,' he adds, pointing at a well-known TV columnist. The guests watch in awe as the number on the screen climbs and climbs before finally settling on an impressive seven-figure number. The Krug has obviously loosened some purse strings.

Unable to stomach the mutual backslapping while the hor-rifying footage of starving children continues to play on the screen, I head to one of the pop-up bars.

'Vodka, please,' I ask the bartender. 'Actually, make it a double.' What's my problem tonight?

She pours Grey Goose into an iced glass and I knock it back straight, shuddering as it joins the Champagne already swilling around in my otherwise empty stomach.

'That bad?'

I look up to see Charlie has joined me at the bar. He's taken his glasses off now and looks even hotter than before. I really need to slow down on the booze.

'Oh hey. Aren't you supposed to be up there doing your master of ceremonies thing?' I nod to where James is still stood, soaking up the attention of the crowd.

'Nah. Some things are better left to the professionals. So why are you back here drowning your sorrows instead of getting the party started with your friends?'

There's something about the way he says 'friends' that makes me think he doesn't think too highly of us.

'I'm not really a party person. Well, not tonight.'

'So, what kind of person are you? Because, and sorry if I'm speaking out of turn, you don't seem to be the kind to be downing straight vodka on your own.' He looks pointedly at the empty shot glass next to me.

I sigh. 'It's just all this.' I nod towards the party. 'Rich people stuffing their faces and getting drunk in the name of charity. It doesn't feel right.'

Charlie looks at me, waiting for me to say more.

'Oh, ignore me, I'm probably just hungry. And a bit drunk.'

'Didn't you like the food?'

'Actually, I'm vegan. All that offal and flesh weren't appealing to be honest. Sorry.'

'No way,' he says. 'You must be starving! Right, don't move an inch.'

He disappears into the crowd and returns about ten minutes later – just as I was starting to think he'd bailed on me – with a paper plate stacked with plant-based loveliness.

'Oh good, you're still here. I told them to offer a vegan option when we were menu-planning but was *assured* that no one would want that. It's not much, but it should keep you going.'

'Thank you!' I say through a mouthful of falafel.

'Are you all right for a drink? Or would you like some more neat vodka to cleanse your palate?'

'I'm fine. Thank you. You really didn't need to go to all this trouble for me.'

Charlie grabs a stuffed vine leaf from the plate and smiles at me. 'I didn't do this for you, Kitty Collins, I did this for me.'

My confused face seems to amuse him.

'I'm a Boy Scout, you see. And I think you've just helped me earn my – very hard to obtain – feed-a-hungry-vegan badge.'

We sit there smiling at each other and munching through the plate of food until Hen comes over, trying to drag me back to the party.

'Kitty! There you are! Daddy is insisting you bring your new friend over to the table for a drink and stop being so unsociable already.'

She's unsteady on her heels as she grabs my arm and tries to grab Charlie's too, but stumbles into him instead.

'He's hot,' she tries to whisper in my ear.

I look over her head at Charlie, who's smirking.

The party is in full swing back over at the table. Maisie and Rupert are seemingly joined at the pelvis as cheesy pop songs – mostly from bands on James Pemberton's label – blare out.

Laurelle is flitting among her three children, but seems most attached to Antoinette, the baby of the family at eighteen and enjoying her last summer at home before she heads off to university. Poor Antoinette is clearly trying to shake her mother off as Grut's bandmates arrive.

Hen skitters off back to her boyfriend as soon as we arrive at our table, apparently forgetting she's been on a mission to get us there.

Charlie and I stand awkwardly looking on until I feel

a hand on the small of my back. It makes me shudder. And not in the good way.

'Well, look who's decided to grace us with her presence after all.'

I don't need to turn around to know that it's James Pemberton's hand on my back.

'James!' I say as he envelopes me in a one-armed hug, not wanting to spill his drink. 'Great speech. And look how much money everyone is giving.' Tor was right. Ignore the virtue signalling and remember what it's all really for.

I've known James since I was a toddler but I still brace myself as he moves in for the requisite kiss on each cheek, his hands gripping my shoulders too tightly. 'You know Charlie, of course? He works for The Refugee Charity?'

I didn't expect James to be too bothered about Charlie. He's only really interested in men as rich and important as himself, much younger women, or naive pop acts who can make him even more money. I have an image of him swimming around in a room of cash, like in a cartoon I watched as a kid.

But instead of dismissing Charlie and his off-the-peg suit, James lets out a bray of laughter – the exact same laugh as Ben's. 'Darling girl,' he says. 'Charlie doesn't *work* for The Refugee Charity. He *is* The Refugee Charity. Owner, founder, CEO – whatever you want to call it. Did you *really* think he was some lowly underling?'

Turning to Charlie he adds: 'Son, I warned you about those suits!' He gives him a big clap on the back. 'Well done,' he says to him but winking at me. I shudder as he stumbles drunkenly away to talk to someone else.

Charlie and I turn to face each other.

'So, you run the show?' I say.

'Well, I have a *lot* of help from my wonderful team, but yeah, it's my baby.'

'That's amazing.'

'My dad doesn't think so, sadly. He's basically cut me off because I didn't follow in his footsteps and go into the family business of finance. He's good friends with James. You know, with money being involved.'

'Jesus, that's horrible. I'm so sorry. You think he'd be proud of you doing something so wonderful.'

Charlie looks at his shoes.

'What about your mum?'

He shifts awkwardly from one foot to the other.

'My mum's dead,' he says eventually. 'She died when I was thirteen.'

'Oh.' I don't know what to say. 'I'm sorry.'

His eyes move back to my face. 'Hey, it's okay. Don't be sorry. Unless you killed her, of course.' He gives me a sad smile.

'My dad went missing when I was fifteen,' I say. 'No one knows what happened to him.'

'The Mystery of the Missing Meat Mogul.' Charlie uses the phrase the tabloids loved around the time my dad disappeared. 'That must be hard?'

It's my turn to stare at the ground. I don't want to look him in the eye while I lie to him.

'It's the not knowing that's the worst,' I say. 'If he's dead or alive, you know?'

I feel Charlie's hand on my arm and am momentarily mesmerised by the fact I don't flinch or try to shrug him off.

'I can't even imagine how tough that must be for you. How do you cope?'

Stop talking about it, I think. Talking about it means I could slip up. Especially as I seem to have lubricated myself quite well with free booze.

'Because I have to. What's the alternative?'

'Yeah, I get that.'

We stand in silence for a moment.

Charlie shuffles his feet and starts picking at a piece of lint on his jacket. 'Listen, Kitty, I've really enjoyed talking to you tonight. I don't suppose you'd like to do it again some time? Maybe somewhere a bit less . . . um . . .' He looks around the garden at the rich and fabulous laughing and drinking and taking selfies next to the screen displaying the obscene amount of money that's been donated. I bet the bloody party's trending on Twitter. I don't want to be here anymore.

'Yes, somewhere *much* less would be great.'

21

KITTY'S APARTMENT, CHELSEA

When I get home later, I open my laptop and log into Instagram to have a look for Charlie on there. Before I get that far though, I spot the little icon telling me there's a message waiting for me.

A picture has been forwarded. It's of me and Charlie at the pop-up bar, laughing and seemingly unable to take our eyes off each other.

The message is short.

'I'm always watching you Kitty.'

I slam the computer shut. What the fuck? The picture could only have been taken from someone inside the party. And not more than a few hours ago. This is getting seriously weird now and I don't like it. I double-check all the locks on my door before I go to bed.

My sleep is broken with disturbing dreams about my dad and parties he used to throw at our old house when I was growing up. My parents were *extremely* social when my dad was around. Our house was always full of people. They threw lavish parties that impossibly glamorous people would turn up in droves for.

Real Gatsby stuff.

I'd dive through the skirts and heels of the women, all mingled in together, and feel giddy from their perfumes. Even my mother would make an effort when there was a party and wear one of her incredible dresses.

'You look like a princess,' I remember telling her once as she danced me around her bedroom in a clumsy waltz while she was getting ready.

'No, honey, I'm the queen and you're the princess. My perfect little princess.' And she'd cover my face and head in kisses.

I loved these moments with my mother, but they always felt like I'd stolen them from somewhere I wasn't supposed to be. They never lasted long either. Usually, a day or so after the last guest had gone home, she'd take to her room again, refusing to come out or let me in. I'd sit by her door. Like a live-action version of *Frozen*.

The guests were always delighted to see me, lavishing attention and kisses on me before I was ushered off to bed by the nanny. I remember thinking how incredibly happy grown-ups were at parties. It was only as I got older that I realised it was because they were all drunk or high.

My dad was always the life and soul of the parties. I remember his big laugh echoing around the rooms of our house. His laugh made me feel safe. My father. My protector.

I don't want to think about this shit anymore. I check the time on my phone and it's 2.40am so I head to the bar area and pour myself a massive shot of vodka. Then I go back to my bedroom and pop three zopiclone out of the blister pack on my nightstand and into my mouth. I wash them down with the vodka.

I wake up the next morning, late, my head throbbing from nightmares and the various drugs and drinks I'd used to knock myself out. The memories from my childhood are still swimming around in my head, gurgling around in the pit of my stomach.

I crawl out of bed and head to the en suite where I throw up in the toilet. There was a time when being violently sick would make me feel cleansed, better, but now it does nothing, except make me need to brush my teeth four times. I'm restless and I urgently need a distraction from this feeling.

I go to the kitchen and make myself the strongest black coffee imaginable, before I open Tinder on my phone. Maybe disembowelling a sex offender is what I need to cure this particular hangover.

I've already picked out a couple of contenders. But just as I'm about to message one of the unlucky matches, an iMessage notification pops up.

It's from Charlie. My stomach does something. It's sort of similar to the anxiety I've been feeling since the message from The Creep last night, but a more pleasurable version. Are these those *butterflies* I've heard people talk about? I shake the thought away and open the message.

Hey Kitty, really hope I come across as cool and not too keen and stalky, but I was wondering if you're busy tonight?

> I've got tickets for the launch of an art exhibition I've been
> involved in. It's a charity thing but I think you might find it
> interesting x.

I'm pleased at the lack of text speak in his message and suddenly remember that with all the stalker drama, I'd totally
forgotten to check Charlie out on social. I scroll to the
Instagram app and type his name into the search. There are
a few Charlie Chambers but it doesn't take long to find him.
He's very clearly the best looking of the bunch, his profile
picture a candid black-and-white shot of him laughing. Those
dimples. I just want to stick my finger in them. He's only got
around 2,000 followers, which is basically none.

Annoyingly, his page is private. Having a locked account is
something that is totally unheard of in my world and usually
means you've done something so humiliating, which has made
it onto the sidebar of shame on MailOnline. I very much
doubt this is the case with Charlie though and consider the
possibility that he's actually a private person.

I know I'm meant to wait like at least an hour before I reply
to him, but I think fuck it.

I text him back.

> Hey! It just so happens that I'm free tonight. Exhibition
> sounds fun. Anyone I would've heard of?

The little dots that tell me he's replying appear straight away.

Absolutely not! It's very much an art student vibe so don't expect too much. And. Are you willing to slum it east :0)

Oddly, his use of the smiley face emoji just makes me smile instead of wanting to throw myself right off my balcony.

Me: How east are we talking?

Charlie: Lewisham?

Me: That I can do.

I'm glad he can't see my grimace through the texts.

Charlie: Good. I was worried you might melt like the Wicked Witch if you left SW3.

22

LEWISHAM, SOUTHEAST LONDON

We arrange to meet at the venue, which is a pop-up gallery in a shopping centre. I try to stifle my inner snob as my car drops me off outside the building, which is like something from Ken Loach's nightmares, quite frankly. There are groups of teens loitering around the front, but these aren't the glossy and groomed teens that I get accosted by in SW3. There's a smell of damp and weed hanging in the heat. I hop from foot to foot, unsure what to do with myself and am relieved when I see Charlie walking towards me. I'm a little unnerved at how vulnerable I feel in my nude Louboutin flats and red Ted Baker skater dress.

He looks gorgeous in a pair of dark jeans and a black linen shirt, with the sleeves rolled up. It's a bit rubbish for men when it's this hot. I mean, what are their choices? They either have to sweat it out in jeans or look like they're on a fucking 18–30 holiday in shorts and vests. And don't even get me started on men in sandals. Some things just shouldn't be seen out in public and hairy toes are one of them.

'Kitty!' He gives me an awkward peck on the cheek and I feel my skin prickle as he lightly touches my bare arm. God, I've missed skin-to-skin contact. 'I'm really glad you could make it.'

He looks like he's caught the sun in the twenty-four hours since I last saw him, a light tan has brought out a smattering of freckles across his face and his eyes are even brighter than I remember.

'Yeah, me too.'

'So, it's actually pretty interesting,' he tells me as he places a hand on my lower back and gently guides me past the feral children and into the centre. 'All of the pieces are made from bits and pieces the artists picked up when they helped clean up the old Jungle camp in Calais. It's called *Privilege*.'

To my shame, I'm not an art fan. I mean, I like it and everything and can appreciate a good painting. But I probably couldn't name you any contemporary artists. Well, Banksy, I suppose. And I'm really not on board with a lot of modern art. I just don't get most of it. I glance at Charlie's exuberant face as he leads me into the gallery and start to worry. I hope he doesn't ask me to make insightful comments or anything like that.

'So, this is the main piece,' Charlie says, as he leads me over to a huge, dirty white canvas, spread out over some trestle tables and encased in glass. The white is covered with flecks of ash.

I stare at it for a moment, trying to think of something to say.

'It's quite abstract I know,' he says, saving me. 'Most of

the stuff on display is. But each one of those specks represents a woman or child who has fled Aleppo to escape the war.' He gently takes hold of my elbow and guides me over to the next piece, which is exactly the same, but with far fewer flecks. 'This one shows the families that actually made it to a safe place alive.'

I shiver. 'That's so awful,' I whisper, knowing my words just aren't enough.

'Yes, it really makes you think when it's actually laid out like that. In literal black and white. All that wasted life. It's such a precious thing.'

We stand and stare in silence for a few moments.

'Hey, it's not all doom and gloom in here though,' Charlie says. 'Come and look at these.'

He leads me over to a wall that is covered with bright pictures. There are rainbows, suns and unicorns and wishes written in the unmistakable scrawl of children.

'This is our wall of hope. Each one of these drawings was done by a child while they were living in the refugee camp. These kids have literally had to leave their lives behind and live in the worst conditions imaginable. Yet, they still manage to draw stuff like this.'

I stare mutely at the pictures, colourful fanfares dedicated to simply being alive.

'How old were the kids who did these?'

'Most of them were done by the really little ones. Eight and under.' He runs his fingers across a particularly beautiful rainbow chalk drawing. 'This one was done by a little girl called Yara,' he says. 'She was only five and had been separated from both her parents on the journey to Calais. But she was the bravest little thing. With the biggest heart. And she didn't doubt for one second that she'd be reunited with her family.'

'Was she?' I ask.

Charlie's face takes on a steely look. 'I don't know,' he says after a pause that feels like forever. 'The next time I went back to the camp, she was gone and no one seemed to know where.' He chews the inside of his lip, lost in another world for a moment. 'Jesus, sorry Kitty, I don't know why I thought it was a good idea bringing you here. It's not the jolliest of first dates.' He attempts a smile.

'Is this a date?'

'Well. It was supposed to be. In my head it was a lot more romantic than this though. Sorry.'

'You've got nothing to be sorry for. It's fascinating to see all this. And it's obvious how much your work means to you. Thank you for sharing it with me.' I give his arm a reassuring squeeze. 'I feel honoured.'

'Really?'

'Really.' I nod.

'Then you won't mind hanging around for a bit while I do my speechy CEO bit. Don't worry, it's not too formal.'

'Of course not!'

He claps his hands together and the sound is so loud it actually makes me jump. I watch, a bit in awe, as everyone turns to face him. But something ugly rouses deep within me at the same time. It's a bit too much like the Adam situation for my liking. What am I even doing here? Why am I making myself vulnerable?

'So,' Charlie starts his speech. He looks far more relaxed here than he did when he was talking at the party last night. 'First of all I want to say thanks to all of you for coming here tonight instead of the nearest pub garden.'

'I just wanted to get home and stand in front of the fridge,' a skinny blonde girl says and pretends to swoon. Everyone laughs.

'A good point about global warming, Jenna.' Charlie gives her a wink. 'Imagine how unbearable this type of heat is in a camp with no air-con. Or many fridges. Anyway, I hope you like the display. As most of you know, it's mostly been made from rubbish collected at the former Jungle camp site in Calais. Most of the artists are around if you want to grab them for a word. Jenna here,' he points at Blondie, 'is the brains behind the main piece, which I'm sure you'll be moved by when she explains the full story to you. As always, we're grateful for any donations you can hand our way. We hope to get back out to the Greek camps when autumn eventually arrives. I'll leave you in Jenna's hands now. And once again, thank you so much for your time this evening.'

Charlie gets an impressive round of applause and then Jenna begins talking about the dots of ash thing. He heads back over to me. 'Wanna get out of here?' he whispers.

'Yes please. If that's okay?'

'Hey, babe, you're with the boss. Everything's okay.' He winks again, but it's far more suggestive than the one Jenna got and my soul is immediately soothed. 'I've just got to say a few goodbyes and we can go.'

The 'few goodbyes' actually take forty-five minutes as

Charlie flits around and says goodbye to everyone on the planet while I nurse a glass (paper cup) of warm white wine and watch him. He's so easy-going and it doesn't escape me how many of the women look at him with doe-eyed admiration.

Adam, Adam, Adam, my brain screams at me out of nowhere. I imagine there are amber warning lights flashing around in my head too. I shake the memories away.

Eventually Charlie makes his way back over to me and hustles me out of the door.

'Quickly, before anyone else tries to talk to me,' he whispers in my ear, close enough for me to feel his breath on my neck.

'So, what would you like to do now, Kitty Collins?' he asks when we're back outside in the sticky evening air. It's so humid, it feels like trying to breathe in soup. 'A drink? Do you have a glamorous event you need to attend? A photoshoot?'

I laugh. 'A drink sounds good. But could we go somewhere a bit less . . . ?'

His turn to laugh. 'Yes, let's definitely go somewhere a bit less.'

We wave down a black cab and have it take us into the centre of town. We stop by Green Park, deciding to walk until we find somewhere 'less' enough.

'So, what did you think of it?' Charlie asks, smiling, those dimples making me feel like the most important person in the world.

'It made me feel quite uneasy actually,' I answer, honestly.

'Yes!' He turns to me, those green eyes sparkling. 'That's *exactly* the way it's meant to make you feel. That and

124

fortunate, spoiled. We see so much of the suffering on the news that it's easy to become desensitised to it. What the pieces do – especially the one with the kids – is show it to us simply. It's even more awful in a way, don't you think?'

I nod. He's right. I feel ignorant and spoiled.

'What happens to the others? The ones who don't make it?' I ask.

'The kids? Well, lots of pretty terrible stuff can happen. They can be kidnapped and trafficked, some are subjected to horrific abuse and killed, others just don't even last the boat journey to safety.'

'And you help them?'

'We try to. We do as much as we can to educate, to help get mums and kids to a safe place and to reunite anyone who's been separated. It's hard though. It's a very corrupt world and obviously funding is an issue.'

'Do you get very hands-on?'

He takes a deep breath, which he exhales quickly, making his cheeks puff out.

'Yeah, I spent quite a lot of time in Kos helping with the refugee crisis over there, as well as in Calais. We set up some places to feed them, made sure there were warm blankets and clothes for when they arrived. But it wasn't easy. Seeing families torn apart, people having to leave lives, careers, relationships they've been building for years, it's horrible.' He looks at me, concern etched on his gorgeous face. 'You've gone quiet. What's wrong?'

'Nothing, it's just very humbling, I guess. It's hard when your privilege hits you right in the face.'

'True – it can be. But you also have to realise that everything is relative. You could have and be everything you want in the world and still be unhappy.'

I shiver.

'Look,' he says. 'There's a pub there. Let's go and get a drink. This really has been far more righteous than I intended.'

23

THE GRAPES ON THE VINE PUBLIC HOUSE, W1

We head into a smallish pub, one of the only places that isn't bursting at the seams with Londoners and tourists making the most of the long evening and beer garden weather. Of course, there's a reason this particular venue isn't packed and that's because it smells very strongly of damp. Which, mixed with a long humid summer and bodies everywhere, isn't very nice.

'We can go somewhere else?' Charlie says as we take our drinks to a table with actual seats, sniffing the air and making faces.

'And trade the luxury of space for standing room only and being squashed at the bar for forty minutes trying to order? No thanks.'

'Well, if you're sure you can stomach the stink. It smells like something died in here. I got you something, by the way.' He grins in a way that makes him look like a shy schoolboy as he fishes around in his pocket. 'Here. They were selling them on one of the stalls on Oxford Street. It's silly really.' He hands me a small paper bag with the Union Jack emblazoned on it.

I open it and pull out a key ring. It's a small, white cartoon kitten, wearing a Union Jack T-shirt, with a pink bow on her head.

'Hello Kitty!'

'I warned you not to expect much.'

'No! It's cute. I love it. Thank you.'

There's a moment of silence. Not exactly awkward, but loaded with . . . something. 'I haven't got you anything. Sorry.'

'God, don't be. Obviously, I didn't expect you to.' He smiles into his pint, those dimples, those freckles, those eyes. I know I'm on dangerous ground here.

'You've gone quiet again. What is it? Is the tacky gift offensive?'

I smile. 'No. It's lovely. I think I'm just nervous.'

'Why are *you* nervous?' he asks, face a picture of innocence.

It's hard to explain to a date that he's the first man in a long time that you haven't imagined dicing into parcel-sized pieces and feeding into a meat grinder.

'I don't know. I just don't get why you messaged me. I mean I'm pretty much everything you go against, aren't I? Spoiled and ignorant?'

He has the decency to look horrified. 'I didn't mean *you* when I said that! Jesus, anything but. You surprised me. At the gala, I mean. I expected you to be like Hen and the others, but you're not. You're layered. You're interesting. You shook my world a bit to be honest. I didn't think I was the sort of person who made presumptions about people. But it turns out I do. And I was wrong.'

'You thought I was like Hen?'

'Yeah. When you came over to talk to me while I was trying to memorise my speech. Remember? I just thought you were going to be another shallow rich girl.'

'Hey!' I nudge his foot with mine under the table. 'Those shallow rich girls are my lifelong friends.'

'You're not like them though, are you.' It's a statement not a question.

I have a gnawing need to turn the conversation away from myself. 'Why did you go down this road? The charity one? Why was your dad so cross?'

His eyes narrow slightly as if he's considering something, but he quickly shakes it off. 'Jesus . . . I don't know where to start really. I guess I've always been a bit "worthy".' He does the finger-quotes thing that usually makes me want to tear my own skin off, but he does it with a self-deprecating half grin that makes me melt a little bit. 'You know the sort of thing: "Save the Ozone Layer" at school, militant household-waste inspector at home. Made my parents move from one bin to three. I think they assumed I'd grow out of it. But I never did. I've just always felt that unfairness. Why some people have everything and others have nothing. Does that make sense?'

I nod, captivated by his passion.

'And I guess I very much felt that people like me, like *us*, can do so much more, you know? I don't need all the money my family were offering. It doesn't make me happy.'

'What makes you happy?'

'Helping, I guess, making a difference. I was a very deep and troubled soul as a kid. I grew up seeing humans doing awful stuff everywhere. God, oil slicks, fox-hunting, recycling aluminium cans. I clearly watched too much *Blue Peter*. But it had an effect on me. All life deserves a chance. Don't you think?'

I almost choke on my drink.

'*All* life? You don't think there are any exceptions to that? Don't you think there are some scumbags crawling the earth who deserve to be six feet under it? What about that girl you were talking about? Yara? If she was taken, trafficked, wouldn't you want those responsible to pay? Imagine you were there with a gun, knowing what they'd done to her. There must be a part of you that would want to avenge her?'

A cloud passes over his face and he looks down at the table, chewing his bottom lip. 'Fuck. I don't know. Obviously, I *should* say I'd try to make sure they got justice the proper way. But when you put it like that . . .'

'Imagine the rage you'd feel,' I push. 'That animal part of your brain wants to hurt them.'

'Jesus, I really don't know. If we're talking about that primal part of our brain that we can't control, I think it's impossible to say how *anyone* would react in a situation like that. Fuck, this has got really heavy again. Aren't these the sort of topics everyone says to avoid on a first date?'

'Okay.' I nod. 'So, what's your favourite colour?'

He laughs.

We have a wonderful evening when we stop talking about all the most serious things in the world. Plus, I beat him twice at pool (a secret skill of mine), which impresses him no end. He's such easy company, funny, clever and obviously not offensive to look at. I'm pretty gutted when he says he needs to get home as he's got an early meeting.

'One of those things I can't excuse myself from,' he says as he waits with me for my Uber. 'So, let me know if there's anything I can help you with? I can send you some shots of the exhibits if you want to post them on Insta? Hashtags and all that.'

Wait, what? WHAT?!

'Is that the only reason you asked me out?' An overwhelming mix of hurt and fury begins to pulse through my veins. 'So, I'd take some photos and hashtags of your exhibition and post to my followers? Bit of free PR?'

Charlie stares at me, his eyes pools of confusion. Or something resembling it. 'Kitty! No! I didn't mean it like that! I just . . .'

'You just what?'

He opens his mouth to give me an answer but I don't wait for it. A car pulls up and I don't even bother checking if it's for me before I get in.

I seethe all the way home, that old adage on repeat in my head. When something seems too good to be true, it's because it is.

Fuck you, Charlie Chambers. Absolutely fuck you.

24

KITTY'S APARTMENT, CHELSEA

I nod to Hakim, who's on the desk, before skulking up to my apartment like a wounded animal. Charlie tries to call me twice, but gives up when I cancel both. I pour myself a Grey Goose and gulp it down neat, following it with another.

I try to calm myself by imagining ways to kill Charlie. But even that doesn't help. In fact, it just makes me more antsy and I eventually knock back two of my special elephant-dose Valiums and pass out on my bed.

I'm not feeling much better when I wake up some ten hours later, the sun aggressively edging its way into my room.

I'm hungover and agitated.

I look at my phone, which surprisingly still has some battery considering I forgot to charge it before succumbing to unconsciousness. There are voicemails and texts from Charlie but I ignore and delete them. In an attempt to soothe myself, I try the treadmill in the room I've made into a personal gym. It just makes my legs hurt. I attempt the Mindfulness programme I've paid a small fortune to have some guru from Thailand teach me. Nada. In the end I pour myself a giant glass of Chablis, collapse on my sofa and pick up my phone.

I scroll through the gossip apps, check out the weather for next week – fucking hot – before opening the news app. And that's where I find exactly what pulls me out of this horrendous mood dip.

His name is Daniel Rose. He's thirty and from Catford. Recently released after spending some time at Her Majesty's pleasure and already familiarising himself with the world of online dating apps, according to MirrorOnline. Nothing wrong with that, apart from the fact he's just been released after a five-year stretch for two rapes. According to the report, he is a signed-up and paid subscriber to Tinder. It's almost too easy.

As is finding Daniel Rose's Tinder profile. Daniel Rose. He sounds so innocent and pure. The rage is already building up inside me and I have to take a few deep breaths to steady myself as I glance through his vital statistics.

Daniel, 28, London

'I'm just a normal bloke looking for someone similar. I like a laugh. I enjoy the simple things in life, good food, good wine and good company.'

And that's it. Funnily he doesn't mention forcing his cock into women who don't want it in the list of simple things he enjoys.

I close the app and reopen the *Mirror* report. Daniel was

arrested six years ago after raping a woman he met on a night out. He'd managed to talk his way into her home – on the pretence he was keeping her safe – and she'd tried to call her boyfriend several times but he didn't pick up. According to the report, the woman had repeatedly spurned his advances, before asking him to leave. Daniel Rose had ignored her, telling her he knew she wanted it, before forcing himself on her. She had spent the entire seven-minute ordeal crying and begging him to stop.

He pled not guilty, forcing the victim to relive the entire thing in court. She refused to give evidence from behind a screen, wanting to look him in the eye as she told the jurors what he'd done to her. She wanted to see if he had any remorse.

He didn't.

He even smirked at her from the dock as he was taken down.

He was released after three years and immediately broke his parole terms by sexually assaulting a female family friend. Apparently, he used the excuse that he hadn't 'seen tits in years' and couldn't help himself.

The judge sentencing him described him as 'a master manipulator and a very dangerous man'.

Showtime.

I open Tinder and swipe right on his face. Predictably it's a matter of minutes before a notification pings telling me I've got a match.

I've changed my name and photo now, obviously I'm too easy to detect if I'm myself. This time I'm a flirty student called Camilla looking for 'fun, dates and a little-bit-more-than-mates'.

Camilla clearly appeals to the sexual predator inside Daniel as a message pings in straight away.

'Why hello there Miss Fun and Dates and Maybe More. How r u doing?'

His lack of proper grammar makes me seethe. I try to think of what 'Camilla' would reply. An innocent who doesn't know this scumbag has raped and groped at least two women and is now trying to get back on the dating scene.

'Hi Daniel! Nice to cyber meet you. How's ur weekend going?' I shudder at the ease in which I let my own grammar slip into text speak.

'It's good. I've been away for a while so I'm getting back into the swing of things lol'

'Haha. Where have you been? Anywhere nice?'

'Just staying with friends for a bit while I sorted some things in my life out. It's good to be home though. So, do you want to move over to WhatsApp so we can ditch this shitty app?'

Urgh. I certainly do-fucking-not. Especially as my WhatsApp came complete with my real picture and a little bio about Kitty Collins.

'My phone's being repaired at the moment and I have this crappy old handset that it won't download on. Sorry.'

'Well how about we cut the crap and I take you out for a drink instead. I'm Catford. Are you local?'

'I can be. Where shall we meet?'

He messages back with the name of a pub that sounds suitably grim enough to not have any state-of-the-art CCTV, and in less than forty minutes I'm there, even managing to find a parking spot almost directly outside.

25

THE CATFORD INN, CATFORD

It's exactly as expected – a dartboard-and-pool-table affair stinking of day-old beer and carpets that haven't been replaced since before the smoking ban. I'm going to need several showers after this.

I clock him straight away, sat at a table, tapping away on his phone, no doubt wondering what he's going to be doing to poor Camilla as soon as he can. I order a house white, which comes straight from a not-very-cold cellar. Luckily, I have no intention of drinking it. I position myself at a nearby table – which isn't difficult as the place is practically empty – where I carry out the full Ritual of the Stood-up Female. Heavy sighs, lots of phone checking and longing glances out of the window.

After about ten minutes I let my eyes meet Daniel Rose's. I've felt them boring into me since the moment I sat down.

'Guess he forgot,' I say, offering a little self-deprecating smile.

He grins back at me. 'Mine too. Fuck it, eh? Their loss.'

I nod, standing up, gathering my phone and keys from the (sticky) table and make out I'm getting ready to leave. I smile at him again.

'Well, I hope she turns up.'

I turn to go but Daniel shouts after me.

'Let me buy you a drink?' he says. 'We're both in the same boat after all.'

And it really is that easy.

I wait for a beat. Not *too* keen.

'Why not? No point in wasting a whole afternoon now I'm all dressed up.'

'Come and sit with me.' He holds his arms open wide, indicating for me to join him. I shuffle into the chair opposite. 'So, what's your name and what are you drinking?'

'White wine please,' I say. 'That's what I'm drinking I mean. My name's Kitty.'

He laughs along with me at my shit attempt at a joke and then holds out his hand. 'Well, it's very nice to meet you, Miss White Wine. I'm Daniel.'

His hand is hot and clammy and I wipe him off me and onto the table, as I watch him strut over to the bar. He manoeuvres past two old timers who've clearly settled in for the long haul, and returns with a pint for himself and my wine. I take the chance to get a really good look at him. He's thinner than his Tinder profile and the photos on the news report. That'll be the portion control courtesy of Her Maj.

He doesn't *look* like a monster though. But they don't, do they? Otherwise, they'd never get the opportunity to be monsters. His brown eyes crinkle when he speaks. He's got freckles on his nose and cheeks that make him look like nothing more dangerous than a naughty schoolboy. He's not big or overbearing. He's just a guy.

The devil wears many guises.

He talks. A lot. Mostly about himself and how he's currently job-seeking after being furloughed but has some 'exciting logs on the fire'. He drinks easily, spreading himself out a little bit more after each pint. Arms wide, legs wide, taking up as much room as possible.

'Who were you supposed to be meeting?' I ask. 'Your girlfriend?'

'No, no. Just a first date. Someone I met on an app actually. I've been out of the game for a while. To be honest she wasn't really my type. A bit too nicey-nicey.' His eyes linger on my chest and I feel a twinge of loyalty for poor non-existent Camilla.

When he excuses himself to go to the 'lavs' I take my chance and dispense a few drops of liquid GHB, which my usual meds-contact kindly provided, into his drink. The report I read online pops back into my head, particularly the bit about smirking in the dock. Fuck it, I pour the lot in. Remorseless bastard.

Half an hour later, as his words begin to slur and his head starts to droop onto his chest, I realise it's time to get Daniel Rose home. To my home, that is. I need my knives.

'Where are we going?' he drawls as I sling his arm around my shoulder, making sure that no one in the pub is paying attention to us. The two old timers are well and truly sloshed by this point, one has fallen off his stool at least twice. That's going to cost the NHS a new hip. There's no sign of the barely legal boy who had served the drinks either.

'We're going to get you somewhere nice and comfy,' I tell him. 'You're very drunk. I think you need to sleep it off. Let's get you to bed.'

'Yes, let's go to bed.' He makes an attempt to leer at me, but he just looks like he's having some sort of seizure.

I half lead, half carry him to my car and usher him into the passenger seat.

26

'I don't feel well.'

Daniel Rose is looking quite sickly actually. Really pale and his eyes keep rolling from side to side like he's trying to focus on something that keeps slipping out of his line of vision.

'Who are you?' He has a sudden moment of lucidity and lurches forward, staring menacingly into my eyes, feebly grabbing at my arm as I try to strap him into the seat.

Safety first.

'Your worst nightmare.' I shake him off my arm and give him a shove, which makes him immediately slump into the seat. Then I hop into the driver's side and start the engine.

He's now looking over at me with a mix of confusion and fear as we pull away from the pub and begin our journey back to SW3.

'It's not nice, is it? Feeling helpless and like your own body is out of your control. Do you think that's how your victims felt? You know, the women you *raped*?'

Daniel pales to the colour of weak tea and sweat starts to run down his face, pooling in a rancid little puddle in his clavicle. He may be off his tits on GHB, but he knows the game is up.

'I didn't rape them,' he wheezes. 'They wanted it.'

My blood feels like it's burning my skin.

'Liar!' I slam on the brakes, hard, letting the motion of being flung forward at force but held in place by his seatbelt wind him.

'Just admit what you did. Apologise. And this doesn't have to be painful. You might even get a few thousand years in purgatory instead of going straight to hell.'

He tries to lift his head enough to look at me, the film of sweat over his face like a caul. 'I. Didn't. Do. Nothing. Wrong.'

I suppose an accidental double negative is about as close as I'm likely to get to a confession from him.

I look at him. Pathetic. Shrivelled up and sweating like a, well, like a fucking *rapist*. I suddenly can't wait to get him home, to watch that fear in his eyes grow into complete and utter terror when he realises what's about to happen.

But when I glance at him again, while I'm stopped at some roadworks where no one appears to be working but the temporary lights have been left on anyway, I can see that something is very wrong. The look of fear has disappeared. In fact *all* looks have gone. His eyes are glassy and staring. But they're staring at nothing. Because he's dead as fuck.

Shit.

Maybe giving him *all* the GHB was a bad idea. I didn't

think it could *kill* someone though. Jesus Christ. I'm going to have to do some research on date-rape drugs. Maybe he was allergic to it? I don't know. I'm not a fucking paramedic. All I know is that he's dead. In the passenger seat. Next to me.

Fuck.

27

Okay. Don't panic.

The problem here is that while I'm used to getting dead bodies out of my apartment, I've never actually had to get one *in* before. And it definitely isn't something I'd choose to do in broad fucking daylight.

I pull over into a smaller road as soon as I see more prams and trees than drunks and tramps. I need to think.

So, I could take him home and leave him in the car until it's dark. But I'd have to somehow cover him up and with the heat it's not going to be long before he starts stinking like the rotten bit of meat he is. I could take him straight to one of the abattoirs, but the workers would be there. Plus the nearest one, in Hampshire, is still a forty-five-minute drive away. That's quite a long time with a corpse next to you. Also, I need my tools. My only real option is to try to get him past whichever concierge is working and up to my penthouse.

I glance into the backseat and thank God (or whatever)

that I'm a nightmare when it comes to cleaning out my car. The entire back is basically my emergency wardrobe. You never know if disaster of disasters could strike at an event and you turn up in *exactly* the same Ghost dress as someone else. Even though your stylist *promised* you it was one of a kind. Anyway, the point is I have hats, cloaks, coats aplenty. And I'm going to have to get creative. I head back to Chelsea, park the Evoque in the underground car park and get to work.

I park an oversized Miu Miu bucket hat on Daniel's head (thank you, Nineties revival) and wind a Madeleine Thompson wrap around his torso. Then I remember the random roller-skates in the boot back when I was stuffing Joel's suitcase in there. They'll help.

Not only does Daniel Rose look stylish(ish), he's also now much easier to manoeuvre.

Luckily for me – I really must've been born under a lucky star – Rehan's working. He's not at the desk, but several feet away in the delivery room. He gives me a big smile and wave as I slide Daniel Rose through the foyer. With some difficulty, admittedly. Even on wheels, he's not light.

'Hello, Miss Kitty!'

'Hi, Rehan, how are you?'

'Very well, miss. Your friend,' he indicates the corpse I'm trying to smuggle in, 'she is not so well?'

'Very sick,' I say. 'She's had one too many, again! Taking her upstairs to sleep it off.'

'She is a very naughty girl.' Rehan nods in recognition. 'And she will fall down dead on skates!' He laughs and I fake laugh while pretending to whisper sobering words of advice to the dead body I'm dragging into the lift.

Once we arrive at my floor it's pretty much plain sailing and Rehan doesn't even notice when I leave the next morning with bits of Daniel Rose packaged neatly in shopping bags. Gucci, Tiffany, Chanel.

'Just off to do some returning.' I smile, handing him a coffee I'd made along with a blueberry muffin. 'Say hi to your girls from me.'

I also slip him a smaller Tiffany bag, which contains two white gold bracelets with tiny diamonds that twinkle like fairy lights in the sun. Rehan's daughters are back in Pakistan with his sister. His wife died in childbirth with his youngest, he told me as I gave him a coffee on one of his first days in the job – around three years ago now. He sends almost all the money he earns here back home to them, to put them through school. He's kind and I like to give him gifts for his girls whenever I can.

I hand him an envelope as well. 'And something for yourself too.' Later, when his shift is over, he'll open the envelope and find it stuffed with twenties. Nothing wrong with reminding people what an absolute sweetheart you are from time to time.

I mean, yes, you *could* call it bribery. But I don't like that word.

After I've disposed of Daniel Rose (a factory in Swindon this time), I check my phone and see that Maisie's requested a conference at The Lost Hours later tonight. I've got about enough time to shower and change, while I try not to think about Charlie. There are no more calls or texts from him. My stomach dips and I register this emotion as extreme disappointment.

28

THE LOST HOURS, KING'S ROAD

Maisie arrives late and slips into her seat at the table silently, three pairs of eyes looking at her intensely.

'What?' she says, frowning. 'Pour me some of that.'

Tor fills her wineglass up with the open bottle of Chablis.

'Come on then,' Hen says. 'Spill the beans. All of them. You summoned *us*, remember?'

Maisie is blushing. 'Oh yeah. I need to talk sex.'

'Urgh. Really?' I say. 'Can you spare us?'

Hen shoots me a look. 'Speak for yourself. I want to know everything. You've hardly told us a thing about Roo's bedroom prowess.'

'Objection overruled,' Tor says, using her wineglass as a gavel before she and Hen chant: 'How big is his dick?'

Neighbouring tables look over at us, but fortunately, it's a Thursday evening, everyone is already pretty tipsy, enjoying their pre-kend drinks. There are a few laughs and one man, wearing a waistcoat for no apparent reason, stands up and gives them a round of applause.

Maisie nods her gratitude to him before rolling her eyes and turning back to us.

'Yes. I'm getting laid on the reg. I don't know why there's this big fanfare about it though. It's not like I've been going through a dry patch or anything. Not like *some* people.' She moves her face close to mine. 'Not that I'd be uncouth enough to name any names, Kitty Collins.'

'Leave her alone,' Hen says. 'If Kitty wants to keep her kitty drier than a Ryvita, then that is her decision. Anyway, she's got Charlie Chambers in her web now so her drought is practically over. We're talking about you. Now, out with it. What's he like in the sack?'

'Just the usual really.' She shrugs, fiddling with a non-existent bit of fluff on her skirt.

Tor pulls a face. 'That is not the response of someone who had their chakras realigned last night. What happened?'

'Nothing. Well, nothing unusual. Just the normal stuff.'

'Okay, so we've established he hasn't showed you his private torture garden yet,' I say. 'But it doesn't sound like you were swinging from the light fittings either. Bad foreplay?'

'*No* foreplay?' Hen's eyes are wide in horror. 'Did he do that awful thing where they just stick their fingers in you, like they're trying to get hair out of the plughole?'

Maisie laughs. 'No. It was nothing like that. It was fine.'

'Fine. Fine sex.' Hen's laughing.

'So, you have to tell us more than that. Did he go down? Was it awful?'

'Does he have a tiny cock?' Tor asks.

Maisie is hiding her head in her hands now and shaking with laughter. 'No. Stop asking me. I don't want to talk about it. I've changed my mind. Let's just get drunk and gossip like usual.'

I gasp. 'Micro penis?'

She keeps giggling. 'No! It's normal size and everything. It's just that . . .' She takes her hands away from her face and looks at us. 'No. I can't. It's too mortifying to even repeat.'

'Well, you *have* to tell us now!' Tor says. 'Or Hen will make up her own version of what she thinks happened and tell everyone that.'

Hen nods. 'That *does* sound like the sort of thing I'd do.' She picks up her iPhone and opens her Twitter app.

'No! Stop! I'll tell you. I'll tell you. Just give me some more of that first.' She points at the wine and Tor fills her glass to the brim. Maisie has to move her mouth to the glass so it doesn't spill. She looks like a little kid with a McDonald's milkshake.

'Okay. So, last night, we're at mine. We'd been out to a couple of bars so were feeling quite drunk by this point and things were getting, um, heated on the sofa. Clothes had started to come off.'

She pauses and takes another big slug of wine. I don't think any of us are breathing.

'I suggested we take things upstairs. You know I'm funny about getting any stains on the sofas. So, we headed up to my bedroom. More clothes were shed along the way. Jesus, we almost ended up fucking on the stairs, but you know, carpet burn. So, we're in my room and we're kissing and his mouth starts to head downwards. By this point I'm almost clawing at him, I'm so close to coming. And it's amazing. I'm there in seconds, gripping the sheets and all that. So good. Anyway, I'm lying there, you know, recovering. He's looking pretty pleased with himself – and rightly so. Then he begins to edge up the bed, his groin getting closer to my face. And then he . . .'

Another pause. Another gulp of wine. The suspense is palpable. This woman should get a job reading audiobooks. You know, if she wasn't already completely loaded and didn't need to work.

'And then what???' Hen almost screams, making Maisie jump and spill some wine.

'And then he,' her voice is a whisper now, 'and then he asked me to suck his willy. His *willy*.' Her head is back in her hands and she's shake-laughing silently again.

I look at Hen and Tor for the correct response. Hen's mouth is agape while Tor is also silent laughing, but repeating the word 'willy' every time she stops for breath.

This sets Hen off into a fit of laughter too and I join them.

'He had on his T-shirt and socks,' Maisie continues once the laughing has calmed. 'He looked like a fucking potty-training toddler as it was, without sounding like one.' She pauses and puts her hand over her mouth. 'Poor Roo. I couldn't stop laughing.'

'Oh dear,' Hen says, holding her pointer finger erect and letting it drop, flaccid, into her palm.

Maisie nods. 'Yes. Exactly. Anyway, he put his trousers back on.'

'The red ones?' I ask.

Maisie gives me a side-eye. 'Yes. If the detail is crucial, they were red.'

Tor snorts.

'And then we went downstairs.'

'I thought he'd already done that bit?'

Hen can't stop laughing.

Maisie is getting annoyed now. I can tell by the little pink spots that are rising high on her cheekbones. 'Down the *actual* stairs to the sitting room, where we were then forced into a discussion about what to call genitalia in a sexual situation.'

'Oh my God, no. Continue.'

'So, I told him "cock" is fine. "Dick" is acceptable. And then I sort of got stuck. After that you're heading into some terrible erotica language. "Throbbing member" and shit like that.' She's giggling, almost choking on her wine. 'I honestly didn't think I'll be able to have sex again ever.'

'Did you get down to it in the end?' I ask.

Maisie nods. 'Yes. Funnily enough all the talk about cocks and cunts got us really turned on and we ended up fucking on the sofa.'

'But the *stains*!'

'Well. What are cleaners for if it's not to mop up sexual bodily fluids?'

The three of them cackle like witches and I feel a prickle of something unpleasant at their laughter.

Tor notices my clear discomfort.

'Come on, Sour-Kits, she's just joking. Don't let your moral compass burst her bubble.'

'Kitty is the only person I've ever met who cleans for the *cleaner*,' Hen says.

'I'm going to the loo,' I say. Hen boos me as I walk away.

I'm only in there for a moment, looking at myself in the mirror, when Tor follows me in.

'What's the matter? You're not your usual self tonight.'

I sigh. 'I don't know. I just feel like we take all this for granted. Like *too* much sometimes. The world is a really shitty place for most people.'

She puts her arms round me and pulls me into a hug. 'Oh, you. And that's exactly why we need to enjoy what we have. God, I could be living in some awful orphanage. I appreciate the life I have, babe. And you know they're just joking. They're good girls. You know that.'

'The thing with Charlie isn't going anywhere,' I confess, glumly.

'Babe. What? Why? I thought there was genuine connection stuff there?'

'I thought so too.' I hoist myself up so I'm sat on the vanity unit. 'He took me to this art exhibition, which was all put on by his charity. There were some amazing things and then we went to the pub – just a regular old man pub but it was so fun and normal – and chatted about everything. I thought it was going so well. He gave me this.'

I pull the Hello Kitty key ring out of my pocket and show her.

'That's so cute. What went wrong?'

'He had to be up early for a meeting so called me an Uber. I was about to invite him up when he dropped in that I can have any images I want from the exhibition if I wanted to highlight it on my Insta.' I feel my face drop. My heart goes with it.

'Oh, Kits, no. Are you sure you didn't take it the wrong way?'

'Pretty sure. And I've not heard from him since last night when I ignored his calls. So I guess I was nothing more than a PR opportunity for him. It reminded me of Adam.'

Tor rubs my knees. 'Come on, let's get a car back to yours and eat loads of chocolate and bitch about men. Leave those two loved-up idiots to it. No doubt we'll be picking up the pieces when it all fucks up eventually.'

I give her a weak smile and let her lead me out of the loos. She tells Maisie and Hen – who are now talking about penis girth loudly and animatedly – that we're leaving.

'Actually,' I tell Tor when the cab we flag down arrives at mine, 'do you mind if I just go home alone? I sort of want to wallow and go to bed.'

'You do you, honey.' She kisses my cheek. 'Shall I take this one?'

'Text me when you're home safely,' I say and watch as she waves from the back window until the cab is out of sight.

29

I plan to spend the rest of the night moping about Charlie and how stupid I was to think a man could actually like me for *me*, rather than what I can do for him, in front of the TV. But I've barely picked out a true-crime series that looks vaguely interesting – women who kill for money – when my phone starts vibrating.

It's Charlie.

I mean to ignore it – I *want* to ignore it – but either curiosity or that tiny flame of hope I've stupidly left unattended in my heart wins over and I answer. Well, I accept the call.

I wait for him to speak first.

'Kitty? Kitty, are you there? Hello?'

'Yes. I'm here. Hello. What do you want? My email address so you can send some high-res press shots to me? Or shall I just give you the number of my press officer?' I don't like the way my voice sounds, clipped and bitter.

'Please don't be like that,' he says. 'I'm really sorry. And I'm sorry I've upset you. I've been an unforgiveable dickhead.'

'You're not denying it then?'

'That I'm a dickhead? No, I clearly am.'

'You know what I mean.'

'I'm not denying it. I *did* think that you posting some stuff online would get some good PR for the charity. But it only came to me as I said it, I swear. I wasn't trying to groom you.'

I can almost hear him cringe at his choice of words.

'I had a really good time with you. And I've been kicking myself all day that I fucked it up. But much more that I'd upset you.' His voice lowers. He's almost whispering when he says, 'I mean it. I'm really sorry.'

He's Adam-ing me, I know he is. But I can't help myself. 'Okay,' I sigh. 'Apology accepted.' Why am I doing this to myself?

'Thank you.'

'I get a bit touchy about who I can trust and who I can't,' I say. 'I've been burned before.'

'I get that. I really do. I just opened my mouth before my brain was in gear. Have I ruined any chance of seeing you again? Because I'd like to. No catches. Promise.'

'You haven't ruined anything,' I say. 'In fact, what are you up to tomorrow night?'

'Hopefully spending the evening with the most adorable and sexy woman on the planet?'

'Correct answer. I'll text you the details later.'

'Okay. Well, I'll say goodnight now as I'm just in bed. Long day.'

The image of him in bed lodges itself in my mind.

'Sleep well,' I say.

Urgh. What am I doing?

30

I PLANT BELIEVE IT, W1D

As promised, I text Charlie the following morning the details of where and what time to meet me. It's an event I daftly promised the PR I'd go to because she had just started the job that week and was so ridiculously sweet that by the end of the call, I was promising her basically deliverance of not only myself, but the moon and stars too. Chloe. She'll go far.

Anyway, it's the opening of this new vegan restaurant that is totally my 'thing', according to the PR, in Soho. I was planning on bailing but I'm looking forward to it now. We'll get to sample various bits from the menu as well as bottomless vegan cocktails.

He's there before me and is breathtaking in a black T-shirt and jeans. He's sat at a table, nibbling the skin around his thumb, like the first night we met. I wonder briefly if chewing your own flesh is considered vegan friendly. His other hand is on the back of his neck, ruffling his hair as he looks around the vast dining area with wide eyes. He's nervous. How cute.

'Impressive, isn't it?' I startle him as I slip into the chair opposite.

A spark dances in his eyes when he sees me.

'Hey!'

He stands up, meaning I have to stand up again, and we do a funny little dance where he tries to kiss me on the cheek but I move my head the wrong way so he gets my ear instead. We laugh and I internally marvel at how adorably awkward we both are.

'Yeah,' he says, looking around. 'It's not what I was expecting at all. Not that I'm sure what I was expecting.'

This place has really gone big on the animal-slash-planet love theme. There are enormous murals with every animal that's ever existed staring out at you. It's weird. The bar, in the centre, is shaped like an ark and the tables are set on a blue floor, like we were cast out at sea.

A blonde waitress with huge tits comes over to us with two cocktails on a tray.

'This is our signature drink,' she tells us. 'It's gin and tonic with a touch of CBD oil. See what you think.'

She plonks the glasses down in front of us and saunters off again.

'Cannabis cocktail? Are your launches usually this bizarre?' Charlie asks as he eyes the drink. 'Did she really say this was drugged?'

'And what's with all the religious undertones?' I nod towards to the ark/bar.

'Yeah, it's not subtle, is it?' He goes to take a sip of his drink but suddenly lets out a pained squawk and buries his head in one of the menus. Which are shaped like giraffes, by the way.

'Too late, old boy, too late,' booms a voice from behind me. I swear I hear Charlie whisper 'fuck sake'.

He sits upright, putting the menu back down on the table, a tight smile on his lips. 'Harry. How are you?'

A man larger than Charlie with a shock of orange hair and the tell-tale braying laugh of someone with far too much privilege in life, claps a hand – with some force – on Charlie's back, knocking him slightly forward. With him is a minuscule brunette, whom I definitely recognise but can't place.

'I didn't think this launch party type thing was your scene, Charlton?' the stranger says, then appears to notice me for the first time. 'A-ha!' he says with a lascivious wink. 'Say no more.' He stands there, grinning and looking back and forth between me and Charlie. After a few uncomfortable beats of silence, he asks: 'Aren't you going to introduce me?'

Charlie rolls his eyes. 'Kitty, this is my brother Harrington. Harry, this is my friend, Kitty Collins.'

Harry's eyes grow as big as the side plates. '*The* Kitty Collins?' He's talking to Charlie more than me. 'Bit of a laugh you being in a meat-free place with your family history!' He brays like a donkey.

'Hi, I'm Kitty.' I hold my hand out to the malnourished brunette whom Harry is clearly in no rush to introduce.

'Bridget.' She places a limp hand in mine – tiny, like a child's hand, groomed enough but so weirdly small – and allows me to shake it. I try to smile, but she manages to avoid eye contact completely, keeping her sights firmly on Harry.

'Well,' Harry booms. 'Isn't this nice?' He clicks his fingers at the waitress, who, in all fairness to her, doesn't let her plastered-on smile waver even a micro-millimetre. 'Be a good girl and grab us two more chairs, doll. May as well park ourselves down with Charlton and his *friend*. Not often that I run into my little brother on a night out.'

He does another hee-haw of a laugh, while Charlie mouths 'sorry' at me.

As if he suddenly remembers I'm there, Harry turns to me. 'I follow you on Insta actually. Loved the recent bikini shots.'

'What are *you* doing here anyway?' Charlie changes the subject. 'You're not going to tell me you've given up the steak and burgers?'

'Nope.' He points at Bridget. 'Twiggy over there wanted to come. She quite fancies being an Insta-influencer, Kitty. Perhaps you could give her some tips?'

I look over at Bridget, who's still staring vacantly at Harry. Has he forgotten to charge her up before bringing her out? I smile, aspartame sweet.

'Sure. Is there anything in particular you'd like advice on, Bridget?'

Developing a personality perhaps?

Her smile matches mine. 'No, thank you.'

We sit in a bemused silence for a moment, which is only broken when the buxom waitress comes back, this time with an armful of samples from the taster menu. Harry can't take his eyes off her chest.

'Mushroom and artichoke soup, some mini samples of our Plant Believe It's Not Burger, Plant Believe It's Not Fish goujons with our No-Ta tartare sauce, No-Rat-atouille tart and our beetroot risotto. All of our dishes are created to give you the most exquisite plant-based taste.' She reels her script off with a dazzling smile as she sets a huge platter down on our table.

'I prefer something with a bit more meat on the bones,' Harry says, practically drooling over her boobs. I see the waitress, who, according to her name badge, is called Donna, prickle slightly under his glare. She hunches her shoulders, crossing her arms over her chest.

'Well, this *is* a vegan restaurant, sir, so . . .' Her smile wavers a little.

'I know that! I'm just having a little flirt with you, girlie. Now, be a doll and bring us some more of these wonderful cocktails. There's a good girl.'

Charlie stares open-mouthed at his brother.

When the drinks come, a painful twenty minutes later, it's a male server who delivers them. He isn't nearly as smiley as Donna.

31

UBER CAR, SOHO

'Well, that was pretty hideous,' Charlie whispers as we gratefully step into our Uber an hour later. 'Sorry about Harry. He comes across as a total dick, I know, but he means well.'

'Don't apologise!' I reach for his hand and give it a little squeeze, feeling tension crackle between us. Or it could be static. 'It was nice to meet him. I didn't even know you had a brother.'

Charlie groans, puts his hands over his face and slumps down low in his seat. 'This wasn't exactly how I was planning to introduce him.' He peeks at me through his fingers. 'Do you want to run a mile yet?'

I point at my ridiculously high Jimmy Choos. 'I don't think I *could*.'

'I usually make sure I'm at least ten dates in before I let anyone meet my family.' He takes my hand. That crackle again. 'Can you ever forgive me, Kitty Collins?'

'I should be asking if you can forgive *me* for taking you to possibly the weirdest restaurant in the whole of London,'

I say. 'I still can't get over that giant ark. Whoever came up with that idea should be . . . is there a ring of hell for appalling marketing?'

Charlie chuckles. 'What did you think of Bridget?' he asks.

'Sorry. Who?'

He throws his head back laughing. After a moment he looks at me.

'I wanted tonight to be special,' he says, bringing his finger up and gently stroking my cheek.

'It was certainly a night I won't be forgetting in a hurry.'

He groans again, dropping his head in faux shame. 'So how can I make it up to you?' There's an unmistakable glint in his eyes.

'I can think of a few ways.'

32

KITTY'S APARTMENT, CHELSEA

We arrive back at my building and I instantly feel the energy between us charge with sexual tension. We stand closer than necessary in the lift and I feel my heart galloping with that delicious anticipation as our bodies graze each other, our skin crackling whenever they touch.

As we walk into my apartment, I feel Charlie's hand on the small of my back and almost growl with desire.

'Nice digs,' he says, looking around.

'Yeah. It was a guilt gift from my mother before she fled to the South of France.'

'I mean, as guilt gifts go, it's pretty decent.'

'Hmm. Well, it's all relative, isn't it?'

'Are you close though?'

'No, not really. We speak at Christmas and birthdays, but I think she just wants to forget all the London stuff. She didn't have the greatest of times, even before Dad buggered off. The press were pretty hard on her.'

'Yeah, I have a vague-ish memory that they didn't like how quickly she moved on or something?' He runs his fingers over the dark blue panelled walls, with a look I can't work out.

'There were loads of rumours that she'd been having an affair and that Dad had a breakdown before . . .' I trail off. Charlie walks over to me, purposefully. He presses a firm finger to my lips, a gesture that would usually make me angry. There's a crackle of static again as his skin makes contact with mine.

'Let's not talk about the past.'

I nod.

The less said the better.

A beat passes. We don't break eye contact. My breaths are fast and shallow. That's when he kisses me for the first time. And I kiss him back, enjoying the feel of a warm body pressed up against mine, a body pulsing, overflowing with goodness and life, and I let myself melt into him. My hands in his hair, his thigh between my legs.

I want you.

When we finally break apart, Charlie puts his hands either side of my face and cocks his head at me.

'Anyway. Now that's out the way, I wondered if now is a good time to ask about posting some of the refugee art up on your Insta page?' He smiles and kisses me in between my eyebrows. 'Kidding. Right, am I making coffee?'

What? He actually wants *coffee*?

He follows me into the kitchen, where he looks around in confusion at the menagerie of gadgets that have been sent to me so I can lie about them on Instagram.

'Do you even know which one of these *makes* coffee?'

'Full disclosure?' I say. 'Not a clue. I usually order my drinks in. And yes, I'm fully aware of how spoiled I sound.'

He laughs. 'Well, what are men for if it's not fiddling around with gadgets and tech?'

He does that knuckle-crack thing which is the universal sign that he means business and then busies himself opening cupboards and adding water and sliding little pod-things into hidden drawers on one of the kitchen-contraption things.

While it gurgles and steams at an alarming volume, Charlie checks out the rest of the stuff. 'You've got quite an armoury for someone who doesn't eat meat,' he says, picking up a meat cleaver and turning it over in his hands.

'Ever tried to open a coconut with a spoon?'

He laughs. 'That is something I have never considered. Although I did do it once with an ancient samurai sword in Thailand.'

'Sure, Jan.'

'I did! I swear.'

When our coffees are poured, we move into the living area. Charlie perches on the edge of one of the sofas.

His manners make me smile.

'You're allowed to make yourself comfortable, I won't tell you off.'

He immediately looks relieved and sinks back into the expensive comfort of the cushions.

'Old habits really do die hard,' he says, taking a sip of his drink. 'Furniture was to be admired, not used when I was a kid.'

'Well, you're all grown up now,' I say, sitting at the other end of the two-seater – Lola, Darlings of Chelsea, in Blue Lagoon – tucking my feet under me. 'And my furniture is all definitely here to be used.' I lean over and put my mug down on the coffee table. He does the same. Mirroring. It's a flirting thing.

I feel that jolt of pleasure again.

He likes me.

'So. Is this furniture being used by anyone else at the moment?' he asks.

'Just you and me.'

'No other men in your life?'

I think about Tinder. The bodies. The crunch of metal against bone as they go through the grinders. 'No other men.'

He's staring at me again, his pupils black and ravenous. He leans forward and his lips are on mine again. His kiss is deeper this time, one hand cradling my face, the other gently pushing the small of my back into him.

I want you.

And I know this is it. I move towards him, my hands on each side of his face. Then his hands are on my hips as he lifts me onto his lap. He pulls me in closer so I'm straddling him, before sliding a hand underneath my Missoni top and pulling it over my head. My fingers are trembling as I begin to unbutton his shirt but the feeling when we're actually skin to skin is so incredible. And we shed our clothes, bit by bit, kissing and biting the newest part of exposed flesh, until we're there. Naked. And he pulls me down, making me gasp as I sink onto him and dig my nails into his back. And we fuck right there on my sofa.

Charlie ends up staying the night and we have sex three more times before he leaves around lunchtime the next day.

'One of the perks of being the boss,' he says as he kisses me goodbye.

'Ooh, The Boss. I like that.'

'I'll call you later. I've got plans for you.'

'Yes, Boss.'

I stretch out in the bed, luxuriating in post-coital bliss, when my phone beeps. It's Hen reminding us she's booked a table at Zuma for lunch. I'd forgotten we'd all planned to meet today and am tempted to cancel.

Although I'm excited that I'll get to tell them about Charlie and all the sex I'm having for once.

33

'But there must be something wrong with him?' Maisie's sipping on iced water, attempting to stay as sober as possible for her date with Rupert later.

'Not one that I've discovered so far,' I say. 'Can we stop coming here by the way? If I have to eat another bloody edamame pod I think I'll die.'

Hen does the thing with her eyes where she rolls them so far back into head that all you can see are the whites and she looks possessed.

'There must be something.' Her eyes are back in place now but narrow.

'I just told you, edamame pods.'

'You know what I mean, Kitty.'

'It's still early days,' I say. 'We're still on our best behaviour around each other.'

'I bet you haven't even had a poo at his place yet.'

Tor and Maisie laugh.

'Is that the bar now?' Tor says. 'Whether you've had a shit

at his place? Stop it, girl, you're going to give me pre-age wrinkles.'

'But *have* you?' Hen's determined.

'Why is it with anyone else, you all want to know the sex details but with me, you want to know if I've pooped at his? What is *wrong* with you all?'

They're laughing now.

Hen actually has a point that isn't one I'm happy to confess to these women. Lifelong friends or not, women are piranhas when they smell blood.

'We've been seeing each other for about five minutes and I've not actually been to his yet,' I say. Quietly into my wine. 'Now can I just tell you about the sex?'

Hen's brows move at least an inch up her head, which, considering her dedication to keeping the Botox trade in roaring business, is impressive in itself.

'Excuse me?' She picks up an empty Champagne flute from the table and points it in my direction. 'Could you repeat what you told the table just then, Miss Collins? You've not been to his?' She says it like she's in *Line of Duty* or something.

'No,' I confess, mostly to my glass again. 'But it's not that big a deal, my place is here, it's amazing, all my things are there. My people are here. We can walk home from most places. Which is romantic,' I say as Maisie pulls a face. 'And there are four separate loos in my apartment for those of you so concerned about pooing. Plus, it's still super early days. We've only been on like three dates.'

'But why wouldn't he want you at his?' Hen's found her bone and she won't drop it without a fight. 'You know all that Englishman crap is his castle stuff. Why's he keeping his drawbridges oh-so-tightly up?'

'Maybe he's got flatmates. Urgh.' Maisie shudders and I give her bare ankle a quick kick under the table.

'Ow. Bitch.'

'*We* used to be flatmates. Was I "urgh" too?'

She laughs. 'No! You were the best. I mean apart from the knife obsession, which is a bit weird for a 'vegan pacifist'. But we were like kids or something. It was party central and none of us had jobs then.'

'None of us have jobs now,' Tor muses.

'Who lives with roommates in their thirties? Unless they're like super poor. I know he turned his back on all that money from his dad. Is he really poor? He doesn't look like a hobo. And he always smells good.'

'Wow. Thanks for your very concise summary, Maisie. He doesn't have roommates though.' Well, none he's mentioned. I suddenly have images of half-naked Zooey Deschanel and Megan Fox in *New Girl* fighting for space in the bathroom in my head. 'I'm pretty sure he hasn't got flatmates.'

'I bet he has terrible interior design and is all embarrassed because your place is all swishy,' Maisie says.

'Oh Jesus,' Tor gasps. 'Imagine if you walk in and he's got one of those New York skyline prints on the wall.' She shudders and knocks the rest of her drink back in one. 'I think I'd rather see a MAGA poster.'

'He could be a killer,' Hen says. 'Imagine that. Your own personal Joe Goldberg. And you *have* got a stalker. Maybe it's Charlie. Maybe he's creepy Dan Humphrey from *Gossip Girl*.'

'Hen!' Maisie is outraged again.

'It's not the craziest theory,' Hen says. 'I mean he's basically the Mary Poppins of boyfriends but you've not seen his home.'

'He hasn't invited me yet. As I *keep* saying, it's early days. And you're all idiots. Please let me talk about the sex now.'

'No. Not until you've been to his and checked the Dyson for bits of bone. Ligament. You know what you're looking for, Queen of Abattoirs.'

'It *is* a bit weird he's not even invited me,' I say, spearing some vegan sushi.

'It's been a while since you've been in a long-term relationship, Kits. And we all know how much Adam hurt you and your daddy issues blah blah. But trust me, you really should've boned at his place by now.'

Hmm. Yet again, Hen may have a valid point. Time for a plan.

34

'So, this is intriguing.'

'The Overground? Surely you've been on a train before?' Charlie gives me a sideways look and a half smile.

'Maybe once when I was a child. Is it *always* this hot and clammy? Anyway, I was talking about where you're whisking me off to. I'm assuming there's more to it than just making me live out childish nightmares of public transport.'

Charlie laughs and pulls me into him.

'Come here, Princess.'

We're standing because, even though I agreed to go on a train, I absolutely draw the line at sitting on one of the threadbare seats that probably have faecal matter like compounded in. It smells gross too, sort of like stale cigarettes and body odour. But it's okay because every time the train jolts forward – which is a lot – we bump into each other, which isn't the worst, and I get a lovely waft of whatever fragrance my very hot date is wearing. We've stumbled into each other so many times that Charlie is now half steadying me with his hand on my lower back and I've buried my nose into his T-shirt. Which, also, is not the worst.

The train pulls into Vauxhall and Charlie grabs my hand.

'Come on, my lady, this is our stop.'

Vauxhall? Really?

'You really take me to all the nicest places.'

We walk along for a bit and I'm glad Charlie at least gave me a heads-up to wear something comfortable on this date. I'm wearing my Prada trainers with black faux leather leggings by Karl Lagerfeld – which are a tiny bit sticky in the heat but as David Bowie said, 'Ooh, *fashion!*' – and a cute Missoni vest top. Charlie's looking super sexy in dark jeans, which I think are Tom Ford, and a slouchy khaki T-shirt. He's caught the sun and the light tan shade to his skin suits him. I mean *really* suits him. He catches me looking at him and winks.

'Are you checking me out, Kitty Collins?'

'Maybe. A bit.'

'Do I pass?'

'You'll do. I suppose.'

He laughs. 'Better than a flat no. But can I say that you look incredible?'

'You can.'

'You look incredible.'

'These old things?'

We share a smile and I like the way we are with each other. Teasing but flirting at the same time.

I like it.

I like who I am when I'm with this man.

35

RANDOM AXE OF KINDNESS, VAUXHALL

We walk a bit further, not speaking or blurting out ridiculous and annoying anecdotes to fill the void. Instead, we're catching each other's gaze every few steps and sharing that smile again, like we have a secret. It's incredibly sexy. Eventually we stop outside what looks like a sort of boarded-up warehouse.

It's incredibly *un*sexy.

'You've brought me to a factory,' I say. 'Not only have you made me go on public transport, you've now brought me to a factory. What's the date? Am I going to be stuffing giblets into chickens or something?'

Charlie laughs and ruffles my hair, which would usually be at least a maiming offence but I like the frisson I feel when he touches me.

'You are so cynical.' He presses a buzzer and a girl in her early twenties, with one side of her head shaved and a digital clipboard thing dangling precariously in her left hand, opens the door.

'Hi, guys,' she says with an I'm-brutally-hungover-but-

I-need-this-job lilt to her voice, which I like. I'm always immediately distrustful of people who are too fucking jolly when they're at actual jobs. There's something just not normal about it.

Maybe I *am* cynical.

'Have you booked?'

'Yep,' Charlie says. 'Two in the name of Chambers.'

Clipboard girl frowns at her clipboard for a couple of seconds.

'Great, there you are. Right follow me upstairs and we'll sort out your axes.'

I raise an eyebrow at Charlie. He reaches over and pinches my cheek as we head up some steps after Clipboard's bum.

'You look adorable when you're confused.'

'Dare I ask why we need axes? I'm guessing this isn't a Michelin tasting venue?'

'Axe throwing.' He wiggles his eyebrows at me. 'What d'ya reckon? Loser buys dinner?'

The stairs lead us to a huge room, which is divided into long sort of booth things. Each booth has what looks like a dartboard at the end of it. There's an umbrella stand full of sharpened axes at the entrance to the booth. Clipboard lifts one out and brandishes it at us.

'So obviously, these are extremely dangerous,' she says. 'I know you're not idiots but I do need you to both sign a waiver just in case there's an accident. Or it turns out you're an axe murderer or something.'

I laugh.

Clipboard and Charlie stare at me.

'It was a good pun. Axe-ident? It was funny.'

Charlie does a little laugh, but Clipboard is still staring at me. I guess health and safety isn't something to be joked about here. Or maybe she's heard the same thing a gazillion times.

'So, have either of you ever done anything like this before?'

I want to laugh again.

'No. Kitty?'

I shake my head, not trusting myself to open my mouth.

Clipboard gives us a short chat about getting a spin on the axe being key and to not stand behind someone if they're waving an axe around in the air. I wonder if there's a story behind her having to point this very obvious thing out. She makes us sign something on the clipboard, which I realise is actually an iPad, and then saunters off. But not without giving Charlie's arse a good ogle as he bends down to pick an axe out of the stand. Not that I can blame her. I give her a wink and she scurries off.

'So, this is an odd choice for a pacifist,' I say to Charlie, who's weighing up two axes.

'Yeah. I'm still a man though. Got to find an outlet for all my hunter-gatherer instincts somewhere.'

'Throwing axes at an oversized dartboard is definitely the solution you've been looking for.'

'Indeed. Well, ladies first. Are you ready?'

'You go first. I want to see what I need to beat.'

Charlie flexes his arms, takes a big backwards stride and swings the axe at the target. It spins a couple of times before falling limply on the ground.

'Hmm. I really thought I'd be a natural at this.'

'Based on what exactly?'

'Man. Man use axe to kill food for woman.'

I laugh as I pick up an axe.

'It's all in the posture,' Charlie says.

'Well, I am not taking advice from someone who can't even hit the target, am I now?'

'Fair. At least be careful of your nails though. If there's an emergency nail bar visit on the cards, you're on your own.'

I roll my eyes at him and get ready to take my swing. It spins through the air like a shuriken, straight into the centre of the target. I turn to look at Charlie next to me. His jaw is on the floor.

'Still want that bet?'

A man from the adjacent booth is watching through the chicken wire wall. He does a sharp intake of breath and shakes his head at Charlie.

'Out of your depth there, mate,' he says.

I can almost see Charlie's male bravado scuttle away. Maybe I've played this wrong. Is he angry? I feel my anxiety prickle the base of my neck as I wait for him to react. What the fuck is that about?

Charlie shrugs and laughs. 'Well, at least I know someone's got my back on the mean streets of London. I'm glad I'm on her side.' He turns to me. 'So, what's that about? Do you slay vampires in your spare time or something?'

'Abattoir Princess,' I remind him. 'Not my first rodeo with an axe.'

'Ahh. Of course. I didn't realise you still, er, kept a hand in?'

'I don't. I suppose axe throwing is just one of those things.

You've either got it or you haven't.' I give my hair a pretend toss. 'The secret's in the wrist.'

'That' – Charlie ushers me to the side and goes to collect our axes – 'is something you can show me later.' He pauses, mid-stride, staring at the target. 'Less aggressively though.'

The rest of the evening is pleasant enough, but we both decide after about an hour and a half that throwing an axe at a target has a certain time limit on how entertaining it can be.

'What do you want to do now?' Charlie asks as Clipboard marches us down the stairs and ushers us into the London night. 'Food somewhere?'

'How about we just go back to yours?' I say. 'We're closer here anyway. And I want to check out your crib.'

He pulls a face. 'Really?'

I nod as I slip my arm through his. 'Really. I mean, Jesus, what are you hiding in there?'

'Urgh. Fine.' He looks at me, brushes a stray hair out of my face. 'You're lucky you're so hard to say no to.'

'Speaking of hard.' I run my hand down his torso, letting it linger at the top of his jeans before sliding it inside them.

Charlie smiles as he tries to pull up the Uber app on his phone. He gives up after a couple of seconds of my stroking him.

'Whoever said men cannot multitask was absolutely fucking right.' He drops his phone into his pocket, before turning to me, grabbing my hair and pulling me in for a kiss. But this is a different side to Charlie. The axe throwing and alfresco hand job have clearly stirred something in his animal brain. The kiss is almost aggressive in its need. His teeth grip my lips as he pushes me up against the wall. With his left hand, he pins my arms behind my back and his right hand slips into my leggings, then into my underwear. 'You're so wet already.' He bites my earlobe as he whispers to me, before continuing the assault on my mouth. He pulls away for a split second, looking into my eyes. His pupils are so huge his eyes look completely black. 'Is this okay?' I nod, wriggle my hands free and pull him closer to me, hooking one leg around his waist to give him better access. 'Fuck, I love feeling how turned on you are for me.'

Within minutes, I reach a shuddering climax and feel myself clench around his fingers, leaving them drenched in my appreciation. I pull his hand out of my trousers and hungrily lick myself from him, not dropping eye contact.

'Hmm,' he says. 'It really *is* all in the wrist.'

'You wait.'

'I can't. You're a bad girl, Kitty Collins.'

'Just order a bloody car already.'

36

CHARLIE'S FLAT, CLAPHAM JUNCTION

'I really don't know why you've been so funny about me coming round,' I say later, as we're lying naked in Charlie's bed, the very last of the light sneaking in through the Venetian blinds covering the big Victorian bay window. 'It's lovely here. Perfect.'

'It's rented. Mostly cold. There's a definite damp issue and I'm pretty sure I share it with a family of mice.'

'You say all of those things like they're bad. Rented? Jesus Christ, my apartment is paid for from blood money. Literally. Cold? If you hadn't noticed we're in the middle of a quite impressive heatwave. Damp? Everywhere has damp. And as for the mice? I think they're cute.' I reach across to his cheek and turn his face to mine. 'You were really embarrassed? Why?'

'I want you to be impressed by me.'

I sit up. 'Charlie. I *am* impressed by you. I don't give a fuck where you live. I'm impressed with you. *You.*' I reach for his hand. 'You're funny, kind, compassionate, sexy as fuck. And as for this guy,' I put his fingers in my mouth and gently suck them, one by one, 'we definitely need to spend more time getting acquainted.'

He looks at me. 'Really?'

'Yes. Really.'

'Comparing myself to some of your exes is an interesting experience.' He frowns. 'Not a nice one.'

'Absolutely do *not* do that. For a start most of what you've read online is utter bullshit. And secondly, you are a hundred times, a thousand times the man any of them could ever be.'

He still looks sulky.

'Look at you. Can you imagine Ben or any of his ilk walking away from daddy's money? Setting up on their own? And doing something to actually help other people? I thought women were supposed to be neurotic and jealous.'

'So, just let me get this straight, you really don't care that I basically live like a student?'

'No. And I'm horrified that you thought I'd judge you like that.' I fake pout.

'Looks like I've got some making up to do then.' He leans over and kisses my lips. 'You really have a beautiful mouth. I mean, your face is obviously gorgeous, but your lips. I need to kiss them.' He kisses them. 'And taste them.' He gently suckles on my lower lip. 'And bite them.' His hands urgently reach round my back and he pulls me closer to him, his teeth nipping my mouth. 'And fuck them.'

I mean, he's already miles ahead of Rupert.

37

I'm on a Charlie-high for the next few days and am delighted that I can tell Hen and everyone that I've now been to Charlie's place. And it's not a drug den, portal to an evil dimension or brothel.

'Not even some mysterious stains that could be blood? Or a dodgy-looking shed with an industrial lock?' Hen's WhatsApp seems disappointed.

'Nope. Not even a murder cage. He's just normal.'

'Oh.'

She may be disappointed, but I am very much not. Not until he tells me that he has to go away for a work thing for a couple of nights. We've basically spent every night together for the past week and a half, so it's not a bad idea to get some space, but a loud thumping starts in my head. This is what happens when I get attached to people. This is why I haven't had a relationship since Adam. And this is why, an hour or so after Charlie leaves for his trip, I find myself scrolling through my phone again. Agitated. I know I'm going to end up driving myself crazy, convincing myself that he's secretly fucking Jenna or someone. I need a distraction, so I open Tinder.

I know who I'm looking for this time. A personal trainer called Niall King. Like Daniel Rose, I spotted him in a news report a couple of days ago. He'd been let off by the judge after following a woman home and attacking her. Fortunately, she managed to escape but the next one – and there's always a next one – might not be so lucky.

According to the report, they'd met on Tinder but she didn't want to see him again after their first date. Obviously, this was too much for his fragile ego and he decided that stalking her would convince her to change her mind. I blame Hollywood for this. There's still some notion that continually trying to win over a woman who has quite clearly expressed having no interest in you is romantic.

The judge didn't feel it was necessary to send Niall to prison, despite admitting he 'posed a threat to women'. Instead, he was ordered to attend a behavioural programme and do two hundred hours of community service.

A fucking behavioural programme.

Well, if the law isn't going to get this man off the streets, then I certainly will.

It's time for me to get creative and make myself another new Tinder profile. This time I pick a photo from Google of a doe-eyed blonde, whom I call Kelly. Kelly is recently separated from her partner, whom she has three little kids with, and is looking for someone understanding and patient to help rebuild her life.

As usual, it doesn't take long for Niall to bite. He slides

into Kelly's DMs like a rat up a drain. At least sociopathic sex offenders are predictable.

Niall – it turns out – isn't one for 'long, drawn-out chats' on the app messenger. He much prefers meeting in person.

Kelly replies: 'I'd love to meet you in person. The trouble is though, I find it hard to get out for an evening because of the kids. They're pretty good sleepers though. So maybe you could come to mine for a drink? I'm not doing anything tonight.'

Niall can hardly believe his luck. 'That would be great. But only if you're sure? I don't want you to be worried about putting yourself in danger.'

I grit my teeth as Kelly replies, 'Lol that's so sweet, but I trust you.' Then she gives him my address and tells him to come over around 8pm.

I prepare for a kill in much the same way I'd prep for a date. I always make sure I've been waxed and threaded and often have a professional blow-dry beforehand. I like to look good while I'm telling them exactly what I'll be doing to them for the next few hours.

My make-up is minimal, a teeny bit of foundation and some mascara. As I watch the clock tick its way around to 8pm – Kelly's 'kids' are sound asleep by then – I feel the delicious pounding in my chest, knowing it's almost time.

Niall doesn't disappoint, and I hear a knock on my door at exactly eight o'clock. I smooth my skirt down, hide the syringe up my sleeve and get ready for the show.

'Oh,' Niall says, clocking that I'm not Kelly when I open the door. 'I'm looking for Kelly?'

'You must be Niall? Kelly's told me all about you.' I give

him a flash of my Insta-famous smile. 'She's in here, I said I'd stay for a few minutes just to check you're not a serial killer.'

We both laugh.

I stand aside to let Niall walk into the apartment and he gives a low whistle just as I plunge the syringe into his neck. He falls – like the sack of shit he is – to the floor. I can't help but give his overpumped torso a quick kick while he's down there.

I didn't really think things through however and when it comes to moving the piece of steroid-infused shit, I get myself quite puffed out and sweaty as I try to drag him to the kitchen where I've laid out my tools, and lined the floor with pages from *Vogue*.

In fact, I can barely shift him at all.

It quickly becomes obvious that I'm going to have to do him right here in the hallway. I glance around at the newly painted walls and grimace as I realise I've got a lot of work to do to get the place kill-ready. And with about two hours before Roid Rage wakes up, I'd better get cracking. It's a tiresome task moving all the magazine pages from the kitchen into the hallway and I am really loath to use the duct tape on the solid oak floors.

The walls are an issue too. Ideally, I'd like them free from blood spatter if possible. Blood spatter is definitely not hashtag stunning décor. I gingerly use tape to stick the pages over the walls, cursing myself for not foreseeing the potential problems of moving an eighteen-stone man.

I'm finally done when I hear some movement from Niall on the floor, where he's lying duct-taped at the wrists and ankles. And mouth, of course.

I'm looking forward to this one.

As I head into the kitchen where my freshly sharpened Shun knife is sitting, waiting to slice its way through some rotten flesh, I hear a knock at the door.

What?

I grab the knife, shove it up my sleeve before heading back to the door.

Shit.

It's Charlie.

With flowers.

I glance back at the hallway – the walls and floor looking like an explosion in a newsagent and there's a semi-conscious body builder coming out of a GHB coma in the middle of it all.

It would be quite tricky to explain this.

Maybe I can pretend to be out.

Charlie knocks the door again. 'Kits? It's Charlie. Open the door. Rehan told me you're in.'

Damn you, Rehan.

I tentatively open the door an inch and peek out.

This is extremely inconvenient.

'I know I should've called first, but I wanted to come over and talk to you about the James stuff. So, can I come in?' He raises one eyebrow half a millimetre, barely detectable but enough to make the gesture suggestive.

'Um. It's not a great time right now if I'm honest.'

He looks crestfallen yet still devastatingly fuckable. He tries to peer through the door. 'It looks like you've got at least half an issue of *Elle* on your walls. What are you up to in there?'

'It's *Vogue*. And I'm getting ready for some decorating. Next week.'

Charlie looks puzzled. 'But you've covered up the walls?'

Niall chooses this moment to make a grunt from the corner. He's almost fully awake now and is battling with his bonds, clearly unimpressed with the piece of tape over his mouth.

'What was that?' Charlie asks, craning his neck to see into the apartment. 'Are you okay?'

'Hen's here,' I say, giving Niall a warning kick to the groin. 'We're trying out a new waxing technique. It's pretty painful.'

Charlie pulls an uncomfortable face. 'Okay, girl time. I get it.'

I'm not sure he's convinced.

'Maybe we can catch up tomorrow?' he asks.

'We can definitely do that.' I give him a lame wave.

He walks a few steps away from me before he turns back. 'It's funny. But I'm sure Hen's Instagram said she was away with Grut tonight. I must've got it wrong.' He turns and heads towards the lift, without a glance back.

I close the door and sink back against it.

Fucking social media.

I have to deal with the Charlie stuff later though as, at the moment, Niall needs my undivided attention. He's fully with it now and is staring at me with that mix of fear and bewilderment I've grown to love so much.

'That was my boyfriend,' I tell the man mountain. 'He's a good man. There really aren't that many of them about. And now, thanks to you,' I give him another kick in the groin at this point, 'he probably thinks I'm fucking someone else.'

I straddle Niall and get my knife out before I rip the duct tape from his face. It's pretty industrial stuff and he gets a mini facial wax at the same time.

'Fucking ow,' he hisses and I hold the knife right against his Adam's apple.

'Did that hurt? Only speak when you're spoken to from now on, or I swear, I will cut your voice box right out of your throat. Understand?'

Niall nods weakly.

'So, you're probably wondering what's going on here, aren't you? You're probably wondering how you went from meeting a lovely little single mummy online to being drugged and held hostage by me.'

He nods again and that fear in his eyes is really starting to turn me on.

'I think you probably know what's going on, deep down, Niall. Have a little search of your soul and tell me what you think.'

He frowns and deep lines appear across his forehead. He's either spent too much time in the sun, or he's lied about his age online.

'I don't know what's going on here apart from the fact you're obviously batshit crazy,' he says. 'Where's Kelly? Who the fuck are you?'

I rap my knuckles on his head.

'You really are a meathead, aren't you? There is no Kelly, you sweaty fucking sociopath. I made her up! She was a ruse to get you here so I can hurt you and kill you. Now, have a think about why a woman who doesn't know you might want to do that.'

I can almost see the switch click in his head. 'Are you related to one of them bitches that's tried to stitch me up or something? Which one put you up to this? They're all fucking liars!'

'All five women, who have absolutely no links whatsoever to each other, all made up shockingly similar stories about how you violently beat them, did they?'

He nods.

'Stop with all the nodding before I cut your spinal cord. Answer me. You're saying they all made it up?'

'They were pissed off when I finished things with them and reported me over something and nothing. That Beth one was a psycho. *She* attacked *me*. Like I told the police, she came at me with a wooden spoon. It was self-defence, what I did to her.'

I pull up the news report on my phone.

'It says here that you broke her nose in two places, fractured her jaw and tore her right rotator cuff so badly her shoulder came out of its socket. She couldn't hold her baby daughter for six weeks. And you're claiming self-defence? You're about three times the size of that woman.'

He's silent. He knows he's fucked.

'And what's the single mum thing all about? Why do you always go for women with kids? Get some extra kick out of having an audience?'

'They're easier. Most of them are so desperate to have a man in their life they'll put up with anything.'

That's more like it. I run the tip of the knife slowly down the side of Niall's face. It glides through his skin as if it were butter, leaving a rivulet of crimson trickling from his cheek.

'Just tell me this, Niall, do you enjoy hurting women? You

can be honest. It's not like you're getting out of here alive either way,' I say.

'You're all fucking mental. I'd happily fuck you up if I had the chance.'

I lean in closer, the sharp smell of his sweat almost makes me heave, but that delicious look in his eyes that doesn't match his fearless words spurs me on. I press my hips into his.

'Tell me what you'd do to me.'

A second passes before he answers.

'I'd start by grabbing your hair and smashing your head into one of your marble tables. That'd stun you, maybe even knock you out. Then I'd just fucking kick the fuck out of you, you mental bitch.'

That does it for me. I plunge my knife deep into his neck, twisting it around as it goes in. The edges are serrated so I know this will make the experience that bit more painful. Niall gurgles and gargles as his blood gushes from the wound in his neck and starts to collect in little red pools on the magazine pages on the floor. I forgot that *Vogue* isn't actually very absorbent. The pages are so glossy that the blood just sits on top of them. I really must use something a little less coated next time.

I stay straddling Niall as the life ebbs out of him. Sometimes I wonder what it would be like to tell the victims of these men what I've done. I wonder how they'd react. Would they thank me? As I gently pull Niall's eyelids down over his eyes, I remember how many future Kellys and Beths I've just saved from this brute.

I'm going to enjoy watching him go through the grinders.

*

The next morning, which happens to be Sunday, meaning I can use the slaughterhouses during the day, I take my bags containing the carefully wrapped packages of Niall's remains down to my car. I'm just opening the boot when I feel a tap on my shoulder.

'Could we possibly have a word, miss?'

I spin round and feel my heart almost leap through my throat when I come face to face with a two uniformed police officers.

'It won't take a moment.'

I smile sweetly even though I can feel my cheeks trembling slightly and my heart feels like it's trying to break out of my ribcage.

'Of course, officer. How can I help you?'

The first officer – middle-aged, crinkly eyes, beardy – looks at his colleague before giving me an embarrassed smile.

'You're that Instagram girl, aren't you? Kitty Collins?'

'That's me.'

He looks back at his colleague – a tall brunette with an insanely pretty face – and gives her a curt nod.

'Told you.' He turns back to me. 'My girls are big fans of yours.' He pats himself down before taking a phone out of his pocket. He quickly swipes a few times before turning the screen to me and revealing a picture of two young teenage girls, with big smiles and blonde curls.

'They're pretty,' I say.

'I know this is a bit awkward, and feel free to say no, but

is there any chance I could get a selfie with you? They'd go nuts.'

My heart is banging like a drum in my chest and he wants a fucking *selfie*?

'Of course. No problem at all.'

We stand there on the street, him trying to get the best shot of us, while the dissected remains of a man sit patiently at our feet, hidden in designer shopping bags.

'Thanks so much,' he says when he's satisfied he's got a photo that will thrill his teenage daughters sufficiently. He nods at the bags on the street. 'Off shopping?'

'Just doing some returns.' I smile, all charm, as I reach down for them.

'Oh, allow me.' And he picks up my bags and loads them in the boot. 'Well, you have a nice day now. And thanks again.'

Then, along with his colleague, he heads off into London, totally unaware he's just helped me load a chopped-up stiff into my car.

I stand, blinking after them for a moment.

38

COLLINS' CUTS SLAUGHTERHOUSE, HAMPSHIRE

I get a text from Charlie around mid-morning asking me if he can come over to talk. I'm halfway through putting the remains of Niall through the grinder when my phone beeps and I manage to smear blood over the screen as I tap out a reply.

'Sure, I'll be home after lunch xx'

'See you then.'

No kisses.

I know this isn't a good sign and I'm going to have to come up with something convincing to explain what was going on last night.

Charlie arrives at around 2pm and he doesn't return my smile when I open the door.

This is worse than I thought.

'Do you want a drink?' I ask, leading him through to the kitchen. 'I've got some vegan sushi that I was just about to have if you want to share . . . ?'

He sits down at the kitchen island and shakes his head.

The silence between us ripples with tension. I can tell it's not the good kind either.

I sit opposite him and steel myself for what's coming next.

'This is about last night, isn't it?'

He nods. 'I'm not an idiot, Kitty. It was quite obvious you had a man here.'

I open my mouth to say something but he cuts me off.

'I know we've not said anything about being exclusive, but it made me feel jealous. I hated it. And I hated that you lied. Although I shouldn't have dropped over unannounced.'

'It's not what you think . . .' I start, cringing at the cliché.

'It doesn't matter,' he sighs. 'What matters is that it drove me mad, thinking about you here with another man. About what you were doing in here.'

An image of Niall's head lolling lifelessly to one side with a knife sticking out of his neck pops into my mind and I almost laugh.

'Anyway,' Charlie continues, 'I guess what I'm trying to say is that I'm not ready for this. I like you, Kitty, a lot. But I'm just not at a point where I can risk myself getting hurt. And you obviously aren't ready to be involved with someone seriously. I'm sorry, but I don't think I can see you again. I just wanted to speak to you face to face. Not be a dick about it.'

I don't know what to say. What does one say while getting dumped?

'It really wasn't what you think,' I try.

'So, tell me then?'

I shake my head. 'I can't.'

'If I'm with someone, I'm all in,' he says. 'I don't do half measures or open relationships or anything like that.'

I nod.

Charlie leans in and kisses me on the cheek. 'Be happy, Kits.'

And then he's gone.

Ten minutes later, my phone beeps and I look to see that I've got a message on Insta.

'Boo hoo for you. At least this one escaped with his life.'

The Creep. With the excellent timing only an internet stalker can pull off. I try to ignore the rising fear that someone, somewhere seems to know every move I make.

I spend the rest of the day in bed, with a bottle of wine.

39

KITTY'S APARTMENT, CHELSEA

I feel like I can't breathe at the moment. The apartment is making me feel claustrophobic and everywhere I look there seem to be reminders of what I could've had with Charlie. And with the stalker on top of everything else, I feel like my nervous system has taken a huge battering. I'm suffocating here.

'You need to get away,' I say out loud, which freaks me out even more. Since when have I become the kind of weirdo who talks to herself?

I WhatsApp Tor, determined that a few days by the sea with an infinity pool, butler service and a swim-up bar is exactly what's needed.

'Few days in Mykonos?' she suggests.

'JFC YES!' I reply.

I book flights for the next morning.

40

Sipping the first glass of Champagne on the plane, I can feel myself relax, like sinking into a warm bath. Plus, Champagne always tastes better when you're flying first class to a luxury destination.

'Come on, spill,' Tor says once the extraordinarily handsome flight attendant has done his thing and the seatbelt light goes off.

'What do you mean?'

'You're seriously trying to tell me that you've booked a spontaneous holiday for no reason? I know you, Kitty, I can tell there's something wrong. Is it Charlie?'

I nod, dumb with a sudden overwhelming feeling of sadness. 'He's ended it.' My voice wobbles and I take a gulp of Champagne, hoping to swallow my grief along with it.

'Why? I thought you guys were solid? It seemed to be going so well.'

'He thinks I cheated on him. He came round to the

apartment while I had another man there and I wouldn't let him in, but it's not what he thinks.' Not that I could explain.

Tor is staring at me wide-eyed. 'So, what were you doing if you weren't cheating?'

I sigh. 'It's personal, but I wasn't cheating. Surely that should be enough? Why wouldn't he trust me?'

She eyes me suspiciously. 'Well, it *does* sound quite dodgy. Especially if you wouldn't let him in.' She puts her hand on mine. 'Look, I believe you and I've known you long enough to know that you're not a cheat and you don't lie. But this thing with Charlie is still new. Maybe some space between you for a few days is for the best?'

I nod, feeling like part of my heart has been scooped out, and rest my head on Tor's shoulder, while she strokes my hair.

'It'll be okay, honey,' she tells me. 'I promise.'

I feel better the moment we step off the plane and the heat envelopes us. It's a different heat to the oppressive humidity of London. I feel like I can actually breathe here. Tor puts her arm through mine and squeezes me tight as our driver takes our bags and ushers us into a waiting car with the best air-con I've ever known.

41

CAVOO RESORT AND VILLAS, MYKONOS

The hotel I book for us is decadent, which is exactly what I need. As well as the personal butler, our suite has a private pool that bleeds into the Aegean. Nothing but pure blue until our eyes hurt from looking. There's a huge magnum of Champagne on ice waiting for us and we giggle like schoolgirls as we drink from the bottle and explore the place that will be our home for the next few days. We change immediately into our bikinis and sink into the cool blue haven of our pool. I'm delighted I chose the Platinum Villa. It's beautiful and so very far away from Chelsea. Exactly what I need.

'Feeling better yet?' Tor asks me, handing me a glass of Chablis fresh from the minibar. We look out to sea in silence for a few moments. I watch an aeroplane split the sky in two with its white tail.

'I had another message from The Creep as well,' I say, breaking the silence. 'I just don't know what he wants from me.'

'Are you going to go to the police now?' Tor asks. 'What did he say this time?'

'That's the thing, he didn't say anything. It was just a photo from the Pemberton party.'

Tor looks stunned. 'What like long lens or something?'

I shake my head. 'No. From inside the party.'

She digests this for a moment. 'But it was only people we know.'

I nod grimly.

'Fuck.' She puts her glass down on the side of the pool. Serious. 'Do you think it could be staff maybe? There were plenty of bartenders. Maybe they think they can make some extra money?'

I frown. 'That's the thing though. Whoever it is hasn't asked me for any money. He's not asked me for anything. It's weird.'

Tor picks up her glass again. 'Well, let's try not to think about it for the next few days. You need to relax. Your chakras are all over the place, babe.'

I smile and clink my glass against hers. 'Yes, here's to forgetting and relaxing.'

Our butler brings our evening meal to our suite at 7pm but the vegan memo obviously didn't get as far as the kitchen. The trolley he wheels in is stuffed with seafood – giant prawns with spidery-legs and eyes that look like tiny black beads, amputated crab and lobster limbs, miniature octopus corpses. It was an ocean massacre on a bed of ice shavings. I snap a quick shot of the gore with my phone and post it to Insta.

'Death in Paradise: Veganism has yet to reach the Greek isles #MurderInMykynos #SaveOurSeas #Vegan #SoNotVegan'

Tor laughs at my horrified face and starts singing 'Like a Vegan', her hilarious version of the Madonna classic. She begins to tuck into the aquatic graveyard while I attempt to call reception and explain my predicament. Eventually the butler arrives again, apologising profusely in Greek and delivering some salad, olives, feta (for goodness sake), bread and oil. I've got so used to the UK having vegan menus pretty much everywhere now that I'm quite disappointed. I feel my mood begin to dip again and pour myself some wine to put the brakes on it.

'I wish I didn't love eating animals so much,' Tor says as she rips the head off a prawn before pulling its legs and shell off. 'You're a much better person than me, caring about life so much. Plus it keeps you skinny as fuck.'

The various eating disorders of our friendship group are unspoken not-very-secret secrets. Tor and I both know that in about twenty minutes, she will excuse herself and go to the bathroom where she'll use the end of her toothbrush to make herself puke all this into the loo. I've even known her to purposely drink tap water abroad to make herself throw up more. Then there's Hen who is very much a signed-up member of the Coke Diet Break, which is kind of like the Diet Coke Break but with Class As. She claims that nothing in the world suppresses the appetite like some good old coke of cane. Shame it also suppresses emotional stability and the ability not to be a total grumpy bitch. Maisie pays through the nose – no actual pun intended here – to have a private doctor come and give her an injection every two weeks, which apparently makes her not want to eat. Which is wonderful and everything, apart from the fact the side effects include the smelliest, eggiest belches I've ever had the misfortune to be around, and spontaneous projectile vomiting. But over the years I've seen them try everything from eating food with baby cutlery to surviving on nothing apart from meat and cream.

'I'm not a vegan for vanity, Tor,' I tell her for the gazillionth time. 'I've seen what happens to animals when they're killed for food. It's not the sort of thing that makes you crave a juicy burger after a night out, trust me.'

'Yeah, but this stuff isn't cute little baa-baa sheep.' She's drunk already. 'Like who even cares if I do this?' She rips the head off another shrimp.

'Tor, stop it now. Please.'

She pouts at me, a little girl reprimanded. 'I'm sorry. Anyway, what do you want to do tonight? Shall we go out for a drink? Or shall we get an in-room spa treatment?'

'I quite like the idea of a massage and a movie?' I say as I throw a tablecloth over the seafood festival of the dead and wheel it outside to be collected. By the time I get back in, Tor has disappeared into the en suite of her room and I'm sure I can hear faint gagging sounds.

Half an hour later, we're lying facedown on some massage beds that have magically appeared from some cupboard in the suite. Two beautiful Greek women are rubbing oils into us. It's bliss and I can feel every bit of the stalker, Charlie and the police being kneaded out of me. Tor has fallen asleep and her mouth is hanging half open as she snores gently. I'm overcome with a surge of affection for her. No matter what other shit is going on in my life, I know I can count on her, Hen and Maisie. They're my constants. The family I was able to choose.

The next morning, the kitchen more than makes up for the previous night's horror show with a fresh fruit platter that arrives along with ground coffee, an array of milk substitutes and a selection of breads.

Tor is almost as happy as me. 'This is amazing,' she says, as she dollops butter and cheese on her bread. 'I can't believe we slept in so late,' she adds between mouthfuls. 'I think I'm jet-lagged.'

'You know there's only a two-hour time difference, right?'

She laughs and shrugs my words off. 'If I'm saying I'm jet-lagged, I'm jet-lagged, okay?'

'Okay.'

We munch away in the kind of silence you can comfortably have only with someone you've known for years.

'What shall we do today?' Tor asks after her third coffee. 'Do you actually want to do tourist stuff or just chill?'

'I'm happy just to chill,' I say. 'I mean it doesn't really get much better than this, does it?'

We both stare at the view, the floating beds that look out over that gorgeous sea, the hazy horizon that could very well be the edge of the world.

'Great spot for some Insta shots too,' Tor says.

We spend the day lolling around on the pool beds, swimming, tanning and draining the minibar. At lunchtime the butler wheels in an array of cold cuts of meat, which makes Tor squeal, hummus, dolmades, salads that are greener and redder than I can ever remember British produce being, a gorgeous rice pilaf, and handmade Greek pitta breads with a fava bean spread. We wash it down with a pomegranate sangria, which is possibly the most delicious thing I've ever tasted in my life.

After our feast we lounge around a bit more and I end up falling asleep in the way you only can when you're on holiday, sun and liquor soaked, relaxed and somehow exhausted despite doing nothing but lying around. I slip in and out of consciousness before falling into a deep and dreamless sleep, the sound of the sea my lullaby.

When I wake up, I'm disorientated and shivering slightly as the sun has begun its golden descent into the horizon. My head is fuzzy from the wine and sangria. I sit up, discombobulated and look around. Tor isn't snoozing on the other pool bed as I expect her to be, so I stumble inside.

'Tor? Tor?' I call out, but the suite is eerily silent.

My phone is lying on my bed where I left it charging. I register an intense stab of disappointment when I see there's nothing from Charlie.

There's a stream of texts from Tor though, who informs me that she's gone out to some bars and that trying to wake me was like waking the dead. She tells me the name of where she is and assures me she's with some girls she met at the hotel bar while I was conked out.

'Come out and play!' she pleads, but I see her messages were sent over two hours ago and she probably gets the hint that I'm not up for a night out.

'Just woken up!' I reply. 'Going to have a swim and go to

bed. Sorry am boring. So exhausted. I want all the goss in the morning okay xxx'

She replies a few minutes later with a sad face emoji and then a selfie with two gorgeous girls she's obviously befriended while I was asleep. I smile to myself. Tor has none of the inner angst that I do. It exhausts me because I have to put on an act all the time, while it comes naturally to her. I send her a line of kisses and tell her that I'll see her in the morning. I then swim lengths of the private pool until my arm muscles simply can't do any more. I shower, pick some nuts from the minibar and fall asleep to an Eighties romcom that I can't remember the name of but has Sarah Jessica Parker in it.

I'm not sure how long I'm asleep for. I'm woken up by an animal-like noise coming from the living area of the suite. My heart pounding, I remember I didn't close the bifold doors before going to bed. I grab the only things that I can possibly use as weapons – a stiletto and a can of hairspray – and gingerly tiptoe into the lounge. But there's no wild animal there, just Tor looking like I've never seen her before. Her make-up is smeared all over her face, her clothes are dirty, her hair is a total mess and she only appears to have one shoe. She's lying facedown on the white sofa, her body convulsing with howls. That's the noise I thought was an animal. All I can do is stare in horror for a few moments before I tentatively walk over to her. I can only assume she's had too much to drink and has had some kind of falling-out with the girls she was with. But I'm baffled as Tor wouldn't act like this. She'd come striding in like Beyoncé circa *Lemonade* and make me sit up doing shots with her until whatever it is didn't matter anymore. As

I put my hand on her arm, she jumps up violently, recoiling deep into the corner of the sofa and staring at me like *I'm* the wild animal. A second or so of confusion crosses Tor's face before she recognises me and her expression changes from fear to . . . something I've never seen on Tor's face before . . . utter brokenness.

'Kitty.' She holds her arms out to me like a toddler.

I go to her, wrapping her in my arms, stroking her hair, letting her sob into my shoulder.

'What's happened?' I glance at the digi-speaker-clock thing. It's 5.30am. The sun is beginning to wake up, casting a golden glow throughout the room.

She doesn't answer for a few moments, just sobs silently in my arms.

'Tor what is it? Has someone hurt you?'

She nods.

'I'll get you a drink.' I head to the minibar and pour two glasses of brandy. Tor swallows hers down in one, then wipes her eyes and takes a deep breath.

'We went out on a yacht,' she tells me. 'The girls I was with had met some lads a few days ago and they said we should all go out on their boat. It was called *Liberty*. It started off fine. We were all drinking and there was coke. But then I started to feel really, really out of it.' She pauses and I hand her my glass of brandy, which she sips more slowly this time. 'You know me, Kits, it's not like I can't handle my drink and drugs, but I was out of it. I could barely even stand at one point. One of the guys, I can't remember his name, seemed nice, trying to help me. He took me down to one of the berths in the boat so

I could lie down. But then he started kissing me. I tried to push him off and tell him I had a boyfriend, but nothing worked. I couldn't speak, I couldn't move. I had to just lie there while he . . . he . . .' She downs the brandy. 'Could I have another one please, babe? I think I'm still in shock.' Her hands are trembling as she hands me her glass.

'Sure.' I head back over to the bar. 'So he raped you. That's what this is?'

She nods as I hand her the drink. 'But that's not all.'

I brace myself for whatever is coming next.

'I must've passed out completely because the next thing I remember is waking up and one of the other men, I think his name was Archie, was in bed with me, touching me. I was too scared to say anything so I pretended I was still unconscious while he had sex with me too.' She breaks down at this point, collapsing in my arms. I don't know any words that can make this better for her, so we sit there as the sun fully rises, me stroking her hair until she cries all the tears she can.

'I need to go to the police,' she eventually says, all the warnings we've heard about not washing away evidence, the internal swabs and exams that feel like being violated again ingrained in her, like for all women. 'While there's still evidence.'

But I stare at her in horror, a news story from a few years ago suddenly popping into my mind. It was a similar situation on another Greek island. But when the woman reported the rape, she was arrested and jailed. It took months for her family to eventually get her home. She'd been accused of lying. Protected from being identified by media law. But not social media. Tor couldn't cope. She's too private. She says being a Black woman living in Chelsea is bad enough.

'Tor, I don't think going to the police is the best idea. This isn't like England. Women aren't treated brilliantly here.' I look up the story on my phone and show her. She crumbles even more.

'So what am I going to do? They can't get away with this! They're probably doing this to different women every night.'

'They won't get away with this. I promise you.'

I spend the day taking care of Tor as her moods swing between desolate and furious and everything in between. I wash her hair for her in the giant bathtub in the main bathroom, wrap her in fluffy robes and towels, order her favourites from room service and pour her wine. Later, we're sat out on the terrace, taking in the last of the sun's rays.

'I always thought I'd fight back, you know,' she says, looking out to sea. 'I didn't think I'd be one of those women who just accept it.'

'You were drugged,' I remind her.

'But not the second time. I just lay there. I was so scared. All these terrible thoughts were going through my head, like he could kill me and throw me out to sea.'

'How did you get away?'

'The boat never actually left the dock. When Archie—' She chokes on his name. 'When he'd finished, I got dressed and made a run for it. They were shouting things after me.' She wipes a tear away.

'What happened to the other girls?'

'I have no idea. They didn't seem to be on the boat when I left.' She looks at me. 'I'm scared to go to sleep tonight.'

'Wait there.'

I come back out a few minutes later with two tiny white pills and a glass of water. Tor looks at me.

'It's okay, it's just some Valium. It'll help you sleep. And I'll be right here.'

She swallows the tablets and heads into her room. I lie next to her, holding her tight, until she starts to gently snore. That's my cue.

An hour later, I'm dressed in a short red sundress and a pair of espadrille wedges. My hair is beach-curly and, thanks to my fresh tan, the only make-up I'm wearing is mascara. I love how getting ready on holiday is just so much easier. Before I leave, through the terrace, not the main foyer, I peek in at Tor, who is still sound asleep. I grab my bag, plus the ice pick from the bar, and head off into the Greek night.

42

MYKONOS PORT, MYKONOS

I march the fifteen-minute walk to the harbour, my heart setting the pace. *Lib-er-ty. Lib-er-ty. Lib-er-ty*, it says in time to my steps. It's dark as I make my way through the town centre, but I don't feel like I even need the cover. Plenty of people see me but there's nothing that makes me stand out. I'm just another woman, in a beach dress, like hundreds of others. I must remember to tell Tor to take down her Insta posts from the island though. The fewer people who know we were here, the better.

I get to the marina super-quickly. It's brightly lit, which makes it easy to see the names on the sides of the boats. It's actually quite a sight, little sailing boats snuggled up next to giant yachts and every single size inbetween. I've always loved sailing. We had a yacht when I was younger and those idyllic days just bobbing along on the water, under the sun, are some of my happiest memories. It's probably nostalgia or false memory syndrome, but I can't remember my parents arguing when we were on the boat. The housekeeper would make us a delicious hamper of food – or pick one up from Fortnum – and we'd sit on the deck eating and chatting. My mother seemed to come alive with the sea breeze blowing her hair, she looked happy, free. I don't know what happened to the yacht. I guess it went with her to Côte d'Azur.

Forcing the thoughts from my head, I refocus. I'm not here to sigh at the pretty boats and get all sentimental about a memory I've probably made up. I quicken my pace and, after about five minutes, I finally see the word 'Liberty' on the side of one of the midsized yachts. I can just about make out three figures on the deck. A bass beat is throbbing so loudly, the mooring shakes. I check the time on my phone, it's not late. This is their pre-game session. I inhale deeply, the smell of seawater helping to put out the little fire of anxiety that's been flickering in my belly since I left the hotel. I want to do this, *have* to do this, but three men is a lot. I have no idea how this is going to play out.

I step up to the prow and shout over the music. 'Are you having a party up there?'

The music is turned down and someone – a man – peers over the edge at me. My skin prickles as he assesses me, weighing up whether I'm worth inviting aboard or not. I pass the test. He smiles, reminding me of a wolf in a picture book I had as a kid.

Grotesque.

'We certainly are. Would you like to join us, beautiful?'

I fake hesitancy. 'I'm not sure. I'm trying to find my friends. They'll be worried.'

'Come on. You can ping them your location from here and

210

get them to come along too. The more the merrier.' I chew on my lip, pretending to mull it over. 'Come up and have one drink at least while you call them. It's not safe for you to be wandering about on your own in the dark.'

'Okay, that's sweet of you.' I smile up at him like I'm the most grateful ever.

'Wait there, I'll come and get you.'

Two minutes later he emerges from the boat. He's tall, easily over six feet. Muscled. Black hair, dark eyes and dark skin. He's wearing a pink polo shirt (Ralph Lauren) and a pair of ecru chino shorts. There are white Birkenstocks on his feet. He lollops lazily over to me and holds out a huge hand.

'Theo,' he says, accent unmistakably London.

'I'm Kitty,' I reply, shaking his hand.

'You coming aboard then?'

I nod and he leads me up the gangway onto the boat.

43

We climb an awkward spiral staircase of about three steps before we're on the main deck. Two other men are sitting on the white leather seats, drinking Champagne. There's a table in front of them with a bottle of Veuve chilling in an ice bucket and a few lines of what I assume is coke chopped up.

'This is Kitty,' Theo says, introducing me. 'This is Archie. And Freddie.'

If Theo is a wolf, then Archie is a spider. A venomous monster, waiting for something to land in his trap.

'Welcome to my humble abode, Kitty, would you like a drink?' He holds out a glass of Champagne to me.

'Thank you.' I take the glass, obviously with zero intention of drinking it.

Archie has slightly thinning red hair, a face full of freckles, a Rolex and is wearing a navy Ralph Lauren polo and cream chinos. Freddie is ridiculously handsome, dark hair (lots of it on his head, arms and poking out of his green Ralph Lauren polo), eyes so blue they are almost navy. I smile at them. Friendly, friendly.

'Chin-chin then,' says Freddie, raising his glass.

I pretend to take a sip of my drink.

'Is this your boat?' I ask Archie. 'It's lovely.'

'Yeah, just bought it with this year's bonus.' Ah. A City boy. 'Do you want me to show you around?'

'Yes, please!' I might need to dial the enthusiasm down a bit. I sound like a kids' TV presenter.

'Then step this way, little lady.' Archie stands up and grabs his glass. He checks that I'm still holding mine.

I follow him, like a good girl, first across to the little cabin where the boat's controllers are.

'This is the captain's quarters. If you're lucky I'll take you out for a spin later.' He laughs. He's not unattractive, but the privilege is dripping from him, twisting him into something ugly. 'Now this way.' He leads me down the little staircase again and we're below deck. There's a living area, with white leather seats that look like they've never been used.

'There's a hot tub up on the deck,' he gushes. 'And look at this.' He leads me over to a bar area and puts his drink down so he can show me how the mini fridge-freezer can dispense ice. 'Cool, right?'

While he's fiddling around with the fridge, I switch my glass with his, dropping a pill of my own into his. This is a special one, for later. He doesn't even notice that his drink has miraculously refilled itself while he was playing with his toy and takes a long gulp.

'Now for the best bit.' He puts his hand on my lower

back and steers me towards the stern. Where the bedrooms are. There are two of them, equally luxurious, with walnut interiors, en suites and huge beds. I feel him peering at me. 'Let me know if you need a lie-down or anything. In case that goes to your head.' He nods at my glass before glugging down the rest of his.

'I will.'

'Drink up then!' His eyes are on me as I down about half the drink.

Archie leads me back up on deck and Theo is immediately on me.

'Got a line ready for you, babe,' he says, handing me a rolled-up banknote like it's the Eighties.

'No, thank you. I don't do drugs. Sorry. Boring, I know. My friends will though.'

'Another drink?' Freddie offers.

'I'm fine, honestly,' I say.

'Have you pinged your friends, doll?' Theo says. 'Not much of a party, is it?' He's getting frustrated. I'm clearly not as much fun as he was anticipating.

'Oh, yes,' I say, taking my phone out of my bag and pretending to text.

Meanwhile Archie is starting to look a little worse for wear. He's sweating, his face shiny with the effort to not fall down.

'You all right, Arch?' Freddie asks.

'I'm actually not feeling too great.' Archie's wheezing now. 'I might go and have a lie-down.' He tries to move to the stairs, but stumbles, clutching at air. Freddie leaps up to help him.

'Fuck sake. How much have you had to drink?'

'Probably sunstroke.' Theo laughs. 'Skin that white can't cope.' He looks at me to check that I'm laughing along with him. 'Sweet dreams, buddy.'

As Freddie leads Archie below deck, Theo moves in closer to me.

'So, what is it you do, doll?'

The ice pick is deep in his neck before he finishes his sentence.

'I kill people,' I say, as I pull the pick out and watch him slide to the floor, blood pooling around him like an oil slick.

'He's out cold down there.' I hear Freddie's footsteps as he comes up the stairs, laughing. He sees Theo bleeding out on the deck and me holding the ice pick.

There's a beautiful moment where our eyes meet and he's momentarily frozen in horror before he turns to flee. It's enough time for me to get some ground on him. I catch him as he reaches the last step, and ram the pick into his back, flooring him. As I pull it back out, he swivels around to face me.

'Why the fuck?'

'Yeah, I wondered that. You should've jumped overboard. Much better chance of escaping.'

'Why did you stab me, you mad bitch?' His voice is little more than a husky growl now. He's in terrific pain. Good.

'You fucking know why. You don't get to drug and gang-rape my friend and continue with your little holiday, you obnoxious prick.' This time I jab the ice pick right in his jugular and watch him gurgle and clutch at his neck.

Two down.

I'm going to need to clean those stairs off before I accidentally slip on Freddie's blood and make myself the third.

I step off the boat, untether it and get back on and head to
the helm to switch the engine on. It's been a long time since
I've piloted a boat, but it turns out it's like riding a bike. Not
literally, obviously.

44

I steer the boat away from the island for about half an hour before I turn the engine off and let her drift. It's really hard work getting massive Theo over the side in one piece. I'm annoyed that I'm not strong enough and have to snap his femurs and humerus bones, before using a broken Veuve bottle to cut through the muscles and stuff.

I reward myself with a glass of Champagne.

It's equally painful pulling Freddie up the spiral stairs and tipping him over too, but luckily he wasn't as stacked as Theo and I'm able to get him over the side in one piece.

It's the blood that proves to be the real problem and, typically for men, there is a distinct lack of cleaning products onboard. There's some bleach, which I pour over the most stubborn of the stains before scrubbing them but the lovely walnut decking is wrecked. Shame.

And now for number three.

I have a little rummage around in the kitchen Archie so proudly showed me and find what I'm looking for. A perfectly sharp, serrated knife. It's actually a Sabatier, which gives me a little thrill.

Down in the berth, Archie is just coming round. He's dazed and confused and seems to think he's in recovery from an operation. Not yet, buddy. Not yet.

His eye catches mine as I head over to where he's lying, prone, on the bed.

'Nurse?' he says, his voice still thick from the drugs. 'I'm really not feeling great. Is there a doctor?'

'I *am* a doctor, Archie.' I smile, and sit on the bed. He smiles back, relieved.

I kneel low down by his ankles, his feet in between my thighs. He tries to lift his head up properly, but his neck control is all over the place.

'What's that? All over you? It looks like blood.'

'It *is* blood.' His Adam's apple pulses.

'Are you hurt?'

'No, no. I'm fine.' I smile at him. 'I had to do some operations.'

He's not looking quite so relieved now. 'This is a boat. This is my boat.'

I nod, encouragingly. 'Yes, I've taken us out for a little trip.'

'Where are Theo and Freddie?'

I shake my head. 'No. It's just the two of us. Isn't that nice?'

Archie, ever ungrateful, clearly doesn't think this is nice at all and starts to scream.

'Shhh, shhh,' I soothe him. 'We're miles out. No one will hear.'

I then shift myself further up his body and begin to undo

his chinos. As expected, the little blue pill I dropped in his drink earlier has done its job and his penis springs from his pants. He stares at it like he can't quite believe it himself.

'What are you doing?' he asks. Nervous, but intrigued. Does he *seriously* think that even in this condition, I'd want to fuck him?

'I'm going to give you the blow job of your life, Archie,' I say. 'And before you come I'm going to hop on that beautiful dick so I can feel you fully inside me when you do.'

His eyes look like they're filling with tears.

'Of course, I'm not. I'm going to saw your cock off at the base. Then I'm going to watch as you bleed to death from your crotch. And then I'm throwing both you and your rapey dick into the sea. Okay?'

And then I take the knife from behind my back and start hacking away at the base of his penis.

It's lucky we're so far out to sea because the screams he makes are real ear-bleeders. I usually enjoy the noises men make while they're being hacked to pieces, but this is pathetic. I tell him to shut up. He tries to fight me off but he's still weak from the Ket, not to mention half his cock is hanging off.

'I suppose you want to know what this is about, don't you?'

'Please stop. Please.'

'Hmm. I think that's what my best friend said to you last night. You didn't stop, did you? So I don't think I will either.'

There's a lot of blood, it really all heads down there when they're hard.

It doesn't take long to saw it off completely. Archie is sobbing like a baby as I hold it close to his face.

'Theo,' he tries to shout.

'They won't hear you, darl. We've sadly had a couple of man-overboard incidents.'

'Please, please don't kill me,' he pleads. 'I'll change. I promise. I'll give money to rape charities. I'll give money to your friend. I'll go to the police.' He looks desperately at his cock, which I'm still dangling in front of him. 'Can you put that on ice or something?'

'Sorry, no.'

Instead, I throw the severed penis next to him on the bed and go back up on the main deck to enjoy the view. I have a couple more glasses of Champagne from a bottle *I* opened and look up at the sky. It's totes a cliché but you really don't appreciate how beautiful all the stars and other space shit is in London. And it really *does* make you feel small and insignificant. Well, it's made Theo, Freddie and Archie insignificant anyway.

I go and check on the patient after about half an hour and he's got that dead sheen/dead eyes thing going on. Not much effort at all really was old Archie. It *is* an effort however to wrap his body up in the blood-soaked sheets and drag it up on deck. Then I hurl Archie into the sea, followed by his penis. I quickly go below deck one last time, to wipe the finger marks from the glasses, etc. I catch a glimpse of myself in one of the full-length mirrors. Luckily, my dress is dark red (see, I plan ahead), but there is blood all over my arms and legs. Annoyingly, I take a quick shower, which I then have to clean too. I grab one of Archie's pink blazers from his wardrobe to throw over the dress.

Then I go back to the wheel and use the navigation app on my phone to return the boat to the harbour, where I tie it up and head to the hotel.

When I'm in my room, I change out of my bloody clothes, shoving them in a bag at the back of the wardrobe, and slide into bed next to Tor.

Then I fall asleep.

The next day, Tor tells me that she wants to fly home as soon as possible.

'I can't stay here. I'm terrified that I'm going to run into *them* if we go anywhere. And I just want my bed. And my mum.'

Obviously, I'm pretty keen to get out of here too. 'Of course,' I say, handing her a chamomile tea and two Valiums.

I spend the next few hours trying to sort us a flight – while Tor packs with a listless energy – and finally manage to get two seats in economy that afternoon. Tor asks for another Valium and sleeps for almost the entire flight home. I look out the window at the Aegean wondering how long it will be before the bodies wash up somewhere. It takes my mind off the lack of space and stench of body odour.

Back in the UK, I drive Tor to one of Sylvie's sprawling mansions in Surrey. Tor's clearly told her most of what's happened and I was fully expecting a showdown with her about letting Tor go off alone. But she doesn't. Instead she wraps us both in hugs. 'My poor babies,' she says. 'Do you want to stay, Kitty? We've loads of room. You're more than welcome.'

I thank her but say no. 'I think Tor needs her mum, for a bit.'

Tor wraps her arms tightly round me and whispers 'thank you' into my neck.

By the time I get back to my apartment, I feel like I have PTSD. I neck a couple of Vallies myself and crawl into bed, exhausted. So much for the relaxing break I'd planned.

It's only when I'm in that beautiful halfway house between asleep and awake that I remember the bloodied clothes in the back of the wardrobe in Mykonos.

Fuck.

But I'm too Vallied right now to care.

45

APPLE NEWS

Police concerns grow for three missing British men on holiday in Mykonos

Concern is growing for three men missing on the Greek island of Mykonos. The men, whose names have not yet been released but are believed to be from London, were due to return from their trip to the popular island earlier this week but have failed to contact their respective families.

It's believed the trio were staying on a yacht belonging to one of the party. The boat has remained docked at the island's main port, with no sign of the men. Witnesses have said the men were familiar faces on the destination's party scene but claim they haven't been seen in any bars or clubs since last week.

Anyone with any information is urged to contact Mykonos police on +30 7732459.

46

Fuckfuckfuckfuckfuckfuckfuckfuckfuck.

It's online now that three men have gone missing from Mykonos and I left a bag covered in a mixture of all our blood in the back of a wardrobe.

I feel like I'm losing the plot.

I can't stop pacing and panicking and pacing some more.

Every time my phone pings I'm certain it's the police. It's been a week since we left the hotel and the suite would certainly have been cleaned by now. I can't stop picturing one of the lovely maids coming across the bag of gore and screaming. They'd have certainly handed it in to the police and that sundress has my DNA, plus the blood of the three missing, no, *dead* men all over it. I can't concentrate on anything. Charlie has called me about ten times, but I can't even bring myself to listen to his voicemails. What's he going to think of me when he discovers the truth? I mean, *I* know that every single man I've killed has deserved it, but I've still murdered people. A *lot* of people. I can't breathe. And I can't wait. I decide to call the hotel.

'Chairete, Cavoo Resort,' the receptionist answers.

I feel my heart freeze. 'Um . . . oh, hello? Do you speak English?'

'Ah English yes, yes. How may I help you today?'

'I was a guest at the hotel about a week and a half ago and I think I may have left something in the room.'

'Ah okay, one moment. I put you through to housekeeping.'

There's an excruciating wait as I'm put on hold, forced to listen to some tinny Greek folk music.

'Hello, this is housekeeping number. How may I help you today?'

'Oh hi, I was a guest a week or so ago and I think I left something in my room?'

'Okay. No problem. You tell me which room?'

'Er, it was a Platinum Villa. Azure, I think.'

'Okay. Azure. You stay there I will look in book. Thank you.'

And I'm back on hold, listening to the ear-bleeding music again. I feel like I'm waiting for ten years before the phone is picked up again.

'Hello miss? There is nothing here from Azure suite. Sorry. Have a good day now.'

'Wait, are you sure? Nothing that might have been given to, I don't know, the police or something?'

There's a laugh from the other end. 'Why we give anything to police? Your room clear. Sorry. What you loss is not here. Good bye.'

'Thank you,' I mumble but the line is already dead. I'm beyond confused. My phone pings and the Instagram app tells me that I've got a DM. I sigh and open it.

'What happens in Mykonos stays in Mykonos. Or does it?'

The Creep is back. This is exactly the opposite of what I need right now. I grab three Vallies, knock them back with a neat shot of vodka – I'm still working with Greek measures – and head back to bed.

An almost continuous ringing eventually brings me out of my drug coma. I don't know what time it is, but it's dark. It takes me a few moments to realise the ringing is coming from my door buzzer. Police? Wouldn't they just let themselves in or get one of the concierges to? I stumble blindly to the door and see Tor standing outside. Or a version of her. She's in flat shoes, jogging bottoms and a cap.

'Kitty. Open this door now.'

Urgh. I rub my eyes and open the door. Tor storms in, switches on lights, heads to the bar, pours two glasses of expensive Sauvignon Blanc and parks herself at the kitchen island before she even speaks to me.

'Sit,' she orders.

Not really understanding what is going on, I pull out one of the bar-stools (Danetti, lime green faux leather) opposite her and sit down. I take a sip of wine and Tor slams a bag on the island between us. It's a plastic bag from one of the gift shops in Mykonos.

'Go on,' she says. 'Open it.'

I don't need to open it to know what's inside. But I go along with her anyway. Tor is clearly not in a mood to be messed with. I unwrap the bag and pull out a red sundress and pink blazer covered in dried blood. Tor is eyeballing me like a psychopath. But I could still kiss her.

'What the fuck?' she says. 'And don't bullshit me, girl. I *know* you.'

There's silence while I weigh up whether to tell her the truth. But before I can speak Tor is scrolling through her phone and starts reading a news report out to me, the one about the three missing men.

'Tell me that *this*' – she gestures at the dress – 'has fuck all to do with *this*.' She waves the phone in the air. 'No bullshit, Kitty.'

And so, I take a deep breath.

And I tell her everything.

47

That's what I let her think anyway. Of course I didn't tell her *everything*.

'I had a miscarriage,' I say, stunned at how easily the lie comes out as we sit in the late afternoon sun. 'I didn't want to tell anyone because I hadn't even told Charlie and didn't know what to do about it. It's partly why I wanted to get away. To think. He thought I was cheating on him, I was going to tell you. But then you were attacked and this happened that night after . . . and I couldn't say anything then. Not after what you'd been through. I didn't know what else to do, so I just shoved the clothes I was wearing into the wardrobe.' I've managed to make myself cry, probably because I'm such an awful person. Who lies to their best friend about something like this?

I suspect a monster.

'Kitty, you should've told me.'

'You'd been raped, Tor. It was hardly the time to make it about me.'

'So you went through it all alone. Don't ever do that again.'

228

'Sorry,' I mumble. And I am. For letting her believe something that wasn't true.

'Are you okay? Now, I mean. How do you feel?'

I sigh. 'I'm okay. Please don't tell any of the others though. I don't want it getting back to Charlie and him feeling like he *has* to talk to me. It was obviously not meant to be. I don't want to dwell on it. It's gone.'

Tor keeps staring at me and tops up my wine. 'I wish you'd told me.'

'I wasn't even very far gone. It can't have been more than four weeks or so.'

She looks at me for a long time. I can't figure out the expression on her face. Eventually she slides nearer to where I'm sat and puts her arms around me.

'Oh, Kits,' she says. 'I'm so sorry. What a horrible thing for you to go through.' She kisses my head and pulls me close again. 'Worst holiday ever.'

We light the little fire pit I have there for chilly nights. It's anything but chilly at the moment, the weather still not having broken while we were away, but we drop the dress and blazer into it and watch them burn.

'Lucky we're not New Look girls,' Tor says. 'Or they would've gone off like a polyester firework.'

I smile and she hugs me. But then a look of something flickers across her face so quickly, I can't work out what it is. She stares at me for a long moment as the smoke blows out into the London afternoon.

'Thank you,' she whispers, so quietly I could have imagined it.

As full(ish) disclosure seems to be where we're at, I should probably take this moment to confess something. The drunk bar creep wasn't the first man I've killed. I've always known that there was something dark inside of me, but for the most part I'd been able to push it deep down, like when you try to get the jack-in-the-box back in the box when you're a kid. I first noticed it the night I caught my father with Hen's mother. Even though I didn't totally understand what was going on, I knew it was bad.

It was a few years after that when I first saw my father hit my mum. He'd come home from work in a disgusting mood and immediately locked himself away with a bottle of whisky.

'Stay out of your father's way today,' she warned me. 'He's having a hard time at the moment.'

'What's going on?' I asked, thirteen and thinking I was basically a grown-up.

My mother smiled at me and tapped me on the nose. 'Nothing for you to worry your beautiful and clever head about, my darling. Now, why don't you go and do your homework so you don't have to spend all weekend doing it. If you get it finished maybe we can do something fun together at the weekend. Just us.'

I loved the idea, hugged her and raced up to my room, determined to work my way through the horrible maths assignments we'd been given.

At 5pm one of the housekeepers brought a tray up to my room with my supper on it.

'Your parents have asked that you stay up here, doll. They're having a grown-up discussion. I'm off home now so mind you do what they've asked.' She gave me a sad look and squeezed my shoulder gently. I think her name was Moira, but I can't really remember. I recall her eyes though, big, brown and sad. And I wondered what had happened in her life to cause such sadness. I had no idea at the time that it was me.

I ate my supper and battled on with my homework but I was distracted by noises from downstairs. Raised voices. The sound of something smashing. A bang. A scream. Even though I'd learned not to sneak around spying on people, the scream scared me. I raced down the stairs to the main living room. My mother was cowering in a corner.

'Please, Robert, it's not my fault.'

They hadn't seen me so had no idea that I saw my father draw back his right hand, curl it into a fist and slam it into my mother's face. Again and again and again. These weren't even slaps, which still couldn't be forgiven, but full-scale punches, the kind I'd seen on TV shows I wasn't supposed to watch but did anyway. My mother's face began to look like a bruised piece of fruit, but one eye was still open enough to catch me staring, horrified. I could sense the fear in that look and without words, she told me to go.

Go or he'll come after you too.

48

THE PHENE, CHELSEA

Sunday roast at The Phene has been one of our traditions since we've been legally old enough to drink alcohol. We used to think we were proper adults then. I think back to being eighteen. I'd not met Adam yet. The press interest in my missing father had all but disappeared. I was a lot calmer inside back then. Not always. I remember Hen having to stop me from heading to the offices of a particular loathsome lad's mag, armed with an axe I'd stolen from one of the meat houses. Their crime? They'd put a countdown ticker on their equally disgusting website.

The first was bad enough: 'XX days until you can legally give meat heiress your meat'.

The second one made me see red: 'XX days until you can legally get meat heiress so smashed, she'll be begging for your meat'.

'It's basically encouraging men to get me pissed and *rape me*,' I remember screaming at Hen, who was the only person brave enough to come near me while I was brandishing an axe.

'Kits, it's just a website, darling,' my mother said, attempting to soothe me. 'We'll put in a complaint and make them take it down.'

'It's not just a fucking website though, is it?' I was seething. 'And it's not just me. It's this fucking disgusting culture that is telling men that it's okay to get girls drunk so they will have sex with them.'

I raged and ranted and swung the axe around so much that my mother gave me two pills from her special stash. When I finally calmed down, she and Hen sat with me.

'I'm already so tired of it,' I'd said. 'It's disgusting.'

Hen smoothed my hair, while my mother made a very angry phone call to the mag's head office.

'And tell them I would *never* be drunk enough to fuck one of their knucklehead readers anyway!' I'd yelled.

I had to start seeing my therapist three times a week after that and 'Kitty and the Axe' became part of our lore. I never forgot though.

But we're adults now. And we're more than capable of seeing something bad online, and controlling our tempers.

Except this time.

'You have got to be fucking kidding me.' Tor is looking at her phone. 'What the actual fuck?' She turns to me first, eyes already half full of tears.

'What's the matter?'

She thrusts the phone at me. Twitter.

I look at her phone. It's a screenshot of a message from

233

a footballer called Raphael Reynolds. He's young, good-looking, world at his feet plus other football puns. And also, a massive fucking dick, by the look of things.

'If you don't reply I will come to your house myself and rape you. Hahahahaha.'

'Is this for real?'

I stare at the message in shock, look at Tor, who nods. I pass the phone to Hen. She does the same and gives it to Maisie, until all four of us have seen the screenshots.

'Wow,' Maisie finally says. 'Care to share the backstory to this?'

'I don't know much more than this,' Tor says. But she hands the phone back to me and I swipe through several more screenshots. There are about five in total showing him threatening and slagging off a girl who'd clearly turned him down.

'And they're for real? Been verified?' Hen asks.

A heavy, world-weary sigh from Tor. 'According to Emily (one of the Extras), yes. But he's been released on bail. Probably won't even get charged if he says he's sorry.'

We all sit in a stunned silence. A bar worker comes over and asks us if we'd like any more Prosecco. Maisie shakes her head and asks for the bill.

'The trouble with men like Raphe,' Tor says, 'is that they think they're untouchable. And to be honest he is. He just does whatever the fuck he likes and leaves his managers to sort out the mess.'

'Who's the girl?' Maisie asks, 'Do we know her?'

Tor shrugs. 'It won't be long before she's called out on Twitter though. And *obviously* subjected to a witch hunt.'

We pay up and leave, each of us equally disturbed by the Twitter revelations. But even before I reach the lobby in my apartment building, a plan is starting to form in my mind.

49

KITTY'S APARTMENT, CHELSEA

It's not often that the Extras play much of a part in our lives, but one thought has been sitting in my head, growing, tentacle-like branches stretching out across my brain. I detest the football groupies. They make me want to grab their silly little heads and shake some sense into them. 'This isn't a career choice,' I want to scream. But they would never listen. They all want to be the next Victoria Beckham.

I grab my phone and scroll through my contacts until I find the name I'm looking for. Jodie Jones, Queen of the Extras and the most desperate of the WAG wannabes. I need to make a super-quick new best friend for the night. The football season hasn't kicked off yet, which means the little dickheads will still be hanging out in nightclubs, getting papped cheating on their partners or driving while clearly half-smashed from the night before.

'Hey Jodz! Are you out tonight?'

'Kitty! Hey babes. Yes, we're going to Raffles. Coming?'

'I'll see you there.'

Urgh.

But. It is time for kick-off.

50

RAFFLES, KING'S ROAD, CHELSEA

I hate nightclubs. I remember this fact as I'm stood at one of the bars in Raffles, desperately trying to order myself a vodka to take the edge off and make myself feel less self-conscious. I've already had to bat off unwanted attention from three men and I've only been here half an hour. My head is banging, I feel claustrophobic, there are too many bodies and not enough air conditioning. Some of the Extras are here and have been milling round me, trying to engage me in conversation, but a) I can't really hear them and b) I don't want to spend my night listening to them vacuously gossip and bitch.

'Amber's been cheating on Jesse with Andre,' one of them, I think she's called Emily, tries to tell me.

'I don't give a fuck,' I say.

'What? Can't hear you?'

'I said "what rotten luck!"'

Even though we don't have much to do with each other, I'm quite pleased the Extras are here. It makes me look less of a saddo, propping up the bar alone. Even better is the news that they've got a table. My feet are fucking killing me. Am I getting old?

'Come and sit with us, Emily's got a table.' I thought I *was* talking to Emily. Anyway, she links her arm through mine and pulls me over to where they're sitting.

'Look who I found at the bar,' Not Emily says.

'Well done, Emma,' says someone else. 'Hey, Kits, who are you here with?' She's probably hoping that Ben and some of his crew will turn up later. He's very popular with them, although I can't work out who's getting the worse side of the deal.

'I was waiting for Jodie,' I shout. 'But it doesn't look like she's coming.'

'Ah don't worry, hang with us. Tasha, pour Kits a voddie would you, babe?'

The girl called Tasha pulls a bottle of Grey Goose out of the ice bucket on the table and sloshes some in a glass for me.

'Mixer?' she asks.

I shake my head. 'That's fine, babes. I like it neat.'

She grins as she passes the glass over, like she's in the company of the Queen or something. I'm trying to keep my eye on who's coming in and out, but the Extras keep firing questions at me.

'Love your dress, babe, who is it?'

'Paloma Wool.'

'Is Ben coming tonight?'

'No idea.'

'Is it true that Maisie is seeing Rupert now?'

'Er . . . yeah.'

'Did you know he used to go out with Sophie?'

239

'No, I did not.' Who the fuck is Sophie?

I sort of tune out after this and the Extras get bored of the novelty of having me at their table. I'm too busy scouting the place to see if any footballers have turned up yet. I mean, that's why I assume the Extras are here. I'd bet a kidney – not one of my own – that becoming a WAG is as ambitious as they get.

Sure enough, about ten minutes later, there's a huge squeal from Emma/Emily/Tasha/whoever.

'Look. That's Raphe Reynolds, isn't it?'

I glance over and see someone who looks barely old enough to even be in here move through the crowd, which parts for him like the Red fucking Sea. He's undeniably good-looking but after seeing the hate-filled bile he'd sent, his attractiveness level had dropped to sub-zero. His eyes are already darting around the club, taking it all in, searching for his prey. His gaze meets mine for a split second, then I look away. When I turn back a couple of beats later, he's still watching. This time he breaks our shared gaze first. We are engaged in a game of eye tennis, the first step of flirting. This is good. When his eyes return to meet mine again a few seconds later, I reward him with a flirty smile, before I pretend to spot someone I know. This time I don't look back. If he thinks pulling me is too easy, it will lose the appeal for him. A phrase Ben or one of his friends coined springs to mind, 'A worthy cunt needs a hunt.' I know, delightful. But it's true, I need to let Raphe think he's chasing me. I need to be the prey right now. I pop a straw in my drink and take a sip. The straw draws attention to my mouth, which will apparently get him thinking about the other things I can do with it. Thanks for that tip, *Teen Vogue*.

I try to involve myself in what the Extras are talking about. They're all sneaking looks at Raphe and the guys he's with. I presume they're all footballers too, but I'm not sure. I'm not like these girls. Being a WAG holds absolutely zero appeal for me.

Emma or Emily is talking about Raphe in a low whisper. 'You know he treats women like absolute dirt apparently? Did you see all that stuff on Twitter?'

The brunette I think is called Tasha shrugs. 'I don't even care. It's all been taken down now anyway so was probably nothing. Look at him, what I wouldn't give for one night with that. What do you reckon, Kitty?'

'He's cute, I guess.'

The girls giggle as Raphe struts over to the table.

'Ladies,' he says, holding his glass up like he's Leonardo DiCaprio in *The Great Gatsby*. If you think extremely average white men have a confidence they don't deserve, imagine one with money who has been gushed over since he was about twelve.

The Extras titter and giggle, but I stay cool. And, as predicted, it gets Raphe's attention.

'Kitty Collins,' he says and squats down next to me. 'Don't often see you here.' His hand is on my right thigh and he's leaning in close to talk to me.

I shrug. 'A change is as good as a rest, so they say.' I hold his gaze for a bit longer than feels comfortable, then look away. 'I'm actually just leaving, to be honest. It's not really my thing.'

'Oh, come on, stay. For me.' He puts his hands together in a pleading gesture and makes puppy-dog eyes at me.

I fake a laugh. 'I've had too much to drink already. I need to get to bed. It was nice talking to you though.'

With that, I say some quick goodbyes to the Extras and leave, hoping my trail of breadcrumbs will work. Sure enough, just as I step outside, I feel a hand on my shoulder.

'I can't let you go home by yourself like this,' Raphe says, all caring gentleman.

'I'm fine,' I say, adding a little stumble to my walk. 'Oops.'

'See, you're not fine. At least let me get you a ride or something?'

'Or *something*?' I turn the flirt dial up to full.

'Why don't you come back to mine for a coffee and I'll get a driver to take you home safely later? I couldn't forgive myself if anything happened to you. You shouldn't be stumbling around alone like this.'

I give him a nod. 'Okay. But no funny business. Got it?' I prod him playfully in the chest. 'And you'd need to drive my car. I can't leave it here.'

'As long as it's nothing made by Germans, I'll happily drive it.' He grins. 'They beat us last month in a friendly,' he explains. 'I'm not a racist!' It would have been quite sweet if I didn't remember the horrendous Twitter grabs Tor showed us.

'It's a Range Rover Evoque.'

'That one?'

I nod and pass him my key fob, wobbling a bit as I cross the road for effect.

'Come on then, you, let's get you sobered up.'

51

RAPHE'S APARTMENT, CHELSEA

It takes about ten minutes to get to Raphe's building, which actually isn't too far from mine. He parks the car in the underground car park and we head up the back steps to his flat.

'I know it sounds bad but I just can't be bothered making small talk with the concierges every single time.' He does a funny little eyeroll at me because I know that exact feeling.

And so we walk all the way up to the penthouse – what else? I take the opportunity to look at him. I'm not sure if it's the lighting but he looks much younger now than he did in the club and seems less sure of himself. He senses me looking and turns to me with a big smile. I notice he's wearing a garish chain with a diamond-encrusted R on it.

Footballers.

No class. Zero.

'This is where I live Monday to Friday, pretty much,' Raphe tells me as I walk through a long corridor lined with signed pictures and football shirts in frames. 'I've got a house down in Surrey, which is for weekends and holidays. And parties.' He flashes me a smile. 'Come through to the lounge, I want to show you something.'

I follow him through into a huge open-plan lounge area, which includes a bar and full-size pool table.

'Do you play? Do you want a game?' he asks.

'Er . . . no. I'm okay thanks. Is that what you wanted to show me?'

He stares at me, blank for a couple of beats. 'Oh. No. It's this. Look.' He walks over to the far wall and waves his hand in front of what looks like a hat in a frame. I move closer to get a better look and realise that it *is,* in fact, a hat in a frame. I look at Raphe. His grin is wilting a little. 'It's an England cap,' he says.

'It's nice.' I'm not sure what the correct response is here.

'I got it when I made my England debut last season. Did you know I'd played for England?'

What *is* this? Why is this supposedly cool footballer, lauded up and down the country for his skills with the ladies as well-known as his skills on a pitch, acting like an awkward sixth former who's alone with a girl for the first time?

'Er . . . yes. I knew that. Well done. Very big achievement.'

He's almost giddy with pride. 'And look over here. This is my trophy cabinet.' I trot after him as he leads me to a glass casing that displays a variety of trophies – young player of the year, blah blah blah.

'Did you say something about a drink?' I can feel my face giving away how bored I am.

'Oh. Yes. Sorry. Where are my manners? Sure. Erm . . .

wine? Something else? I've got Champagne. Lots and lots of Champagne. A whole fridge of it. Probably enough to bath in. I mean, not that I'm saying we should. Just that, we could.'

'A bit sticky, I think. Wine is lovely.' Why do I feel like I'm babysitting?

Raphe disappears into what I assume must be the kitchen and I take a chance to look around the rest of the room. There are lots of photos of Raphe. Raphe with some famous old guy who played football, I think. A teenage Raphe, holding up a team scarf. There's a collection of guitars on one wall but that is basically the only thing that suggests there is any actual depth to this two-dimensional football cliché.

'Sit down.' Raphe comes back into the lounge carrying two glasses of white wine, almost filled to the brim.

I walk over and take one from him as it looks perilously close to spilling out onto the oversized rug, which is no doubt worth thousands. I then head to the sofa – a monstrosity of a silver crushed-velvet L-shaped thing – and sit down.

'There's a hot tub on the balcony,' Raphe suddenly says, as if he's only just remembered. Is he high?

'I don't have a swimming costume with me. Sorry.'

'Oh. We could skinny dip? I bet you look hotter with nothing on anyway.' He scoots across the sofa so he's closer to me. I scoot further away and take a long swig of wine.

'I think I'd rather stay clothed and dry.'

His face falls in disappointment and I have a weird sensation, like I've kicked a puppy in the face or something.

'How about some music?'

'Sure.'

He grabs one remote from a pile of about twenty and starts jabbing at the buttons. The TV comes on.

Loudly.

We both jump and Raphe laughs nervously as he stares at the remote in confusion.

'Sorry!' he shouts over Charlotte Crosby, who is shouting at another drunk Geordie. 'I thought this was the stereo!'

'It's not!'

'No! I can't turn it down though.' He looks back at the remote, perplexed. I guess footballers aren't known for their brains.

'Give it here.' I snatch the remote from him and turn the TV off. 'Jesus Christ. My ears. You really shouldn't be listening to it that loud. It's not good for you. You'll get tinnitus or something.'

Raphe picks another remote from the collection and presses a couple of buttons. He's hit the jackpot this time as the lights dim and some R&B music, which sounds like it's probably from a playlist called Now That's What I Call Date Rape, starts up softly. 'There we go.' He looks extremely pleased with himself. I guess this is what happens when people tell you you're amazing and throw money at you. 'Let me get you some Champagne. You'll love it. It's really good stuff.'

'Okay, sure.'

He disappears and comes back with two wineglasses of Champagne. 'I couldn't find the proper long ones.'

'Flutes.'

He looks at me, his brow furrows slightly.

'Champagne glasses are called flutes.'

'Oh. Right. Yeah. Them. I couldn't find them.'

'It's fine.' I take a drink from him and take a sip. He's right, it's delicious. I need to keep a clear head though so can't get too used to it. Although I really don't feel like I'm in the company of a dangerous sexual predator. More like a child.

Raphe scoots along the sofa, closer to me again.

'So. What's it like being famous?' he asks.

'You probably know more about it than me.'

'Why would I?'

He really was at the back of the queue when the smarts were being handed out.

'Well, you've played for England,' I say. 'All I've done is post some photos on Instagram.'

'Oh *yeah*.' He laughs. 'It's a different kind of famous. You're really pretty. Even prettier in real life.'

'Thanks. That's sweet.'

'You've always been my favourite Instagram model. Your bikini pics from Marbella were hot!'

'That's really nice of you to say. I'm not a model though. I'm an Influencer.'

'Are you seeing anyone at the moment then?'

'Er. No. I've actually just broken up with someone.'

'Looking for some rebound action then?'

'Sorry?'

'That's what you girls do, isn't it? Get over one man by getting under another and all that?'

'That's actually really disrespectful. And no, I'm not look-ing for some "rebound action" as you put it. Maybe I should leave?' I stand up.

He looks mortified. 'Oh God, no. Sorry, I honestly didn't mean it like that. I didn't mean to upset you. I'm just a bit nervous. I always get like this around beautiful women. Please don't go yet.'

He looks so earnest that I actually *do* sit back down.

I need to get a grip on myself.

He is *not* a nice man, he is a sexual predator. Those messages Tor showed us were disgusting. That's why I'm here, to get justice for that girl and the hundreds like her, not to sit here chatting about how to get over a break-up.

'Could I use your loo?' I ask.

'Sure.' Raphe hops up and leads me back down the corridor. 'Shout if you get lost on the way back.'

The cloakroom is as opulent as the rest of the place, all white marble and chrome fittings. I rummage around in my bag until I find what I'm looking for. Then I head back into the living room. Raphe is sat with his back to me. His neck prone.

'Didn't get lost then? Did you decide you wanted a dip in the hot tub after all?'

'Not quite,' I say as I plunge the syringe deep into the skin at the back of his neck.

He's confused when he comes round and keeps looking at me like a dog who can't understand what he's done wrong. He's fighting against his duct-tape restraints. Or duck tape, as he would probably say if it wasn't over his mouth too.

'Don't pretend you don't know why this is happening,' I tell him as I stand over him, twirling my knife. 'I know all about you and how you treat women.'

He's grunting against the tape, shaking his head frantically.

'Oh yes, I saw the disgusting messages you sent. All of Twitter did before your manager magicked them away, am I right?'

He's squirming harder now, shaking his head, his eyes huge with fear. Good.

'Scared are you? You think money and power gets you everything. Well not this time.' I straddle him and feel around his neck for the vein I'm looking for. He's struggling harder now, which is starting to annoy me, desperately trying to tell me his lies through his gag. Tears are running down his cheeks. I make one swift incision in his neck and watch in morbid glee as his pulse pumps spurts of blood all over the white floor. I'm mesmerised by it for a bit. The contrast of the red on the pure white marble is quite beautiful. I'm brought out of my reverie by a grunting and gasping sound. I'd almost forgotten Raphe was here.

He's still trying to say something.

I turn away and clean up as I wait for him to bleed out, getting rid of any sign I was here. This includes washing the wineglasses.

'Flutes,' I tell the mess on the floor. 'That's the trouble with footballers. Money can't buy class.'

When he eventually stops gurgling and squirming, I crouch down beside him on the floor and pull his lids over his eyes. He really does look so young. It's difficult to equate him with the disgusting potential rapist from the Twitter screenshots.

Satisfied that I've got rid of all traces of me being there, I head out of the front door and back down the stairs to my car. As I drive the short distance home, I wait for the euphoria to hit me. That wonderful buzz that comes with the kill. The pure, unfiltered joy of knowing I've rid the world of one more sexual predator.

But it doesn't come.

52

Even when I get home and pour myself my celebratory glass of Chablis, there's nothing. I just feel empty. And there's something else. Something I can't quite get a handle on that's creeping through my veins like a thousand spiders.

Is this guilt?

Remorse?

Fear?

Or am I coming down with something?

I take my wine to the sofa and switch on my TV, which comes on at a nice, sensible volume. The news is on. Two men are debating the pressure on young footballers. Apparently, there's been an incident in a hotel in Puerto Banús where some of the young England stars have gone on holiday. There appear to have been a couple of arrests. Do absolutely none of them know how to behave? Cross, I gulp down the rest of the wine and head to bed, the feeling of unease still lurking in a dark corner of my brain.

It's still early when I wake up. My head is pounding and

I think I've pulled a muscle in my shoulder, which must've happened when I was moving Raphe around last night. I rub my eyes, grab my phone from its charging dock and wander into the kitchen. The silence, which I usually find soothing, feels like a presence in the room and I wish – for a splinter of a second – that there was someone else here. Maybe I should think about getting a dog. I pop a pod in the coffee machine and head into the lounge, switching on the TV just to stop the deafening silence. It's still on the news channel from last night and I'm stirring soy milk into my coffee when I hear the name 'Raphael Reynolds' from the Sky News presenter.

Has his body been found already? I take my drink into the lounge. But I'm confused. The news isn't showing an expensive apartment block in West London. Instead, the presenter is talking from Marbella, Spain – according to the caption. I turn the volume up.

'Raphael Reynolds remains in police custody in Spain following an alleged bar brawl in the Spanish town yesterday. The England centre-forward is accused of punching a waiter who tried to take a selfie with the star. It's believed that Raphael had been drinking heavily with friends and teammates during a long lunch at the exclusive resort. The England star is already immersed in a story in the UK where he's accused of harassing a teenage fan on Twitter.'

What? WHAT?

The TV is now showing footage recorded on someone's phone of a man – who looks a lot like the man I murdered last night – hitting out at a waiter, while some other men try to hold him back.

'Raphael's spokesperson has confirmed that he remains in custody. With the new football season just weeks away from kick-off, his UK club will be worrying what the future may hold for their breakout star.'

I rewind the news feature and watch it again. I do this four more times before heading to the kitchen, pouring my coffee down the sink and immediately downing a large vodka.

Then I scream.

Okay. Don't panic. There has to be a simple explanation here. Raphe can't be in prison in Marbella *and* dead in his Chelsea apartment. But if he's in Marbella, who is the guy I killed last night? *Did* I kill someone last night? Am I going crazy? I reach for my phone and type out a text.

Me: Hey! So nice to see you last night. Sorry I bailed early. Was a bit drunker than I thought. I hope I didn't do anything embarrassing! (Cringe!)

Maybe Emily (Extras): Oh hey! You missed a fun night. No, you were fine, don't worry. You spent most of your time talking to Ruben, bless him.

Me: Ruben???

Maybe Emily (Extras): Ruben Reynolds. You know, Raphe's little brother. He's super sweet.

Fuck. Fuckfuckfuckfuckfuckfuckfuckfuckfuck.

I open my phone and type in 'Raphael Reynold's brother'

in a search. The first entry is Raphe's Wikipedia page and I scroll down to family. 'Siblings: Rowan, 30, and Ruben, 18.'

Shit.

I've killed the wrong man.

And not just a man. A fucking kid.

I head to the bar and unsteadily pour myself a neat vodka. Then another. Then another. I pop one, two, three Valiums, but my pulse is still thumping out a drum n bass beat through my nervous system. Then suddenly, for the first time in over a decade, I feel the overwhelming need for my mother. It's something that never fails to bemuse me, the absolute most primal needs humans have, no matter who we are. I stalk back to the sofa and grab my phone, my hands refusing to calm. I ineptly scroll through my contacts, before I can steady myself enough to tap my mum's.

It rings about ten times and I can picture her, on the veranda of her Riviera house, holding court with her new friends, looking at the name lighting up her phone. I can almost *feel* her hesitation all these miles away. To answer or not to answer, the temptation to just cut me off almost overwhelming. But she doesn't and – despite the early hour she eventually answers.

'Kitty? What have you done?'

And those five words are all I need to hear.

Suddenly I'm not a twenty-nine-year-old woman anymore; I'm transported back to being a fifteen-year-old girl. A fifteen-year-old girl who has just killed her own father by smashing an antique vase through his skull. And my mother is sat there, covered in blood and brain splatter, staring at me like she has no fucking clue who I am. And even though I know he's dead, even though he's crumpled like gold-plated tin in front of us, I'm still hitting him with the vase. And I'm hitting and hitting until we hear bones crunch and joints pop, and all that's left of the upper quarter of his body is a pulpy mess, like a punched plum. My mother and I look at each other, horrified, for what feels like an eternity before she hauls herself up, pulls her nightwear into place to cover her bruised breasts and thighs, and walks over to me. She takes the vase from my shaking hands and wraps her arms around me.

'Kitty, what have you done?' she whispers into my left ear as I remain statue-still, like a child determined to win the prize at a demented birthday party. 'What have you done?'

I saved you, I think in a daze. *That's what I've done, I saved you.*

She puts her hands either side of my face and turns my head so I'm looking her directly in the eyes. My mother was . . . is beautiful. Her eyes are that very rare colour of blue so deep they're almost violet. She was the absolute queen of London before she married my father and became yet another house-wife. The life she'd yearned for as a child growing up in the poorer districts of London soon became tainted and hated as she realised what it really meant. A cheating husband; regular beatings and sexual assaults; the pity of the women she was supposed to call friends, despite most of them having slept with her husband. Gifted with an ungrateful daughter who was so painfully a daddy's girl, despite the fact her mother had been beaten so badly she could never have any more children when she produced a daughter instead of a son and heir. It was hardly any wonder my mother had collapsed in on herself as she had. And by the time I was old enough to notice the gilding sticking to my fingers every time I touched my father, my mother was already too broken to repair.

She was almost robotic that night as she cleaned and commanded, asking for various knives, meat cleavers and hammers until my father was little more than a bruised pile of meat, wrapped in plastic. She took the wheel of Dad's Range Rover. She drove to one of the abattoirs, this one out in the West Country. She helped me unwrap him and throw the pieces of his body into the mincers. She turned off the CCTV before driving his car to a known suicide spot. Then she took the wheel of another car that had somehow appeared at the slaughterhouse while we were gone, and drove us home.

When we got back, we spent two days in uncomfortable silence, drinking tea, my mother kissing my head and stroking my hair, before she called the police and reported my father missing. I listened in as she lied to them about his depression, about how working in a business that revolved around death had affected him. And she listened in as I told them the same lies. Lies upon lies upon lies and I knew life would never be the same again.

About six months later, my mother announced our house was sold as she was moving to the South of France for a new start. She didn't directly ask me to go with her. Besides, she told me, I had my life here. I had my friends and my schooling to finish, and my French has never really been very good. Instead, she splashed out on one the most expensive Chelsea apartments she could find. Plus I had Hen's family so close, they'd always keep an eye on me. I went on holidays with them. James was delighted to have another daughter around who wasn't 'surly' like Hen or 'high energy' like Antoinette. He taught me to play tennis when Hen showed no interest. Helped me with my sailing when Hen went through a gothic stage where she did little more than roll her eyes and whine that her own family liked me better. That wasn't true. I have never gelled with Hen's mum. I guess you don't gel with women you catch your dad shagging over a pool table.

Anyway, back to now. I find the omnipresent concierges comforting. Almost more than my family ever was. Mum sends me an overly generous allowance each month, but I tend not to touch it; instead I live from my own income from social media. There's an unspoken rule between us that we don't talk about The Thing. Talking could crack the veneer. Could make her remember the look in my eyes as I smashed my father's skull in with that vase.

'Kitty, what have you done?'

I'm transported back to the present day and I suddenly feel childish and pathetic for needing my mother.

'Oh nothing,' I say. 'I just wanted to see how you are.'

'Do you realise the time? Are you drunk? High? Go to bed.'

'Yes, sorry. I couldn't sleep. I'll call you soon.'

'A more appropriate hour next time.'

'Yes, sorry.'

There's a long pause.

'Kits?'

'Yeah?'

'I love you, sweetheart.'

'I love you too.'

Then the line goes dead and that's probably all the contact I'll have with my mother until Christmas, when she'll invite me skiing or something and I'll lie to her about having plans here with a boyfriend. Lies upon lies.

53

KITTY'S APARTMENT, CHELSEA

It's been a week since I killed an innocent man. A week since I snuffed the life out of someone who'd done absolutely nothing wrong, apart from having the misfortune to be related to an absolute piece of scum.

It's all over the news obviously. I haven't been able to get away from it so I've turned everything off and am hunkering down in my flat. I've even disconnected the Wi-Fi just in case I'm tempted to torture myself some more.

I haven't left my bed in three or four days. Apart to get more wine or drugs. I stink. I can smell myself every time I move, which hasn't been much.

The first news report I saw about Ruben's death plays over and over in my mind like a snuff movie I can't walk out of.

The body of Ruben Reynolds, younger brother of footballer Raphael Reynolds, has been discovered in the soccer star's home.

According to friends, Ruben had been enjoying a night

out at Raffles nightclub in the Southwest London borough, before heading home before midnight. Friends said he seemed in good spirits. The alarm was raised two days later when Ruben, 18, failed to turn up to a second dinner organised with his family. His eldest brother, Rowan, and father found the body in Raphael's Chelsea apartment where Ruben was staying while his brother was on holiday in Spain.

An autopsy will determine the cause of death but the Metropolitan Police have confirmed that they've launched a murder investigation and that anyone with any information about Ruben's movements that night should get in touch with them as a matter of urgency.

Raphael has been released from police custody in Spain, where he was arrested following a drunken affray. It's believed he's returning to the UK to support his family.

After the news report come the inevitable back stories about Ruben. About how he idolised his footballer brother. How he still lived with his mum and dad and was thrilled when Raphe asked him to look after his Chelsea apartment. How he would sometimes pretend to be his brother to impress girls because he'd never had a proper girlfriend. I can't stop watching – Raphe talking on the news, photos of their mother, haunted and grey, his father pleading for any information about their son's death. I sit in front of my TV, letting the stories run on loop. Rewinding, re-watching. Rewinding again. I don't move from the sofa for – how long – hours, or it might be days. I'm unable to sleep despite the cocktail of downers I throw down my throat. When sleep does come it's not sweet relief or perchance to dream. It's a nightmarish funhouse of the grotesque. I dream I'm in labour, but the baby's head is torn off during delivery. A faceless midwife puts the decapitated child on my chest and when I look down it's Adam, that rivulet of blood coming from his mouth. He tries to latch on to my breast but I'm screaming, I'm paralysed and can't wake myself up. When I eventually come round, I'm soaked with sweat, shivering and confused.

The only person I have any contact with during this time is Dr William, my meds supplier, who does a weekly drop of pills and potions, like a twisted subscription service.

I keep telling myself it was a mistake, but I can't deal with it. A mistake is picking up dairy butter instead of vegan, not drugging and murdering an innocent man. Then there are more dreams. This time it's Ruben drowning in a sea of blood, shouting for me to help him. I stand on a pier watching him and waving. He gets sucked under a scarlet wave. I'm taking selfies while he drowns in blood. I hear my mother's voice: 'Kitty. What have you done?'

I increase the amount of pills, mix some Diazepam and Zoplicone, throw in some Lorazepam for good measure. I don't want to dream. I want to be unconscious. I don't want my brain spewing up inside my head anymore. I shove handfuls into my mouth like Smarties and wash them down with vodka. I eventually manage to crawl from my sofa to my bed and stay there, the covers pulled over my head. I only leave to get more drugs or vodka.

I think I hear the buzzer go several times, but I'm so in and out of consciousness, I can't be sure. And why would

I answer it? Who would it be? The only people who should be visiting me are the police. I've considered calling them myself. I deserve it.

What stops me?

They'd not stop at Ruben's murder. They'd look at me, put my life under a microscope and find out that I'm not one virus, but many. They'd discover the truth about all the others. All the others and my dad. My mother would get dragged into it, Tor too. And Charlie would see it all. He'd know the truth, which is far worse than my cheating on him. He'd know that I have this monster living inside me that can kill. It wouldn't matter that it was a mistake, that he was never meant to die. 'Yes, I kill men, but only men who deserve it.' The thought of him seeing me like that terrifies me more than prison.

In the rare moments I'm able to drag myself out of my bed, I make it as far as the balcony where I sit, still hidden. Time means nothing and I spend probably hours staring down at the ground. Wondering how much it would hurt to fall on it from up here. My dreams continue and Adam joins Ruben in the sea of blood. But he can't swim. He can't save himself or shout for help. He can only blink.

I think of my expensive knives, my beloved Shuns, and imagine myself cutting through the flesh of my wrists. To press down hard enough that it slices through the delicate butterfly-wing skin into the vein, opening it up like a ziplock, watching the blood flow out of my own body this time. I fantasise about it – I even go as far as the kitchen and pick out a knife. But the complete truth is, even killing myself seems like too much of an effort. I put the knife down and head back to bed, grabbing my self-prescribed cocktail of vodka and benzos on the way.

I'm aware of a few things during this period. I've already mentioned the occasional blare of the door buzzer. Sometimes there's a more insistent knocking. And there's also the heat. It still hasn't broken. I don't open any windows – apart from when I think about throwing myself out of one – so the apartment stinks. My cleaner usually comes twice a week but doesn't have a key. I think briefly that I should pay her anyway; it's not her fault I'm having some kind of breakdown. But then the thought of banking apps and life just becomes too much again and I take more drugs and drink some wine this time and soon it fades away again. A dark black wave washes over me and takes me back out with it. Back to the peace of total oblivion.

54

Before I wake up, I can tell that something isn't right. I'm in a considerable amount of discomfort. My throat in particular feels like I've swallowed one of my knives. Oh God, I hope I'm not getting sick. I feel bad enough as it is without having to deal with actual physical illness. It's too bright as well, which annoys me because I haven't opened the blackout blind in over a week. My eyelids are stuck together, like I've got conjunctivitis. Fuck, it feels like I'm actually going to pull my eyelashes out. That would be far from ideal. When I finally manage to open my eyes, I have to close them again because I'm clearly having one of those weird dream experiences where I think I've woken up, but I haven't. Because when I open them, I see Charlie sat next to my bed. He's reading a book, glasses on. I open my eyes for the second time and he's still there. What's happening?

'Charlie?' I attempt to say, but it comes out as a croak.

He looks up, alarmed. 'Kitty? You're awake? Stay there. I need to get a nurse.' He flings his book down and almost trips over his own feet in a scramble to get out of the room. Nurse though?

I attempt to sit up but realise I'm hooked up to a machine. And this isn't my bedroom at all. It's a hospital and I should've known by that horrible smell. I can feel my heart start to speed up and my breathing getting shallow. The beginnings of a panic attack, but because of my ridiculously painful throat, I can't get my breathing under control. I feel myself beginning to spiral when Charlie comes back in with a middle-aged woman, who I assume is a nurse.

'Shhh, shhh,' she says, obviously sensing my panic. 'Let's sit you up and get your breathing under control. You're safe.' She strokes my hair and holds my hand as she breathes slowly with me. Sure enough, after about a minute I'm feeling much calmer. 'Right, let's get you some water. I bet your throat is feeling awful.' She pours me some water from a jug on the hospital-standard bedside table and I swallow it down urgently, wincing slightly.

'What's going on?' I ask, my voice sounding unfamiliar.

'You're in recovery love, you're okay,' the nurse says.

'Kitty, do you not remember?' Charlie's staring at me in horror.

I shake my head, confused.

'You tried to kill yourself. I had to get Rehan to let me into your apartment because you weren't posting or answering your phone or door or anything for days. We've all been so worried. And when I got in, you were in bed, empty packets of pills and drink everywhere, you were completely unresponsive. I had to call an ambulance.'

The nurse nods. 'We had to pump your stomach, hun.'

Hun? I shake my head again. 'No, I wasn't trying to kill myself.'

'Well, you did a damned good impression of someone trying to. This one probably saved your life,' the nurse says. Charlie does that adorable blushing thing that makes me melt. 'How are you feeling?'

'Tired. Confused.'

'Okay, I'm gonna get a doctor to come and take a look at you. Back soon. You want some more water?'

I nod gratefully and she pours me another glass before heading out the door, humming.

Charlie comes and sits down next to me on the bed and takes my hand. 'Kitty. Why didn't you call me?'

He actually thinks I tried to top myself. Christ.

'Charlie, I really wasn't trying to kill myself,' I say, but I can tell by the look in his eyes that he doesn't believe me.

'I know you've been struggling with . . . stuff,' he says, squeezing my hand.

'But—'

He puts a finger gently to my lips. 'Look I've been in some really dark places too. When my dad cut me off, I was devastated. It was only my brother who kept me going sometimes. I was proper depressed. On pills, the lot. I thought about ending it all too. Lots of times.'

Oh, Jesus. Please stop this.

'What I'm trying to say is I know what it's like. And I'm going to help you through. Okay? I'm here for you. I'm coming to stay with you until you're better. I've told the doctors.

They've been on about admitting you or something if there's no one to look after you at home.'

'Charlie, that's kind but I don't need a babysitter.'

Charlie frowns. 'It wasn't an offer. It's happening. It's that or a psych ward.' He leans forwards and kisses me on the lips, which can't be a very nice experience if the taste in my mouth is anything to go by. A psych ward or my ex-boyfriend who thinks I tried to kill myself.

The lovely nurse comes back in, this time accompanied by a doctor with the beardiest beard I have ever seen in my life.

Surely that can't be hygienic?

My breathing starts to quicken again, but Charlie softly strokes my hand with his thumb and I begin to calm.

'Hello, Kitty.' He chuckles. 'Ah Hello Kitty.' The room remains tumbleweed silent. He coughs. 'Well, you gave us quite a scare, young lady, but luckily there's been no serious damage. One of our psychiatrists will be here later to have a chat with you and we'll go from there. At the moment, I don't think there's any need for you to be admitted. And Mr Chambers here has said he'll stay with you while we help you work through what brought you here.'

I have a sudden flashback of trying to stem the bleeding from Ruben Reynold's neck. I'm really not sure anyone probing into my mind is a good idea. Charlie is nodding supportively.

'I've told Kitty that I'm happy to stay with her as long as necessary. I'll sleep on the sofa. You need someone to look after you. You're fragile.'

'Yes, I think that's a good idea. You're very lucky to have someone who cares about you so much.'

Charlie gazes at me and there is such adoration in his eyes it makes me want to scream. I'm not who you think I am. I'm not *what* you think I am.

'Anyway,' the doctor continues, 'let's leave Kitty alone because the psychiatrist will be here shortly.'

Charlie kisses my hand. 'I'll be right outside, baby, okay? I'm sorry. I love you.'

Fuck.

Does he think I did this because of him? Not that I *did* anything.

I'm left alone for a total of three and a half minutes before a lady, probably in her early forties, clip-clops in. I look at her shoes. Miu Miu. Psychiatry must be well paid. She smiles at me but it doesn't quite reach her eyes and I realise that I'm not being assessed here, I'm being judged. I'm so tired but I know I need to put on the show of my life. I wish I had some bloody make-up on.

'Hi, Kitty,' she says, too slowly. She's trying to make me bite already.

I smile weakly. 'Hi.'

'I'm Dr Jensen, but you can call me Emma if you like?'

'Okay. Thanks. Dr Jensen.'

She pretends to look through my notes, but I know this is just for show as she probably had an orgasm when she was told she'd been assigned a famous patient.

'So, I can see from your history that you've had counselling and medication previously for depression. This was after your father disappeared. Is that right?'

I nod. 'It was a very difficult time.'

'Of course. Do you think this current episode has anything to do with that?'

I hate the way she says 'episode', like my life is a Netflix show.

'I really don't know. Possibly. But in all honesty, I've just been overdoing it. Too much drink. Too many drugs. Not enough sleep. I'm really not here because I tried to kill myself.'

She stares hard at me. Almost *through* me. 'With all due respect, Kitty, I'm not sure anyone ends up in hospital having their stomach pumped because they've OD'd on prescription drugs and alcohol by accident.' Is she trying to gaslight me or what?

'It wasn't that. I was having trouble sleeping and—'

'Why?' Holy fuck, she's in there so fast my head spins.

'Why what?'

'Why are you having trouble sleeping? What's on your mind?'

'Nothing in particular. It's something I've always struggled with—'

'There's nothing in your medical notes about it,' she interrupts again. 'If you've been struggling to sleep long term, why haven't you asked for help?'

I see where she's going. I give her what she wants. 'Because I've been self-medicating,' I say in a small voice.

She nods, satisfied. Scribbles some stuff on my notes. I fight the urge to choke her with the heart monitor wire and take them off her.

'Okay. Kitty, I don't think you've got any underlying mental health conditions. I think you just need to take care of yourself.

I can refer you to a counsellor about the self-medication, but I'm assuming you'll probably want to do that privately as you have the resources?'

I nod.

'Good choice. Also, the online CBT you'll be offered through the NHS will barely touch the sides. It's one of those awful areas where money talks, sadly.'

I nod again, making a note to tell Charlie about this.

'You can go home today as long as you agree to Mr Chambers's staying with you temporarily. And weekly calls from myself. Plus at least weekly sessions with a counsellor or psychotherapist of your choice. I don't think you're a danger to yourself or anyone else. Are you comfortable going home with Charlie? There's no issues there?'

I shake my head. 'God no, nothing like that.'

She watches me for a very long moment.

'Okay, well if you're happy to go home and let Charlie take care of you . . . ?' She leaves a long pause. I wait it out. 'Then I'm happy to discharge you.' She reaches over and touches my hand gently. 'Just please take care of yourself, okay?'

I nod. Of course.

55

'Tor told me about the baby. The miscarriage,' Charlie says as we bump along at the speed of an easily distracted pigeon.

Oh.

Okay.

I'd forgotten about that.

'Why didn't you tell me?'

My head is too woolly for this conversation. 'The last thing you had told me was that you thought I was fucking someone else, so why would I?'

He has the decency to look ashamed. 'You should have told me. I can't believe you were dealing with that on your own. Why didn't you tell me you were pregnant?'

'Can we talk about this later, please?' I croak. I can't remember who I've told what. And I still don't fully understand how I ended up in hospital. An NHS hospital, at that.

My skin is still itchy from the sheets.

'Was it mine?'

The look I give him would curdle milk, as one of my nannies was fond of saying.

He spends the rest of the drive looking out of the window. Even the driver who has been watching us with far more interest than necessary finally starts paying attention to the road.

'We'll talk at mine.'

'Yes, sorry. Sorry. Of course.' He looks utterly heartbroken.

This really isn't my finest hour.

56

We get back to mine, Charlie acting like a mother hen, which I have to say I do *not* find attractive. But when I catch sight of myself for the first time in God knows how long, I see that Charlie probably isn't finding me that alluring either. My hair is greasy and lank and is hanging in knotted rat tails down my back. My skin looks grey, no hint of my Mykonos tan at all. I've lost weight. A lot of weight. My collarbones are jutting out and my face looks gaunt. And not good gaunt.

Amazingly though, the flat is immaculate. There's not one empty bottle of wine or packet of pills in sight.

'Rita came in and cleaned while you were away,' Charlie says, seeing my confusion. 'We didn't think you'd want to come back to, well, it was pretty disgusting.'

I make a mental note to give Rita a massive tip when she next comes in. I head gingerly into my bedroom, where I see myself in the mirror again and almost scream.

I look like the girl from *The Ring*.

'I'm going to take a shower,' I say. 'I feel hideous.'

273

Charlie looks at me, his face a knot of worry.

'Charlie, I can take a shower. I'm not going to do anything to myself. I promise.'

He gives me a sad smile. 'I don't want to feel like your jailer.'

'Then don't act like one.'

I head into my en suite and turn the shower on. I take my clothes off and examine my skinny frame in the mirror. My ribs are showing too. Maisie would be so jealous. I think about taking a selfie and sending it to her, but realise this might be in bad taste. I also realise that I don't actually know where my phone is. I step into the shower, turning the water up as hot as I can bear it. I squeeze shampoo into my hair and rub expensive shower cream over my body and immediately feel more human. I rinse and slather on a handful of conditioner and decide to give my legs a quick shave while it does its job. But as I drag the blade up my legs, I realise my hands are still trembling and I nick my skin several times. I watch the blood make a whirlpool as it runs into the drain. It makes my head swim and I have to sit down on the cold porcelain. That's when I notice that I'm crying too. I desperately swallow the sobs back down so Charlie doesn't hear and burst in, deciding that I've made another attempt on my life. I stay like that for about ten minutes, trying to stop the flow of blood and tears, before gingerly stepping out and wrapping myself in one of my giant bath towels, that are even more giant on me now. I dry off, give my hair a quick blast, put some PJs on and head into the lounge, where Charlie is pacing, reading something intently on his phone. He sees me and immediately clicks the side button and shoves it in his pocket.

He smiles and claps his hands, business-like, which makes me jump. 'Sorry,' he says. 'So, do you want the sofa and duvet? Or bed?'

'Sofa please.' I sit awkwardly on it, while Charlie shuffles around, bringing me pillows and a blanket. He makes tea. I want vodka.

'Do you need anything else?'

'My phone and laptop please.'

He looks at me and there's a beat of silence between us. 'Actually, I've been advised to keep you away from social media.' He sounds awkward.

'What? Why? That's my *job*!'

'Well, considering what you're going through, you probably could do with having a bit of time off, don't you think?'

'I'm not going *through* anything. I'm fine. How many times do I need to tell you that I wasn't trying to kill myself!'

'Kitty. I found you slumped unconscious in your bed, surrounded by fuck knows how many empty bottles of booze and pills. I thought you were fucking *dead*! You had to have your stomach pumped, for crying out loud. That is not the behaviour of someone who is fine.' He runs his hand through his hair, then sits down on the sofa by my feet. 'Is this because of us? The baby?'

Wait. What? He thinks I did this because I was pregnant and he *dumped* me? Men are really ridiculous sometimes. Even the non-sociopath ones.

'Charlie. This is nothing to do with you or the *miscarriage*. I promise. I didn't try to kill myself either, I just overdid it a bit trying to deal with some other stuff, okay? Now can

275

I please have my laptop? I want to read the news and catch up with my life.'

He looks dubious.

'You can sit right there and if I start to spin out, I'll let you know.'

I can tell he's still reluctant, but Charlie gets up, locates my computer and hands it to me. I need to find out what the fuck is going on with Ruben Reynolds.

In all honesty, I was surprised when there wasn't a prison guard sat outside my hospital room. I quickly put his name in the search bar and hundreds of links fill the screen. I head to Apple News. It's not great news.

No leads yet on football star's murdered brother

Police investigating the brutal murder of Ruben Reynolds, younger brother of England International star Raphe, are set to hold a press conference later this week after admitting they are yet to find any strong leads connected to the case.

Ruben was last seen with friends and teammates of his brother in Raffles nightclub in Chelsea, Southwest London. But witnesses say they saw him leave the venue early and alone. CCTV confirmed this but it's unknown how Ruben got back to the luxury apartment he was house-sitting for his brother who was enjoying a pre-season holiday in Spain. Anyone who has any information about Ruben's movements after he left the nightclub are requested to get in touch with the police.

Raphe – who has been capped four times for England – said in a statement: 'We are desperate to find out who killed a much-loved brother and son. Our family is devastated that something so horrible could happen in my home which is fitted with state-of-the-art security. We are determined we won't rest until his killer is brought to justice.'

My stomach rolls over and I'm suddenly light-headed. Press conference. Fucking press conference. Someone is bound to say something about him talking to me. Charlie clearly senses a change in my energy.

'I told you it wasn't a good idea to go on there. Do you need anything? Another tea? One of your pills?'

'Both, please. Thank you.'

As he heads off to get me my supplies, I take a deep breath and open Instagram. As expected, there is a huge number of messages that I can't be bothered to go through. They're from people asking me where I am and stuff. But there's only one message I'm looking for. I'm not left disappointed when I spot it.

The twisted and ugly avatar.

The Creep.

With trembling hands, I open it.

'Your time is running out. Make the most of your freedom.' A grainy photo is attached. It's me and Ruben, some time after leaving the club, in my car.

'What do you want?' I angrily type back, ignoring all the words from the police and victim support. But when I send the message the screen goes weird and tells me that this user does not exist. Charlie heads over with a mug of tea and two small pills I've been instructed to take when I'm overwhelmed.

I could do with taking the whole box right now. He sits down next to me and gently takes the laptop from me, closing it.

'That's enough for now,' he says.

He's right, that's totally enough internet for one day. My brain is already starting to spiral. I need to work out what this fucking stalker wants and how he seems to have constant access to me. I look at Charlie. Could it be him? Have I naively let my enemy into my life? I mean, he's just literally admitted to a dark past. Even if it was a bit lame as 'darkness' goes. But what else could he be hiding? As his eyes meet mine, they soften and twinkle. Of course it's not him. Anyway, one of the photos was of me *and* him so that wouldn't make any sense.

'Actually, Kitty, there's something I've wanted to talk to you about.'

Oh God. 'Okay, what's up?'

He takes a deep breath. 'Okay, well, when I found you here and called the ambulance, I mean, even before that, really. When no one could get hold of you. I was so worried. I just wanted to see you. I didn't care about any of the other stuff.' He pauses and takes another deep breath. 'Anyway, what I'm trying to say, in the clumsiest way possible, is that I missed you very much when you weren't around. And that I love you. And, when you're ready, which I know could be a while because you're obviously going through something major here, I'm hoping that maybe we could try this relationship thing again.' He's looking down at his hands now. 'What do you think?'

'Charlie,' I say. 'I'm ready now. I don't need to wait.' I sit myself up properly and lean forwards. 'I love you.'

He looks up at me and suddenly those dimples are back

and it's like the first time you get to sit outside in spring. 'I love you too.' He moves in closer, cups my face in his hands, stroking my cheeks with his thumbs, taking in my face (which still looks a miserable pale state, I'm sure) before kissing my mouth, softly as a feather.

57

KITTY'S APARTMENT, CHELSEA

Tor comes to visit the night after I get home from hospital. Charlie lets her in and she waves some flowers in his direction. I'm back on the sofa, Charlie still treating me like an invalid. She comes and wraps her arms around me. I bury my nose in her hair and breathe in her familiar, beautiful smell.

'Hello you,' she says. 'You really know how to bring the drama, Kits, I'll give you that.' She sits down the bottom end of the sofa, near my feet. Charlie is hovering. Tor gives him a stern look.

'Right,' he says. 'I'm just going to put these in water and then I'll go for a walk.'

Tor smiles as he heads to the kitchen.

'He's a good one,' she says and I have a warm sensation in my stomach, like it's a freezing cold day and I'm eating soup. 'Now, girlie, you need to talk to me about this situation here. What the hell happened? You know you can talk to me if you're feeling low.'

'I didn't try to kill myself,' I say for the millionth time. 'Seriously. I was just trying to block some shit out and obviously took things a bit too far.'

'A bit too far is throwing up outside a club. It is *not* going AWOL for a week and ending up in hospital having your stomach pumped. You're lucky to be alive. And equally lucky not to have been sectioned.' She reaches for my hands. 'Whatever is bothering you, you need to let it go. Try this with me. Actually, let's go out on the balcony. Be at one with nature.' I puzzle at how 'at one' we can be at nature on the tenth floor of an apartment block in the middle of one of the most over-populated cities in the world. But I go with it.

She leads me outside, arranges herself cross-legged on the Maze sofa and reaches for my hands. 'Now close your eyes and take a deep breath.'

I do as she says.

'Now let it out slowly to the count of eight and imagine yourself in a bubble of shining white light.'

I roll my eyes under my lids, but try to picture myself in a bubble anyway.

'Now imagine a cord linking you to whatever is bothering you. Keep breathing deeply.'

I picture Ruben, looking at me with pleading, desperate eyes as I tell him I can't call an ambulance. I imagine a cord coming from my stomach, linking me to him.

'Now imagine a huge pair of scissors or a knife cutting through that cord.' She takes another deep breath. 'You're free.'

Oh, Tor. If only it were as simple as that.

'How do you feel?' she asks, her face bright with hope. 'It's a cord-cutting ritual to release you from things that have been holding you back.'

I smile back. 'Well, I'll keep trying. Thanks.'

'Charlie was so worried about you,' she says. '*That* is a man in love.'

Tor smooths down her hair and sighs. 'I'm sorry for blabbing to him about the baby. I was just so angry with him. I wanted him to know how fragile you are and how much he'd hurt you. But it wasn't my place to say anything.' I can feel her looking at me while I stare ahead.

'It wasn't a baby,' I say, facing her.

A tiny crease appears between her brows.

'Look, I'm not getting into a debate with you about where life starts, but you were pregnant. And then you weren't. You can't just ignore that and carry on like it's had no emotional impact on you.' Tor's been in very costly therapy since the rape. Which is helping her. But not me. Even so, I can't tell her the truth.

'It was barely a missed period,' I sigh. 'And it certainly had nothing to do with the suicide attempt I *didn't* make.'

She side-eyes me. 'Do you think you might be in denial, Kits?'

'No. I do not think I'm in denial, Victoria. I don't want a baby. And nature took care of that decision for me. And I didn't try to kill myself. I was in a crappy mood, I couldn't sleep and I over-self-medicated. It happens. Why is everyone trying to make me think there's something wrong with me?'

Tor's twisting her fingers into knots. 'Because you could

have died. Because you lost a baby. Because you've been so painfully unhappy for so long. You've not been the same since Ad—'

'Don't say his name,' I snap.

'I don't care what tone of voice you use with me, Kitty Collins, you *need* to let go of the Adam-guilt. It wasn't your fault.' She reaches for my fingers now and knots them in with her own. 'I know you feel bad. I *know*.' She pulls me into her and coaxes my head onto her shoulder, rests hers on mine.

'I feel terrible,' I say. 'I wanted him hurt. I wasn't even sorry when he was.'

'Babes, we all think about awful things happening to people who hurt us. But you're not bloody Carrie. Your thoughts had nothing to do with what happened.'

No. Not my thoughts.

'Anyway, I promise you the therapist will help. The one I'm seeing has been brilliant with me. Really gentle.'

I'm sure a therapist is exactly what Tor needs to help her start to heal from what happened to her in Greece. Not quite sure how they'd deal with a non-suicide attempt, a miscarriage that never happened and the several dead men in *my* recent past. But, it's a good opportunity to change the topic.

'And how are *you* doing? *Really?*'

She pulls her hands away from mine and tucks them under her bottom.

'I don't know,' she almost whispers. 'Some days I'm okay and it's like nothing happened. But then other days, even a car horn makes me jump. Some days I don't leave my bed. Paul says it's PTSD.'

'Paul?'

'Dr Paul.' I swear there's a flush on her cheeks. 'Anyway, he says there's lots we can do to help rewire my brain.'

I bet he does.

'Is he good? Your Dr Paul?'

That's when I see it. It's nothing more than a tiny softening of her expression but she's bloody well falling in love with her therapist and – not having any psychology degrees myself – even I'm willing to bet this is Not A Good Thing.

'What?' Tor asks me, all Victorian churchgoer innocence.

'You're blushing.'

'It's night and I'm Black.'

'I can *feel* you blushing.'

'Oh, Kits,' she says. 'Try eating something. Your cheek-bones are starting to look like Maleficent's. And, for once I'm not saying that as a compliment.'

I shake my head. 'Stop changing the subject.'

'Says the actual queen of the subject change.'

'Okay. Well, when you're ready, I'll be here. Just say the word,' I tell her. 'You're vulnerable. And it would be totally unethical.'

She kisses the top of my head before she leaves. 'I love you, Kits.'

58

For the next few weeks, Charlie and I are mostly alone in our little bubble. I've never lived with anyone before and it has never been something that appeals to me, for obvious reasons. But with him, it just works. He makes sure I eat properly, makes sure I sleep properly and makes sure I keep my screen time down. Which has helped so much to calm my mind. The meds given to me by the hospital are kicking in and I feel myself returning to normal, whatever that is. Non-murdery, I guess.

As agreed with the hospital, I also have twice-weekly therapy sessions. My therapist is a guy called Peter who was recommended to me by Tor's mum. I guess Tor is keeping Dr Paul very much to herself. He's what Hen would call a DILF, which make the hourlong sessions slightly more bearable. We talk a lot about my childhood and my dad. Peter seems to think I'm suffering from a deep-set trauma from all the stuff I saw as a kid.

'It's not healthy to see that much death at such a young age,' he tells me during one session. 'It can desensitise you. I would say your recent breakdown is a repressed reaction to what you witnessed as a child.' I would say my recent breakdown is probably more to do with accidentally murdering an innocent man and leaving him bleeding to death when I could have saved him. But what do I know?

As I open up more to Peter, I find myself opening up to Charlie too. I tell him about my parents' twisted relationship and how I don't miss my father.

'I don't grieve for him,' I say one night as we're sat on the floor eating Japanese takeaway. (NB: I've put back all the weight I lost during my 'episode'.)

'Well, you don't know if he's dead,' Charlie says between mouthfuls of food. 'You're in a kind of limbo in that respect. No wonder things are so tough for you.'

I cringe at my blunder. 'Yeah, but there's still a grieving process to go through when someone leaves your life. Dead or missing or just leave you.'

Charlie puts his arms around me. 'I know. I kind of feel the same way about my old man. And he's not missing or dead.'

'You don't miss him?' I ask, surprised. Since his depression confession, Charlie hasn't spoken much about his family.

He shrugs. 'Sometimes. It's hard because Harry still has a relationship with him. But I don't want someone in my life who can't support me. What's that meme? If you can't handle me at my worst, you don't deserve me at my best.' He pretends to flick his hair. 'None of us are perfect, Kits, we're all human, trying to do our best at life. But we all make mistakes too. We need to learn to forgive ourselves for those mistakes. We're our own worst judge and jury.'

He smiles that dimply-smile and I wonder if I can tell him about Ruben. A huge, devastating mistake, but a mistake, nonetheless.

I think I'll keep that to myself for now.

As I watch him, eating and talking, I realise that this is it.

This is my person.

And I will do anything to keep it that way. That means no more killing. It stops now. If I can make such a massive mistake once, I could do it again. I don't even know if I'm in the clear yet.

59

KITTY'S APARTMENT, CHELSEA

The inevitable knock comes a few days after Charlie brought me home. I'm wrapped up on the sofa in my favourite blanket, watching a show about a serial killer in the Seventies.

'Are we expecting anyone?' Charlie asks and I feel a little frisson of pleasure buzz through me at the word 'we'. I'm no longer just me. I belong to someone. Well, you know, in the most feminist sense of the word.

'Not that I know of,' I say.

We look at each other puzzled for a few seconds, thinking the same thing. No one just drops round anymore, do they? The knock comes again, and it makes us both jump.

'I'll go.' Charlie lifts my feet from his lap where they've been resting, tucking them under the blanket, before heading towards the door. I can feel my hands trembling as the muffled sound of voices echoes down the hall.

Then they're there. Two of them. Not uniformed. A woman and a man. The woman must be around my age. She's pretty and I wonder why she's a police officer when there are a hundred other less traumatising things she'd be able to do with her looks. The man is in his thirties, nondescript. I can already tell from their body language that he is in love with her, despite the gold band on his finger. I may be on a cocktail of drugs that make my head feel swimmy, but I can still spot these things. I wonder if they're actually fucking. Or if it's an unrequited love. That's the tipping point, isn't it? We've all got the potential to do very bad things; it's whether we can control those urges that make us what we are. Would he cheat on his partner? Christ, I'm high.

Charlie's chatting away as he leads them through to me. He's talking too fast and it's making me agitated.

'Kits, these guys want to talk to you about the night Ruben Reynolds was killed. Are you up to it? I've told them you've not been well and have been in hospital. I don't know, maybe they could come back later—'

'No,' the woman says, cutting him off. 'We'd rather get it done now. It's just some questions. I'm sure Miss Collins can cope.' She smiles at me. It reaches her eyes and I can see exactly how she gets people to trust her. It's something I do myself.

'Sure, it's fine. Please sit down.'

The officers sit on the other sofa. There's an awkward moment as someone on screen is violently hacked to death. The noise of an axe ripping through flesh fills the room. I scrabble to find the remote and turn it off. I give the lady officer a winning smile of my own.

'Sorry about that. Just been catching up on some TV. Would you like a drink? Tea? Coffee?'

The man opens his mouth to say something but he's cut

off by his partner. No wonder he's in love with her. She's a phenomenal presence. I'd probably have a crush on her too.

'We're fine. Thanks for the offer though. So, I'm DI Taylor and this is DS Marsden. We're looking into what happened on the night that Ruben Reynolds was found dead at his home.' She eyes me.

I nod, deliberately keeping the silence.

She breaks first and Marsden takes out a notebook.

'So according to witnesses,' he says, in a voice that is clearly being put through its paces with a forty-a-day smoking habit, 'you were one of the last people to see Ruben alive. This was at Raffles nightclub on the night in question.'

I nod again. 'Yes, that's right.'

'A Miss Emily Whitely has said you and Mr Reynolds were chatting for much of the night and she says he left shortly after you. Is this right?'

'I was talking to him, yes, but it wasn't for much of the night. I was only there an hour or so. And I don't know when he left because . . . well, I'd gone.'

'And can you remember what you spoke about?'

'It's actually a bit embarrassing,' I say, pulling the blanket tightly around myself so only my head is visible. 'I was talking to him for about twenty minutes, thinking he was actually his brother, Raphe. That's actually why I didn't stick around. It was pretty humiliating.'

Marsden is scribbling stuff down – do they not have iPhones? – but Taylor is still eyeing me.

'And it was Raphe in particular you wanted to speak to? Why was that?'

'It's quite embarrassing too,' I say. 'Charlie and I had broken up. I wanted to make him jealous. When I saw Raphe, well, who I *thought* was Raphe, come into the club, I thought it would be a good idea to try and get some photos with him for Instagram. It's childish.' I give Charlie big, sad eyes. 'I'm sorry. I was still hurting so much. I wanted you to be jealous.'

He smiles weakly at me. 'Don't worry.'

'Okay. So, at what point did you realise that it wasn't Raphe you were talking to?'

An image of Ruben, slumped on his floor, clutching at his neck as blood spurted out, pops into my head. I have to squeeze my eyes closed and shake it away. The police people are looking at me strangely when I open them again. Luckily Charlie steps in.

'She's had to start taking medication,' he explains. 'She's still getting used to them. They give her brain zaps sometimes. Do you want some water, Kits?'

What I actually want is a fucking huge measure of vodka and some horse tranquilisers. But water will have to do. For now.

'Yes. Thank you. It was about two minutes before I left. He'd topped up my drink. I put my hand on his arm and said, "Thanks, Raphe." He started laughing, said something like "I've just spent twenty minutes talking to someone who thinks I'm my brother". He found it funny. I was embarrassed, so I left.'

'So, it's possible that Ruben left to find you and make sure you were okay?'

I shrug. 'It's possible. I don't know. I've not been very well. I sort of had a bit of a breakdown.'

Taylor is nodding. 'Yes. So we gathered. You attempted suicide, according to the hospital. You must've been in a very dark place to do that.'

'It wasn't a suicide attempt.' I feel like I should get some cards printed with this. 'I was feeling low . . .'

'She was pregnant, she lost the baby,' Charlie says. I let it go this time. I mean, he needs to move on from this though.

'I was very depressed and I must've accidentally taken too many sleeping pills. And I know they say not to mix with alcohol, but I did. I'm lucky Charlie found me.'

'Okay,' Taylor says, standing. 'Well, thanks for your time. We'll let you know if we need anything else.'

'Is that all?' Charlie asks.

Taylor and Marsden nod in unison. Synchronised.

They're definitely fucking.

'We wanted to talk to everyone who Ruben was with that night. Everyone has said pretty much the same thing.'

'What about CCTV?' Charlie, will you shut the fuck up.

'Very strange. The cameras at the club weren't recording that night. And Ruben's home security was all off. We think this made him an easy target.'

'Target for who?' I ask.

'It looks very much like a robbery gone wrong. We think Ruben may well have disturbed them. There were signs of a struggle and forced entry.'

There *were*?

'Anyway, thanks again for your time, Miss Collins.' Taylor

holds out her hand and I untangle myself from my blanket fort to shake it. 'Glad you're feeling better. Hopefully you'll be back online soon? My little sister has been moaning that you've not posted anything for ages.' She smiles at me again, but this time I can feel it's genuine.

Marsden doesn't say anything but nods and they let Charlie show them to the door.

Signs of a struggle and forced entry?

What the fuck? Have I actually gone mad?

I pick my phone up from the coffee table and open Instagram. I've promised Charlie and my therapist that I'd take at least a month away from social media, but I need to look. I open the app and the messages and, sure enough, there's one from him. The Creep. I'd almost forgotten about the bloody stalker with everything else that's going on. I really need that drink now. My hands are trembling and I worry that I'm about to lose the plot. There are too many balls in the air and my hands are slippery with blood.

'Added a few little touches to the Ruben Reynolds scene. When did you get so careless? Don't worry, Kitty I've got your back. But you need to start playing my game properly now. I'll be in touch.'

So, the stalker *does* have plans for me after all.

60

Despite it now being technically autumn, the heatwave is persistent. And now I'm feeling more like I can cope with real life, Charlie decides what I really need is a picnic. I hate picnics, but just to show how much this man is changing my life for the better, I'm willing to do this for him.

'I don't get the point of eating outside with no table service,' I whine as he packs a hamper full of food. 'Sitting on the floor.'

'It's romantic,' he says. 'I don't know how familiar you are with the concept of romance, but trust me.'

'But. Wasps. Ants.'

'I will slaughter them for you.'

'Hello? Vegan.'

'Fine. I'll shoo them away in a humane manner. Happy?'

I pretend to sulk, but actually I am happy. Ridiculously happy.

We head to Green Park in an Uber and set up our picnic in a not-too-crowded spot when my phone buzzes.

It's from Hen. 'Daddy's having one of his parties. He's adamant that you come and bring Charlie.'

James Pemberton's parties are the things of legend. He's always throwing these Gatsby-style affairs, usually when he's signed a naive singer or band he knows will make him a ton of money. Growing up, we used to live for James's parties, they were more raucous than the ones my parents threw – and usually filled to the brim with celebrities and models. And drugs.

'Hen's dad's having a party,' I say. 'He wants us to go.'

'Do you feel up to it?'

I think for a moment. 'You know what? I do. But what about you? I mean, they're pretty wild.'

Charlie laughs. 'Let's go. We've been cooped up in your flat for much too long. We need to remind ourselves how to socialise with other humans. Plus, we're still relatively young, I believe.'

I tap out a reply. 'We'll be there. Any theme?'

James loves a theme.

'Oh yes, Eighties cinema #eyeroll'

Yep. This was going to be pretty painful.

Weirdly, Charlie is more into the idea than I thought he would be.

'I think it would be great to get to know your mates better,' he says.

'Really? I thought you thought they were vacuous airheads who don't care about me?'

He grins. 'I'm always happy to be proved wrong. And you can't go wrong with some Eighties cosplay. So, who are we going as? Two out of four Ghostbusters? Doc and Marty? ET and Elliott? You'd have to be the funny-looking alien, of course.'

'Hilarious. To be honest, anything that involves any kind of heavy make-up or prosthetic is totally out. I'd die in this heat.'

Charlie looks up at the sun, which is angrily glaring down at the planet. 'Yeah, good point. How about Kim Basinger and Mickey Rourke in *9½ Weeks*? They don't wear a lot, from memory.' He wiggles a strawberry suggestively in front of my lips.

'I'll bite your fingers off,' I warn him. 'Seriously though, if you're going to do this, you have to do it properly. People really go all out at James's parties. It's like this huge thing.'

'I am still capable of having fun, Kits. I'm not your carer.'

I watch Charlie for a long time as he eats and pours us sparkling water – I'm off the booze for a while as I'm meant to be letting the anti-depressants I've been prescribed kick in – and make myself a promise. I promise that I won't do anything to wreck this. And that I won't ever kill again. Not only could I not live with myself if I made another mistake, but this wonderful man who has saved my life can never know what a monster I am.

I lean in and kiss him.

'I love you,' I say.

He looks at me, tilts his head slightly and brushes my cheek with his thumb.

'I love you back.'

And just for that moment, everything is perfect. But there are still a few tiny loose ends I need to deal with before I can put this all to bed.

And keep it there.

61

My heart is racing in my chest as I pull into the driveway of the care home. I've not visited before, but I've looked at the Grade II–listed building several times online, trying to imagine him there, imagine his life there. It looks nice enough. Ivy climbs the walls and the gardens are pretty. There are lots of flowers in bloom and the front lawns are startlingly green, even in this heat.

Adam always liked flowers.

It can't be cheap, but I don't think money has ever been an issue.

I take a deep breath in, count to five – and out, count to five, and sit on my hands to stop them from shaking. Of all my demons, this is going to be the toughest one to face. I keep up the breathing exercise as I get out of my car and head towards the double oak doors.

A receptionist is sitting behind a massive mahogany desk, surrounded by fake orchids. There's a large blue sofa in the lobby, as well as a couple of well-used armchairs. The walls are painted a warm yellow and have a scattering of framed prints on them. All warm colours and cosy scenes. It all feels very homely, which is obviously the intention. It feels more like a hotel lobby than a care home. Apart from the smell. The bleach and misery reek of hospital. I walk to the reception desk and the receptionist, younger than me, skin to kill for, gives me a huge but eerie smile.

'Hello,' she says, in a voice a few octaves higher than I am expecting. 'How can I help you?'

'I'm here to visit Adam Edwards?'

'Ah yes, lovely Adam.' She stands up. 'Let me show you through to his room.'

I follow her down a carpeted corridor.

'You've not been here before, have you?' she asks me, not curiously, just making conversation.

'No . . . I . . . well, no. I'm a bit ashamed actually.'

'Okay, well just prepare yourself in that case. He's worked with some of the best physios in the country, but he's still unable to do more than communicate by blinking.' She gives me a sad smile and pats my arm. 'Do you know him well?'

'Oh.' I don't know what to say. 'We were close friends.'

She opens the door of a room and can't help but take a sharp intake of breath. She gives me another pat on the arm, probably trying to reassure me.

'Look, Adam, you've got a visitor. That's the second one this week. Isn't that nice?' She turns back to me. Her name badge says Laura. 'I'll make you a cuppa, shall I?'

I nod, grateful, and watch as she turns, leaving me alone with the most painful piece of my past.

And I'm not prepared for this. My breath catches in my lungs every time I try to inhale.

Adam is propped up in a chair, held up by a kind of harness thing. I haven't seen him since that night at his house. The night I boiled with white-hot fury after seeing those messages from Saskia.

It's been almost eight years since I last saw this man, this man whom I was once so completely besotted with. He is still beautiful, thinner, but it just has the effect of making his cheekbones look even more incredible. His eyes haven't changed, those dark pools that I used to think I'd be able to drown in. But as they fix on me, standing in the doorway, the only expression they show is terror. He has a tracheotomy tube in his neck to breathe, and another in his stomach, which I assume is how he's fed.

I did this to him.

'Hey, Adam,' I say, edging closely towards his chair. He starts blinking frantically, but it's only me and him now and I don't know what he's trying to say. 'Don't be scared,' I speak softly. 'I'm not here to hurt you.'

I sit myself down on the bed, making sure that I'm in his eyeline. We stare at each other for what feels like several lifetimes. A rivulet of saliva trickles from the side of his mouth. I look around the room and see a box of tissues on a table next to his bed. I take one and gingerly wipe the drool from his face. He doesn't flinch – because he can't – but he closes his eyes, trying to block me out. 'Adam. I'm so sorry.'

His eyes stay closed and I wonder if he's also thinking about the last time we saw each other.

I was furious, full of a vicious anger after seeing the messages between him and Saskia. He'd been lying to me for months. Lying, even when I was trying my best to look after him while he was in the depths of depression. I'd dedicated so much time and so much of myself into loving him. The humiliation stung as much as the anger and – when he came back downstairs – ready for our night out, I flipped. I'd already grabbed one of his fucking awful fibreglass trophies – some kind of best debut novel award – as he sat down on the sofa, waiting for me to bring the drink I'd pretended to be fixing, I swung it at the back of his head. There was a crunch as the bone at the base of his skull caved. He howled from the pain and stumbled forward, trying to catch hold of the arm of the sofa. But his brain was no longer sending the right signals to the right body parts and he ended up sliding down until he was slumped against it, his eyes boring into mine, asking me why.

'Fucking Saskia?' I'd dropped down to my knees so I was level with him. 'Fucking. Saskia.' He kept on staring at me. 'Well, at least say something. At least *try* to deny it.'

But no words came. Only a trickle of blood from his mouth. I stood up and backed away, horrified. Panicking, I grabbed my bag, shoved the murder weapon in it. I frantically looked around the room, also grabbed his laptop and a couple of other expensive-looking bits – some headphones I think – and his phone, which he'd dropped during his descent to the floor, and I fled.

I ran out into the street, thinking I should call an ambulance or something.

I meant to.

I wanted to but, in all honesty, I thought I'd killed him. I thought it was too late.

It was Saskia who found him, of course. She'd probably started to panic that he'd changed his mind and wasn't going to break my heart and leave me after all.

But he wasn't dead.

I didn't visit him in hospital while surgeons tried to put his brilliant and broken brain back together. Instead, I read about it online. The police assumed it was a robbery gone wrong, that Adam had disturbed them mid-looting. He'd been attacked and left for dead. But they hadn't hit him hard enough to quite kill him. The blow to the head had caused a massive stroke, which was what had left him like . . . this.

It was sometime later when I read about him again – although I thought about him constantly. An article in a Sunday supplement. A stylised shoot at Saskia's home. It turned out that his brilliant brain wasn't damaged at all. It was fine. But he couldn't walk or talk. Or write. In fact, all he could do was blink and think. And I knew how badly those periods of 'just thinking' got for him. I remember thinking that, for someone like Adam, this was worse than death. All that creativity and brilliance combined with all that darkness and pain. And now without any outlet for it at all. He'd once told me, during a particularly dark depression, that his head was the scariest place to be.

Now he was trapped in it, until death.

Saskia had been his carer for a while, but she soon tired

of having to feed him through a straw and wipe up his shit. I'm assuming his parents weren't keen on it either. Which is how he ended up here.

The receptionist gently tapping the door brings me out of my reverie.

'Here's your tea, love. I put a couple of sugars in there for the shock. You look pale as a ghost. I thought you were gonna pass out on me for a minute.' I notice she has a wisp of an Irish accent. She puts the tea down on the bedside cabinet, between Adam and me. 'You can have a chat with him, you know. We do one blink for "yes" and two for "no", don't we, Adam love?'

Adam blinks once.

'Such a shame, what happened to him. Wrote a great book about ten years ago. They thought he was gonna be the next Dan Brown.' She pats my arm again as she leaves the room. Adam glares after her. I can't help but allow a small smile.

'Still think Dan Brown is commercial bullshit, then?'

Adam blinks once.

'I'm sorry I haven't come to see you,' I say. 'Do you like it here?' The room is nice enough but it's obviously a far cry from his London townhouse. It's a ridiculous question and we both know it. There's a floral throw on the bed, which doesn't disguise the fact that it's a hospital bed. There are a few pieces of furniture – some shelves with his precious books on them. I guess one of the carers must read to him or something. There are a few pictures of his family. None of Saskia. There's a flat-screen TV on the wall. I wonder how he changes channels or if he just has to sit in front of whatever the carers put on.

He blinks twice.

I feel the tears falling from my eyes now and I wipe them away with my sleeve. They're not self-pity, they're tears for this man whom I'd once loved so dearly and completely. Whom I'd danced and drank and fucked around London with, having – what we thought were – the most incredible conversations but were probably bullshit like everyone else's, but it was *our* bullshit and it mattered and I'd ruined it.

I'd ruined him.

'I really am so sorry, Adam. I am. I didn't mean for this. I was just so angry. I loved you so much. I would've done anything for you.' I reach for the tea but the sudden movement makes him look startled, afraid. I'm taken aback. 'Are you scared of me?'

He blinks once.

Shame swallows me. I'd thought this was a fitting punishment for him, but sitting here, looking at the man I once adored with my whole heart, a man who was once so brilliant he could hold the attention of an entire roomful of people, a man now reduced to communicating in blinks, I would do anything to change the past.

'Why didn't you tell anyone it was me?' My voice is childish and whiny. 'I don't understand.'

There's another knock on the door and an older lady pops her head in. She must be mid-forties, her hair is dyed a bright red and styled like a pin-up girl's. She's wheeling in a machine with a bag of fluids attached to it. She's stunning.

'Hello, Adam love, are you ready for lunch? Oh. You've got a visitor. Hello, love. Are you a friend of Adam's?'

'I'm Kitty,' I say.

'Well, it's nice to see someone here. Don't get too many visitors now his parents have moved abroad, the poor love. Talk to him though. He likes that. He likes being read to as well. We're going through the works of James Joyce at the moment, aren't we, Adam? We're on *Dubliners*. Why don't you read him a few chapters? I'll come back in a bit with this. I'm sure he'd appreciate someone other than me or Elise reading.' She hands me a worn copy of *Dubliners* and I can picture where it sat on his shelves all those years ago.

My hands are trembling so much they look like I'm having a seizure.

'Can you ever forgive me?'

One blink and a half. My heart leaps. I love him. And I hate myself.

'This was a terrible idea coming here. I don't know what to tell you apart from that I truly truly am sorry. If I could put it right, I would.'

He just stares at me. Cold.

'Okay, I'm going to go. Can I ask you something before I leave though? Can I come nearer?'

One blink.

I kneel by his feet, my hands on his knees, looking up into those eyes. The man I'd have done anything for. The man who absolutely broke me to pieces.

'Did you ever really love me?'

There's long pause and, for the briefest moment, I see a flicker of something in those dark eyes, a tiny glimpse of my first love. He blinks once.

I don't even realise I'm crying until I'm back in my car.

62

Charlie's cooking something when I get home. It smells wonderful but I know I won't be able to eat. My mind keeps going back to Adam and what I did to him, intentionally or not, it doesn't matter. I've ruined his life because he cheated. Yes, it sucked and it hurt like fuckery, but I could've just keyed his car or slept with his best friend like a normal person. He doesn't deserve to be where he is. Somehow, I need to make things better for him.

'Penny for them,' Charlie says as he comes up behind me and wraps his arms around me.

'Hmm?'

'You were miles away then.' He nuzzles into the back of my neck and breathes me in. 'Missed you. Where have you been anyway? I tried calling.'

I turn around and wrap my arms around his waist, letting my head rest against his chest.

How honest can I be here?

'I went to see an old friend, well, an ex actually.' I look up into Charlie's eyes, gauging his reaction. 'My one ex, actually.'

He frowns slightly, a tiny crease of confusion between his eyebrows. 'Anything I need to be worried about?'

I shake my head. 'No. He's in a residential hospital.'

Charlie's brows shoot up.

'He was in an accident, well, attacked, in his home a few years ago. He's been left with locked-in syndrome. It's awful.'

'I remember reading about this, I think. Wasn't he an author or playwright or something?'

'Yeah. Adam Edwards. I've not seen him since it happened. I couldn't bear it.'

'You weren't with him then? As in together when it happened?'

'No. We'd already split. He dumped me for someone else. It was a pretty shit time to be honest.'

'Who in their right mind would dump you?' He kisses the top of my head.

'Well, many would argue that he wasn't.' I attempt a weak smile. 'He had serious mental health issues.'

'It's the only explanation for picking someone over you that I can think of. So, it was a bit of a shock?'

'Yeah. I wasn't really prepared. The last time I saw him, we had a huge row about him cheating on me. It was weird seeing him like that.'

'He can't do anything?'

'He can communicate with blinks, but that's it.'

Charlie pulls me closer to him. 'I'm sorry it's upset you so much. Glass of wine needed?'

I nod. 'Please.'

He heads over to the fridge and pulls out a bottle of Sancerre. 'Why now though?'

'Why now what?'

'Why did you decide to see him now? After all this time?'

'Guilt,' I say. It's not a lie.

Charlie hands me my drink and looks at me with that little brow furrow thing again, his eyes questioning.

'I feel guilty that I haven't visited him sooner. It's been years and his girlfriend shoved him in this hospital and his parents have moved abroad. He's just been left there. Trapped in his own mind. I feel terrible.'

'You know your problem, Kitty Collins? Your heart is too big.' He pulls me in for a kiss and I let myself melt into his goodness, hoping that maybe some of it will transfer to me.

63

PEMBERTON MANOR, KENSINGTON

'Are you sure you're feeling up to this?' Charlie asks as our car pulls up outside the Pembertons' giant house. 'You still seem low after seeing your ex yesterday. I don't want you relapsing when you're doing so well.'

I look over at him, his nose scrunched up a little. Concern or distaste? I wish I could read people better. 'I'm fine,' I say. 'A party is actually what I need right now. Take me out of my head for a bit.'

He frowns.

'Not *literally* out of my head. I know I need to take it easy.'

'That's up to you. Like I said, I'm not your carer. But I *do* love you and I don't ever want to see you as low as you were.'

I kiss his cheek and let him get out of the car first so he can come around and open my door for me. I'm all for equality and stuff, but there's still room for some old-fashioned chivalry in the world. As he offers his hand to help me out of the car, I feel a jolt of pleasure and proprietary pride shoot through me. Mine.

We'd decided on She-Ra and He-Man and, when he tried his full outfit on before we came out, I was delighted with the choice. His costume consists of red pants, a chest plate – and that's about it.

I wink at him as he puts his arm around my waist and we walk up the drive to the house.

'Stop leering at me!' He laughs. 'I'm not a piece of meat. *You* however look sensational.'

I do a little twirl for him. 'Come on then, Master of the Universe, let's get this over with.'

'Is it wrong that I quite like you calling me that?'

'Don't get used to it.'

The party is as hideous as expected. As we walk in, I feel Charlie's fingers brush mine and our hands slip into each other's.

James – or rather his team – has gone to extreme lengths, even by his standards. Charlie is stopped in his tracks by the actual DeLorean, which is in pride of place in the main hall. There are waxworks of famous people from the Eighties situated around the edge of the room. There's even a huge projected moon on the ceiling, with a real bike suspended to recreate the famous image from *E.T.*

'Why the Eighties?' Charlie whispers as we squeeze past Freddie Mercury deep in conversation with Princess Diana to get a drink from Tom Cruise, who's throwing cocktail shakers around behind a pop-up bar.

'It was when James set up his record label. All of his parties are basically him wanking over his own success. But shhh. We don't talk about it in public.'

'It's pretty authentic. It's a shame about all the iPhones and selfie sticks though. They are kind of killing the vibe.'

'Killing it? They are absolutely murdering it and dancing on its fucking grave.'

Charlie chuckles as I look around the crowd of Ghostbusters and Flashdancers and spot Hen (Eighties Madonna) and Tor (Lisa Lisa) and drag Charlie over to them.

'Hey, Eighties bitches,' I say. 'You look great.'

Hen gives me and Charlie the Chelsea Once Over and smirks. 'Aw, you've come in couples' fancy dress. How sweet. But you know they were actually siblings, not lovers, right?' Her tone is iced with something I can't put my finger on.

'Ignore her,' Tor says. 'She's just pissed off that Grut hasn't messaged her all week and is convinced he's sleeping with one of his groupies. Which he probably is.'

Hen glares at her.

'What? You said it yourself about ten minutes ago.'

'I didn't tell you so you can repeat it to everyone.'

'It's only Kitty, for God's sake. Who's she going to tell? We're both here and Maisie . . . well.' She indicates a corner, where Maisie and Rupert are engaged in what would probably be called 'heavy petting' at a local pool.

'Ah, that's back on then?' I ask. 'After Willy-gate.'

Charlie's eyes go wide. 'I'll get some drinks on that note.'

'I'll have a Martini McFly and Kits will have a Long Island Vanilla Ice Tea. Trust me. They've been inseparable since the shit with Ruben,' she adds as Charlie battles to the bar.

'But no one knows what went on?'

Hen shrugs. 'No one has a clue. You were like the last

person to see him. The general consensus is that it was a break-in gone wrong.'

This was news to me. 'Oh really?'

'Yeah. The police seem to think that whoever killed Ruben obvs thought Raphe was in Marbella. But Ruben was house-sitting and surprised them. So awful. Raphe's setting up a charity apparently, something to do with families affected by grief.' She rolls her eyes.

'There's nothing wrong with doing something for charity,' Charlie says, as he comes back with some alarming-looking cocktails.

Hen knocks back the drink she's holding before starting on another. 'There is when it's ninety per cent for selfish reasons.'

We watch silently as she stalks off to the bar to get another drink.

Tor turns to me and Charlie. 'She is in a *foul* mood. I don't know what's going on but I think there's more to it than her casual shag acting like a casual shag.'

'Do you think she's fallen for him?'

'Hairy Grut? I very much doubt it. I think maybe she's pissed off with Maisie for being so cutesy with Roo. But I don't know.'

'Ah. Okay. That makes sense.' I glance over at the bar where Hen is talking to Jane Fonda, but glaring over to where Maisie and Rupert are sitting. 'I'll talk to her later.'

The party is actually a lot of fun. I'm having to watch how much I drink because of the pills I'm on but I'm quite enjoying seeing the wasted people stagger around. There's a particularly surreal moment where I walk into a bathroom to find a totally pissed Bananaman holding back a Fraggle's hair as she vomits into the loo.

'I'll find another one,' I say to Bananaman, who's starting to look a bit green.

As I head up another staircase, I spot Hen. She's sitting on a step, swirling a glass around in front of her eyes, looking pretty pissed off with life. Which I know is hard to swallow, but even rich girls get the blues.

I drop down next to her. 'What's up?'

She squints at me. 'Where's your sidekick?' She's very drunk. There's slurring and head wobbling.

'If you mean Charlie, he's somewhere around. Is that why you're upset?'

She sighs and slumps against me. 'I feel like I'm the only one who's unhappy. Why does no one love me?'

I hold her head in my hands and look into her drunken, glazed eyes.

'Henrietta Pemberton. I love you. And Tor loves you. And Maisie loves you.'

She scoffs hard at this point and jerks her head away from me. 'You all. With your perfect lives. Perfect love lives. Everything so fucking perfect.'

'Hen,' I say. 'I hate to point out *all* the flaws in your argument. But none of us have perfect lives. I mean, my dad . . .'

'Your dad!' She waves her glass in the air and liquid sloshes out onto the wooden stairs. The wood immediately discolours, which I should try to remember because what the hell is it doing to our insides?

'My dad is missing, Hen. We don't know if he's alive or not. That's pretty much a daily dose of hell.'

She stares hard at me and for a moment it feels like she doesn't like me very much at all. 'At least your dad wanted you,' she finally says before her head drops into my lap. I stroke her hair and let her sob her daddy issues out for a bit. Eventually I hear her take a deep breath, knowing she's giving herself an inside pep talk. She lifts her head up. 'Even *my* dad wants you. I feel like I'm invisible to *him*.'

'What?'

She nods. Wipes her arm over her face.

'Your dad *adores* you. Anyone can see that,' I say.

'He adores money. And power. Not us. Well, not *me*.'

'Hen hun, you're in a bad mood and I think this is the drink and . . .' I pause and take a look at her nose. Sure enough there's a slight trace of crusty white powder around her right nostril. 'Have you thought about maybe getting some professional help if you really feel like this?'

Her sad, tired eyes are suddenly blazing with fury.

Oh God.

She's about to kick off.

I've seen this look *many* times before.

'A *counsellor*?' She rises to her feet, looking down on me like I'm beneath her in so many ways. 'A counsellor? Wow. One failed suicide attempt and suddenly Kitty Collins is a qualified psychotherapist.'

I stand up to face her. 'Hen, you know I didn't mean that in a derogatory way. I just . . .'

'What? You just what? Wanted to remind me of yet another

way that you are better than me? You're so kind and compassionate now?'

'I'm trying to help,' I say, helplessly.

'Ram it, Saint Kitty. I'm going to find some drugs.' She pushes past me and stomps down the stairs.

That was a lot.

I leave it for a couple of minutes, breathing deeply, and head after her, hoping she'll have calmed down enough to let me talk. She's becoming quite an aggressive drunk.

When I catch up with her, she's half dragging one of the Extras out of the front door.

I can hear her yelling.

'You weren't even invited so stop trying to use my party and *my hashtag* to make your sad little account better. You don't even have ten thousand. Why are you even here?'

The girl – Tasha maybe – looks mortified while Tor is trying to calm Hen down. I'm really not in the mood for this.

And I still need to pee.

64

JAMES PEMBERTON'S RECORDING STUDIO, PEMBERTON MANOR BASEMENT

I carry on with my journey towards the basement studio and am pleased to see it's completely empty.

Good.

I could do with a few moments to clear my head after that monstrous row. No one else would dare come down here.

The recording booth looks sad and abandoned, one lonely microphone standing in the middle of it. I head into the bathroom at the back of the studio, pee, flush and wash my hands. I check out my face in the mirror, no mascara under eyes. Good.

I head back out to the main studio, slump into one of the seats by the mixing desk and take some deep breaths. I look down and realise my hands are shaking. Maybe Charlie was right and coming to a massive party was too much too soon. I'm going to go and find him and go home. All I want is my blanket, my head in his lap and some awful TV.

I'm about to stand up when I hear the door close softly

behind me. I spin round, startled when I see James standing there, a glass of something in his hand and a strange look in his eyes. They're slightly glazed over.

'Kitty, Kitty, Kitty. You know you're not supposed to be down here, you bad girl.' He waggles his finger, mock-scolding me.

'I know, sorry. I came down here to use the loo. The others were all taken.'

'Yes, it's starting to get a bit wild up there. My bloody daughter throwing a hissy fit over some girl. I came down for some peace.' He takes a little bag of white powder out of his shirt pocket and waves it at me. 'But you're here.'

'Honestly, I was just leaving. I've literally been in here for five minutes. Sorry.'

'Don't apologise. It was a pleasant surprise. Be peaceful with me for five?' He waggles the baggie again.

'Nah, I don't really do all that anymore.'

'No coke woke enough for you, eh?'

'Ha. It's not that. I just had, I guess, what's called a life-changing experience lately. It's good to see you. Let's catch up soon.'

'No, no.' There's an edge to his voice and I don't like it. 'Stay and have a drink and a line with me. We haven't spoken in ages. I do worry about you, Kitty. Your dad always told me to look after you if anything happened to him.'

He sits down on the leather couch and pats the seat next to him for me to join. I really want to find Charlie and go home but I awkwardly perch myself as far away from him as I can without seeming rude.

'So how are things, Kitty? I heard you spent some time in hospital?' He leans over the coffee table, which looks more like a piece of modern art than furniture, and empties the contents of the bag onto it. He roots around in his pocket again, this time pulling out a bank card. 'Was that the life changer?' He begins to chop the powder, separating it into smooth white lines.

'Yes, but it was accidental. And I'm fine now. Charlie's been looking after me.'

He nods. 'That's right. Little Charlie Chambers. I have to say, Kitty, I always thought you would've preferred a man over a boy.' He leans back into the sofa, crossing his legs so his right ankle is on his left knee. His eyes make their way from my face down my body and then back up again. It's a far more sexual move than the Chelsea Once Over. The hairs on the back of my neck prickle in warning.

This isn't right.

This is James. My surrogate dad James.

'Charlie *is* a man,' I say and stand to leave.

'Hey, don't rush off.' I startle as he grabs my arm and manoeuvres me back down onto the sofa. 'Now. You stay right there. Help yourself to some of that and I'll get us a drink of something special. Then you can tell your Uncle James all your woes. How does that sound?'

'James. I really do have to go.'

'No, no. You came down here, Kitty. You came down here to my *private* quarters, so I have to assume you were looking for me. So, I think I get to say when you go. Okay?' He thrusts a rolled-up banknote into my hand.

'That's not the case. I already explained I needed the loo.'

He narrows his eyes at me. 'Stay. We can have some fun before you have to rush off.' He runs one of his hands up my arm, making me shiver. 'You really have grown up to be a beautiful woman, Kitty Collins. Very beautiful indeed. And I *did* promise your dad I'd look after you.'

I try to wiggle free from his grip, but he doesn't let go. My heart starts to hammer and I'm worried I'm about to have a full-blown panic attack. I've always known James can be quite handsy, but not with Hen's friends, not with me. I'm practically family.

'You really need to let me go,' I say. 'I'll scream.'

He laughs and claps his hands together like I've made a delightfully charming joke. 'But darling, the whole place is soundproof. In my private space, no one can hear you scream.'

I try to stand up again but he grabs my arm and drags me back down. He's more forceful this time and I know I'll have bruises there by morning.

'Now. Behave yourself. Have a line. Then I'll help you relax. It can't be good for your mental health to be so uptight.'

Bastard.

He taps the coffee table and I reluctantly lean forward. Holding my left nostril closed, I put the banknote against the other one and inhale a line. As I do this, James stands up and walks behind the sofa. When I sit back, I feel his hands on my bare shoulders. He's squeezing and kneading my skin. I can't move. He moves his hands over my shoulders, down to my breasts, under my top. He squeezes the flesh there too. His lips brush against my neck. I still can't move. I'm totally frozen in fear.

'I bet I can make this Kitty purr.'

It's the slamming of a door that makes him leap away from me.

'What the fuck is going on here?' Hen's voice is shrill with outrage.

'Just having a little catch-up with Kitty,' James says.

I rearrange my clothes, grab my phone and push past Hen. I heave the door open and run up the stairs, straight into Maisie.

'Where's Charlie?'

'Um. I saw him talking to Roo a little while ago,' she says. 'What's wrong? You look like you've seen a ghost. Are you okay?'

'I just want Charlie.'

I find him in a corner talking to Rupert.

'I want to go home,' I say.

'Oh hey, I wondered where you'd got to. Sure, let me finish my drink and I'll call a car.'

'No, Charlie. I want to go *now*.'

Charlie looks at me, puzzled. 'Kits, what's wrong?'

'I'll tell you later, but please, I really *really* want to get out of here. Right now.'

'Do you have to bring the drama all the time, Collins?' Roo slurs. 'Can you not let the man have some fun?'

Charlie turns to him. 'That's a bit much, pal. She's clearly upset about something.'

'Kitty's always upset about something.' Roo stands up

and holds his hand out to shake Charlie's. 'Well, it was nice chewing the fat with you, old boy.' Charlie ignores him and Roo shrugs before drunkenly bumbling off, singing some old rugby chant.

'Kits? You're worrying me now. Are you okay?'

'I'm fine, honestly. And I'll tell you in the car. But can we get out of here?'

It takes about twenty minutes for a car to collect us and Charlie keeps asking me what's wrong as we wait outside.

'Come on, what's happened? I heard you and Hen had words. Has that upset you?'

Our car pulls up and Charlie holds the door open before slipping in beside me.

'It's not that,' I say as we pull away from Pemberton Manor.

'Then what?'

'I had a run-in with James.'

'James?' There's an unexpected clipped tone to his voice. 'What do you mean?'

'Well, I needed the loo and all the bathrooms in the house were "in use", so I went down to his studio in the basement because I know he has a bathroom down there. I knew it would be empty.'

'Right, go on.' I don't recognise this new tone. And I don't like it.

'I was just about to leave when James came in.'

Charlie's frowning now.

'He was fully drunk and wouldn't let me leave. Wanted me to stay and have a drink, a line and some "fun" with him. I was really scared. I kept saying no, but he wouldn't let me go.'

Charlie's jaw flinches.

'He kept making all these inappropriate comments about how much I've grown up. Luckily Hen came in. I don't think he would've let me go at all otherwise.'

Charlie's expression darkens and he slams his hands against the seat in front of him, making me jump.

'Are you okay? Did he hurt you?' His eyes are furious as they meet mine.

'I'm fine. Just shook me up a little. I didn't think he'd let me out.'

'That man. He never learns.'

'What do you mean?'

Charlie sighs. 'You're telling me you don't know that James has got a bit of a reputation? There are a lot of rumours floating around about him in his industry. And he gave a few women who work for the charity a hard time whenever he came into the offices. I had a number of complaints about his inappropriate behaviour.'

I stare at Charlie in shock. 'What? No. But he's still a patron? Why?'

He sighs again, much more heavily this time.

'Why do you think, Kitty? Because he brings a lot of money in. And gives a lot too. Half of the projects we've done wouldn't have been possible without his money. I'm not proud of it, but our association with James is a huge fucking deal, okay.'

I stare at him, not quite believing what I'm hearing. 'So, in essence, you're saying it's fine for him to sexually harass your staff because he gives you money? You're basically prostituting them?'

He shakes his head. 'No, it's not like that. He's been warned, several times, that he can't act like that. He seemed to take it on board, even apologised to the women in question. But it looks like he can't help himself.'

'And what are these rumours? The ones you said about in his industry?'

Charlie looks pained. 'It's gossip. I hate talking about a person when they're not there to defend themselves. And nothing official has ever been raised.'

'What rumours, Charlie?'

He sighs for the third time. 'There's a lot of talk about him offering women – young women who want to be the next big thing in music – the earth in exchange for various things. Nude photos, sexual favours, that kind of thing.'

'Wow.'

'Yeah. And there's even some chat about him taking it anyway, if the women say no.'

I'm floored. 'And this is a man you choose to have associated with your charity?'

'Like I said, I'm not proud of it. And it's just talk as far as I know. He's never been taken in for questioning or anything like that. No one's come forward. To be honest I thought it was something started by a rival label to sully his name.' He turns to face me. 'But now I'm not so sure.'

'But you believe me? You believe the women who work for you?'

'Of *course* I do.' He cups my face in his hands. 'I've been an idiot, clearly. Look, try not to stress about it too much now. I'll have some sort of crisis meeting with myself in the morning and see if there's anything I can do about James's involvement going forwards.' He kisses the top of my head. 'I love how deeply you care about people. Are you sure you're okay? You don't want to go to the police or anything?'

I shake my head. 'What's the point? He'd just deny it,' I say miserably as we pull up outside my apartment. When we get inside Charlie grabs his laptop and takes himself off to a spare room, which doubles as an office/jumble of clothes, saying he's got to send some emails and make some calls.

I make us tea and scroll through my Instagram messages, skipping the usual flurry of requests asking me to promote a weight loss tea or some other shit, when a notification pops up.

It's from The Creep, of course. I mean, what else could top the night off so perfectly?

'Get a good night's sleep, Kitty. Tomorrow is going to be a busy day for you.'

What? What does that mean?

'What???' I reply, but he's offline already.

Stressed, I swallow a couple of diazepam, knock them back with a gulp of vodka and head to bed.

65

I'm woken up with a start the following morning. I sit up in bed, squinting and trying to work out what woke me. Charlie isn't in bed with me. I'm not even sure he actually *came* to bed last night. I grab a robe and walk through to the living area. He's in the kitchen, sweeping bits of glass from the floor. Something smashed. That's what woke me. I breathe out, slowly. Relief.

'Morning, you,' I say. 'What happened?'

'Dropped a vase. Sorry. Was it expensive?'

'I didn't even know I had a vase. Woke me up though. Did you come to bed last night?'

He shakes his head. 'Kitty, go and sit down. I'll make you a coffee. But please don't look at any news or social media before I speak to you.' He's looking hard at me. 'Please, baby.'

'Is everything okay?'

'Something's happened. It's, er, look, just brace yourself, okay? It's pretty big. Do your breathing for a bit.'

I sit at one of the stools at the kitchen island. Charlie hands me a mug of coffee a few moments later and switches on the Smart TV installed to look like a microwave. A pretty blonde is talking earnestly to the camera from an outside location. I sip my coffee. It takes a couple of moments for me to realise that I recognise the place she's reporting from.

'That's Hen's place,' I say, turning to Charlie. 'What . . . ?'

He nods towards the TV.

'Mr Pemberton remains in police custody this morning. He will find out later today if he will be released on police bail. A spokesperson for the family has declined to comment on the accusations apart from calling them "absolutely ludicrous". We'll have more details as they come in. Now back to the studio.'

What in the name of living fuck?

'What's happened?'

'James was arrested early this morning,' Charlie says. 'He's been accused of some pretty awful stuff.'

'Is this what we were talking about yesterday?'

He nods. 'Someone's come forward and made an official statement.'

I'm stunned. 'I need to call Hen,' I say, grabbing my phone.

Charlie gently takes my hands, removing the phone and putting it on the kitchen island. 'Not now. Let things settle a bit.'

'I need to let her know that I'm here for her,' I say. 'She was there for me when my dad . . .'

'Just have a coffee and something to eat first? I think this could be a long day. For both of us.'

I nod, but as he goes to make more coffee and breakfast,

I take my phone. This is one of my best friends. I can't just pretend that this isn't happening.

I try to call Hen a couple of times but it goes straight to voicemail. I text her instead.

'Hen, I'm really sorry about your dad. Been trying to call. Pls call me xx'

I've got messages from Tor and Maisie too, both gob-smacked by James's arrest. I reply to them both, expressing my own shock.

Charlie and I plant ourselves in front of the TV in the living area and watch as the news plays footage of James being led away in a police car on a loop. There's a major buzz on social media about it, obviously, which Charlie is following on his phone.

'I think this might just be the floodgates opening,' he says, miserably.

He's right.

The first post comes on Instagram later that day, from a beautiful young singer called Maribelle Mason, alongside a picture of a broken and blackened heart.

My heart is breaking as I'm writing this but I know that we need to stand strong together. I can't name this man as I've been gagged by a legal order but everyone will know who I'm talking about. I first met him two years ago when I was gigging around London. He came to see me in a club, he said he'd been tipped off that I was good.

He promised the world, told me I could be the next Ellie Goulding. I was young and naive enough to believe him.

It wasn't long before things took a bad turn. He'd invited me to a hotel to sign a contract. I was so excited. I'd told my parents, they wanted to come into London with me but I thought it would look too uncool turning up with my mum and dad. So I went alone. And it was the biggest mistake I've ever made.

When I arrived at the hotel room, there was no one there but him. No secretaries or assistants, no one. But I still didn't think anything of it. He'd poured two glasses of Champagne and gave one to me, which I drank. I'm not a big drinker and it went to my head quite quickly. I remember asking him why we needed to be in a hotel room and that's when I knew I was in danger. He laughed at me and asked me why did I think we were in a hotel room. I tried to make polite excuses and leave. Even at this point I didn't want to upset him. He grabbed me and pulled me away from the door. Then he tried to kiss me and put his hand down my jeans. I was struggling and crying at this point but he wouldn't let go of me. He put his hand inside my knickers and at least two fingers inside my vagina as I sobbed. He told me to relax and enjoy it and said that there were hundreds of singers that would happily let him do what he wanted, that I was lucky.

When he tired of touching me, he pulled my jeans down and took his penis out of his trousers. I was still too scared to move. He then proceeded to masturbate before he climaxed over my thighs. When he'd finished he even handed me some baby wipes and told me to clean myself up. He told me there was no point telling anyone because

329

who would believe that a woman had gone into a hotel room alone with him and not known what to expect. He made me feel humiliated and stupid at the same time. I didn't tell anyone. I was too scared. And guess what? That contract never appeared. In fact my whole career seemed to just come to an abrupt halt after my encounter with him. It was almost as if he'd smeared my name.

Charlie and I read through Maribelle's post in horror. He grips my hand tightly, holding it between his. 'Fucking hell,' he whispers. 'Jesus fucking Christ.'

Maribelle's post is just the beginning. They're everywhere after that. Instagram and Twitter are soon flooded with women – singers, models, actresses, some going back years – all with stories about James. All under the hashtag #YouKnowHisName. There are rape allegations, tales of unwanted attention, sexual coercion, of him never taking no for an answer. Charlie and I pore over the women's accounts of James's vile, predatory behaviour.

Later comes one, from an anonymous voice.

I've been watching this all unfold and feel nothing but admiration for the women who have stood up and waived their anonymity. You are all so brave. I'm not currently feeling brave enough to put my name and my face out there. But I wanted to share my story nonetheless. It began when I was 14 and I'd gone to watch one of James's label's most popular bands. I won't name them either but it was his biggest boyband at the time. I was near the front with my friend and we couldn't believe our luck when someone from the crew came over and handed us two backstage passes. We watched the rest of the gig from the side of the stage and got to meet the band after. We were so happy. My dad was collecting us from the venue but before we left, James approached me. He asked me if I'd ever considered modelling. I hadn't but he said he could put me in touch with some of the right people if I was interested?

I remember my friend being green with envy when he asked for my number and said he would give me a call when he'd had a word with one of his contacts. It was two days later when he called me. He told me that he'd had a word with a friend of his and he was happy to take some photos of me and help me put together a portfolio.

James even spoke to my mum and arranged for her to be there because I was under 18. We headed to London and I was so excited. Having the photos taken was the best thing ever. We were treated like stars, a car picked us up from the train station. There was food and drink. It was an amazing day, one I'll never forget.

I actually did get a few modelling jobs off the pictures James organised for me. For two years we stayed in touch, he would text me and tell me how special I was and how I was going to be the next big thing in modelling. He told me not to tell my mum about how often we spoke as she wouldn't understand what great friends we'd become.

Then, just after my 16th birthday, James texted me about a party he was having in London. I told him there was no way I'd be able to go, Mum would never allow it. He told me to make something up, say I was staying at a friend's house and he would send a car for me. So I did.

I hated lying to my mum but the party sounded amazing, he kept feeding me little details about who would be there.

Only there was no party.

When the car dropped me at James's house, it was only him there. I felt uncomfortable right away but he told me to relax and that everyone would start arriving soon. He gave me a glass of champagne and – not wanting to look like a little kid – I drank it.

I really don't remember much after that. The next thing I knew I was waking up, coming round would be a better term, in a bed. I was totally naked. There was no one else there. And all I was aware of was this stabbing pain between my legs. I managed to drag myself to the en suite and was horrified to see that I was bleeding.

I cried when I realised what had happened. Just curled up on that bathroom floor and cried. I'd been a virgin.

I don't know how long I was there for but eventually James came in with my clothes. He was acting like nothing had happened. He told me to get dressed and he'd sort a car for me. I was in so much pain and so confused that I just did as he told me.

I was so ashamed. I thought I'd done something to lead him on. But the shame was enough to keep my silence. He didn't even have to threaten me.

I stopped modelling after that because it reminded me of him. I started suffering from anxiety as well, something I still have to this day, over 15 years later.

I should have told someone. I should have gone to the

police. I could have stopped this. I feel responsible for every
woman after me.

We sit in silence, trying to process what we've read. Charlie's
head is in his hands while I let silent tears run down my face
and drip off my chin.

I think about the promise I'd made to myself. The promise
that I made to Adam. The safe and happy future I've planned
with Charlie. But there's no way I can let James get away with
everything, and as Charlie and I sit there, mutely watching
the horrific truth unfold, I'm already sharpening the knives
in my mind.

James Pemberton. I'm coming for you.

66

KITTY'S APARTMENT, CHELSEA

Hen calls later that afternoon. There's a sob in her voice as she tells me James has been released on bail.

'There were so many paps and reporters waiting for him when he came home,' she says. 'They were like a pack of animals. I really thought they were going to hurt him. He's had to go and stay in the Belgravia apartment. We had to send a decoy out in a car so he could be taken there in a van.'

They've managed to outfox the media for now who have been broadcasting trees and rolling countryside from the Pembertons' Surrey Hills home for hours. But it's only a matter of time until someone finds out where he really is.

'What happens now?' I ask her.

'I don't know. I really don't know. The press want blood. We're all probably going to have to go and stay somewhere else too.' I hear her mumble to someone else in the background. 'He's going to have to do an interview, Mum says, or we'll be hounded until the trial. Have you seen Twitter?'

'Yeah. It's not looking great. There's not a lot of support.'

This is clearly an understatement: there is no support at all. Twitter is awash with various versions of the fact James has been arrested.

#MeToo #IBelieveHer #JamesPembertonsOverParty #ReclaimTheCharts are all trending and don't look like they're going away.

'Kits, I've gotta go. Antoinette's having a full-scale meltdown. Keep your phone on. I'll talk to you soon.'

'Okay. Bye.'

'Is she okay?' Charlie says, walking over and wrapping his arms around me.

'Yeah, well no, but considering everything, she sounds like she's functioning. Hen is amazingly adept at handling a crisis. I've said I'll leave my phone on in case she needs me though.' He kisses the base of my neck. 'I wonder who blew the whistle?'

I turn to look at him. 'How will this affect the charity?'

He sighs heavily. 'Well, it won't be good. Obviously. I'll need to speak to Kaitlyn who does the PR as we'll need to put a statement out that we will no longer have him as an ambassador. Which obviously means no money from him.'

'But you've got other ambassadors? And people who donate, right?'

'Yeah, but James has put the big bucks in. Probably because of my dad. But that's not the issue here. The issue here is getting justice. I really should've listened harder to those rumours. I'm sorry. I feel like I've let women down.'

'A lot of this was from a long time ago,' I try to reassure him, but he's right. He *has* let women down. Silence is compliance and all that. 'But yeah. You probably should've.'

'But then none of the women and children we've helped build lives away from Syria and places would be where they are.' He sits down and punches a cushion. I notice how firm and muscular his upper arms are. Which is really not where my mind should be right now. 'It's such a fucking sick tactic.'

'What is?'

'Fucking perverts like Pemberton getting themselves so embroiled in charity work that no one could ever believe they could be as sick as they are. It's a classic move.'

Charlie's face is lined with worry. He can't keep still either. He keeps standing and pacing. Sitting and tapping. Then standing and pacing. I'm getting dizzy just from watching him. I want to sit him down and use my thumbs to smooth the worry from his face. I don't want him ending up with Gordon Ramsay wrinkles either.

I push him gently down onto the armchair – Feather & Black, ecru – kissing his lips, earlobes, nose and lips again as I do. 'You're too stressed, Mr Chambers,' I say, falling to my knees before him. I can see a tiny internal battle going through his mind, but the part I knew would win does, and he sighs deeply as I unzip his trousers and take him in my mouth. At first, his hands are gentle as they cradle my head, but he's soon clawing and pulling me, forcing himself as far down my throat as he can. I'm gagging and my eyes are watering, but my own hand has crept between my thighs and before I know it, I'm coming as Charlie comes deep down my throat.

'Did we just get off after reading some horrible sexual assault confessions?' he asks me about a minute and a half later, upset.

'No,' I tell him, firmly. 'We distracted ourselves.'

'It's just so much to take in,' he says eventually.

'I mean, it's certainly a more-than-average girth.'

He smiles, and pulls me onto his lap. 'I love you, Kitty Collins,' he whispers into my hair. I nod in agreement. He's not the only one feeling torn though. I promised that my vigilante days were over. There's no way I can risk another Ruben Reynolds. It's early days with Charlie, I know, but I'm already learning that he's not Adam and it's not written in the stars that he's going to hurt me. But if there's any chance of Pemberton getting away with this – and he'll be able to afford the best lawyers on the planet, pay people off, etc. – if there is any chance of him doing this to even one other woman, then I have to do my part. And I'm one of a handful of people who know where he is.

He's a sitting duck.

It couldn't be easier.

I can feel my heart starting to thump harder in my chest as I think about how good I'd feel stabbing that man, sending him into a ring of hell saved for monsters like him. I imagine his blood spurting out of his neck, splashing up the white walls of the apartment he's hiding in. I imagine the relief that the heart of every woman and girl he's ever touched would feel knowing that their dragon has been slain and won't be coming after them in their nightmares anymore. It's just *one* more, a sort of last hurrah before I hang the boning knife up for good.

It's a no-brainer.

'I'm going to have to make some calls,' Charlie tells me. 'Is it okay if I use your office? It's mostly damage control from my side.'

'Yeah, of course. I'll bring some food in for you in a bit.'

He kisses my cheek and sort of nuzzles into my neck. 'You're amazing. I love you.'

'I love you back,' I say, watching as he heads into the room I never use as an office. It's late afternoon now and I know that I need to get things moving if I want to target James tonight.

Which I do.

I'm already half-high from the adrenaline rush. I grab my phone and scroll through until I find James Pemberton's number. I tap out a text, holding my breath as I press send.

'I'm coming over tonight. 7.30pm. Kx'

No backing out now.

The reply comes, of course it does, quickly. He might be on bail but it clearly means nothing to someone like James who sees himself as above the law. I book an Uber to the flat for later that evening, under a false name and start getting ready.

Charlie pops his head in while I'm in my robe, about to shower. 'Going out?'

'Yeah.'

Fuck. I hate lying to him.

'We're meeting at Tor's to go through everything and probably drink a lot of vodka. Poor Hen has got a lot to get her head around. You don't mind? I can always bail . . .'

He shakes his head. 'No, your friends need you. I'm going to be crunching numbers and updating websites and other boring stuff for the rest of the night anyway. It's more of a shit show than I realised.' His brow crumples again and my heart tries to jump out of my chest to soothe him. 'I'm going to order a takeout though. Fuck. I might even go all out and have a burger.'

Poor Charlie. I walk over to him. 'Poor baby,' I say, standing on tiptoes so my lips can reach his. He slips a hand under my robe. 'Is there anything I can do to ease *your* stress before I go?' His thumb rubs across my right nipple and it stiffens immediately from his touch. He pulls the cord on my robe, making the whole thing drop to the floor. Then he turns me around and both his hands are on my tits, squeezing and kneading, while his mouth makes its way from my ear, down my neck, down my back.

I suppose I can get ready quickly.

67

THE PEMBERTON APARTMENT, BELGRAVIA

Luckily, I know exactly which Belgravia apartment Hen means. We used to hang out there when we were younger, pretending to be adults.

I've begun to think of my kills as something of a performance. I'd have liked to have been an actress. I mean, it's just pretending, isn't it? And I'm quite good at that. I mean, look at what I've done. What I've got away with.

Every performance needs a good costume. My costume for James is something special. A Victoria's Secret eyelash lace corset, Fleur of England suspender belt and a pair of black Wolford stockings, 20 denier. I round the look up with some classic black Louboutin pumps. I don't go as gaga as my friends over shoes, but there is something about Louboutins that gives me a little thrill. I think it's the red sole. It reminds me of blood. Fresh blood, straight from the body, before it has a chance to darken and congeal. Which, yes, is weird for a vegan.

I've gone to town on my hair and make-up: lashes, glossy

red lips, bouncy hair. When I'm done I take a look at myself in the full-length mirror.

I look like a walking wet dream.

I'm hideous.

Luckily Charlie didn't see me as I hollered a 'bye' and basically ran out of the apartment.

Even in the lifts at the Pemberton apartment – which I still have a key for – the temptation to rub it all off tugs at me. What I really want to do is go home and snuggle up with Charlie. Back in our bubble where men don't lie and cheat and rape and abuse. But I remember the words of Maribelle's victim statement. *He told me there was no point telling anyone because who would believe that a woman had gone into a hotel room alone with him and not known what to expect.*

I check that everything I need is ready: stun gun from one of the abattoirs, the handcuffs, the gloves, the syringes – just a little backup in case anything goes wrong.

This is it. The final one. The big one.

My last hurrah.

I don't use the key. Instead, I knock on the apartment door and James opens it.

'Inside,' he snaps, grabbing my arm and pulling me into the apartment, shutting the door behind him before sliding three industrial bolts over it and punching numbers into what looks like an iPad on the wall. He stares at me like I've crawled out of the sea.

'What the fuck are you doing here? And what are you dressed like that for?'

I'm confused.

'You know why I'm here. We've been texting.' I drop my coat to the floor, revealing myself to him. I can't read the look on his face but it's not what I'm expecting and I'm suddenly cold with embarrassment. There's no way I've read this situation wrong. He was thirsty as a fuckboy in the desert on text. 'Well, aren't you going to come and get your prize?' I ask him, but my voice sounds wrong. It's not husky and sexy.

It's awkward.

'Kitty. As much as I appreciate the effort you've clearly gone to for me – and don't take this the wrong way, you look *incredible* – I really don't think this is the right time for me to be shagging my daughter's friends. Do you?'

'James. We were texting about this. Literally an hour ago.'

'I can assure you, Kitty, whoever you were messaging *wasn't* me. I'm in hiding in case you hadn't realised. Pour yourself a drink or something.' He takes a long, regretful look at me standing there. 'And then fuck off. Jesus Christ.'

'We were texting . . .' I say, more mortified than anything. 'It was your phone. So if it wasn't you . . . then who?'

We both jump as we hear an internal door slam and the click-clack of heels making their way slowly down the marbled floor of the corridor.

'It was me. Now both of you sit the fuck down and I'll tell you how this is going to go.'

68

'Kitty,' Hen says. 'Would you like some wine?'

'No thanks, how about you just tell me what the fuck is going on here?'

She pours a glass anyway and hands it to me. 'Trust me, you will be wanting this when I explain.' Then she glares at her dad. There is absolute hatred in her eyes. 'Fucking *bail*.' She almost spits at him.

James is staring at the floor. He won't look at either of us.

'It's all true,' Hen says, more to him than me. 'Every word of it. And I know that he tried it on with you at the party too.'

'How do you know that?'

'Because I know everything, Kitty.'

'What do you mean?'

'I mean that I know everything from the sleaze that followed you home that night, to Mykonos. I know about it all.'

She can't mean what she seems to be hinting at. Can she?

'What are you talking about, Hen? I think you need to

343

sit down and have a glass of wine yourself. I know it's been a tough day for you.'

'The men, Kits. All the men.' She turns to her dad. 'She's almost as prolific as you but at least there's some purpose behind her crimes. Until poor Ruben.'

Fuck.

'How?'

'Because I'm your stalker, Kitty. The Creep. It was me the whole time.'

I take a big swallow of the wine.

She was right about that too. Clever girl.

'What the fuck, Hen? What the actual fuck? And why?'

Hen stares at me before lighting a cigarette. Since when does she smoke? She offers one to me. I shake my head.

'So, it's been you all this time? You've been the one stalking me, threatening me?'

She shrugs. 'Maybe you're not quite as clever as you think you are.'

'But why?'

'Funnily enough, it started as a bit of fun. Well, fun for me. I wanted to scare you. Do you know how sickening you are? So perfect and so fucking smug with it. I wanted to freak you out a bit.' She takes a long drag of the cigarette, still regarding me. 'And it worked, didn't it? At first? When you went to the police, I could tell I'd really shaken you. But then *he*' – she nods over at James – 'found out. And suddenly it was all "security for Kitty" this and "maybe she should move in here" that.'

'She was scared,' James growls from the sofa, rubbing his

already thinning hairline. 'Do you not think a stalker might not be a bit terrifying, Hen?'

'I wouldn't fucking know. Anyway, it got almost addictive after that though. I knew I should stop, but every time you came and met me for brunch or whatever, it gave me a little kick to see you so jumpy, always looking over your shoulder. Watching that veneer crack was so much fun.' She claps her hands on each of the last three words.

'You need help.'

'But then I struck the jackpot, didn't I? That night when that loser killed himself on the broken bottle. The night you left your phone in the bar? All it took was five minutes to install some spyware onto it – your passcodes are so predictable – and suddenly your entire world was open to me. Let's just say, it's been a bit more cert 18 than I ever expected. I have to admit, I was actually quite in awe of you for a while. Taking those monsters out. I mean, they all deserved it, didn't they? And you were pretty creative with them. It was fun watching you. That's why I didn't say anything. I was biding my time.'

She takes a few steps towards me and then sits down on the floor, inches from where I am.

'I was planning on going to the police. But then the shit hit the fan with my dad and I figured you'd be of more use to me *not* behind bars.'

'What are you talking about?'

'It was me who tipped the police off about James. Me!' She's excited. 'Can you even imagine?' She laughs but it's hollow this time. 'Now I want you to kill him.' She points at her father, who is still clutching his head.

'But he's your dad,' I say, hating how lame I sound.

'Unfortunately, yes. But he's not just my dad though. Are you, James? What else could you call yourself? What else would you say you've been to me since I was twelve? My lover? My abuser? My rapist.' She's glaring at him. 'James Pemberton's liking for young girls didn't even stay outside of his own family, did it? Daddy? Can you remember the first night you came into my room and raped me? Because I can. It probably all blurs into one for you though, doesn't it? All those underage girls. Well, let me tell Kitty all about it because, even though I know everything about her, she doesn't really know a thing about me and my life.' She comes over to me and tops up my wine. 'You'll need to brace yourself for this, babe. It's quite the story.'

What. The. Fuck.

James looks up at me for the first time. 'This is bullshit, Kitty. She's warped.'

'You remember all those parties our parents used to have back in the good old days? My dad was especially known for throwing a good bash. But it turned out that they were not quite as fun as we thought they were. Definitely not for the girls there at any rate. I'm not quite sure I have the words to explain to you what it's like to walk in on your own father getting a blow job from a fifteen-year-old he's promised to make the next big thing in music.' She turns to James again. 'I don't even get why. A fifteen-year-old can't give a decent blowie, she shouldn't even know what she's doing.' She paces back and forth in front of me. 'But that's nothing compared to your own father coming into your bedroom that very same night and explaining that it's very important that I never tell anyone what I saw him doing.' There's an armchair in the corner of the room and she perches herself on that. 'He got into bed with me and told me that I was the most special girl in the world. And that because I was his most special girl, he had a special present for me. Have a guess at what my special present was, Kits, go on.'

I can't answer her.

'I'll give you a clue, then. It wasn't a fucking puppy!' Tears have started to run down her face now, some of them dripping right into the wine.

I begin to stand up to go and comfort her.

'Stay the fuck where you are,' she barks. 'Let this be about someone else other than you, just for once Kitty. Do you think you can manage that?'

'These are lies, Kitty. She's a fucking lunatic.'

'And do you know what the worst thing is? The thing that makes me feel so sick I have tried killing myself. Three times? When I got too old for him, when I saw him start to look at other younger girls – even Antoinette for fuck's sake – in that creepy fucking way, I was jealous. I tried every way I knew how to get his attention, that's why I was screwing Grut and any other one of his acts that I could. How fucked up is that? I wanted my own father to start raping me again so I could be his special girl.' She laughs bitterly.

'Hen, you're not fucked up,' I say. 'You're damaged. What he has done to you, has been doing to you, has damaged you.'

'Can you even imagine what it's like to have that level of self-loathing, Kitty? Even at that fucking stupid Eighties party. It was *you* he sought out, not *me*.'

She nods once, takes a deep breath and hands me my bag. 'So now I need you to kill him. And I'm going to tell you exactly how you're going to do it.'

'Hen, no, I don't do that anymore. I don't *want* to do that anymore. For the first time in my life, I feel like I have something good.'

'You've killed for less,' she says, almost squaring up to me at this point. 'This man is a fucking monster.'

'No, I haven't.'

She glares at me. 'What about Ruben Reynolds then? Don't forget, Kitty, I know *it all*.'

I turn to look at James. He's smaller than he's ever looked. Painfully thin. Everything about him looks grey. His hair, his skin. He wouldn't last two minutes in prison. He'd probably kill himself.

'What have *you* got to say about all this?' I ask. 'Look at your daughter. Look what you've done to her.'

'She's full of shit' is all he manages. He doesn't even uncover his face from his hands. Or look up. The only movement is his shoulders, which are convulsing up and down. Is he fucking *crying*? But when he eventually looks up at me, there aren't any tears. Not one. Instead, there is a big shit-eating grin over his face. He's shaking his head, laughing.

'What have I got to say about this? The same thing my press statement said. The same thing my extremely expensive lawyer will say in court. That there is absolutely no truth to any of the allegations against me. *Especially hers!*'

I'm burning up with fury; it's running through my veins like a fever. There isn't an ounce of remorse in his face.

'And no one would believe her.' He nods over at Hen, who's lighting a cigarette, watching the exchange between us. 'She's going straight to a psych hospital the minute this is all over. All the tales of drugs and underage sex that I'll make sure get leaked to the press about her. She's no threat to me.' He looks me up and down. 'And neither are you. In fact, the only reason I didn't ever go after you was because I had a deal with your father that *you* were out of bounds.'

I swallow down bile. Now is not the time to show weakness.

'It didn't end up very well for him though, did it?' I say. 'You know I bashed his brains in, right?' I turn to Hen. 'I have questions for you. A *lot* of questions. But first of all, are you sure this is how you want it to end? No one will get their day in court. The victims won't see justice.'

'He's pleading not guilty,' she almost whispers. 'They'd all have to relive it. Even the ones who haven't come forward will be forced back there when it's all over the news. You know what this country is like for women. Their entire sexual histories will be brought up, picked apart. They'll be shamed. And those are the ones he hasn't yet paid to keep silent.'

I nod. I understand.

'And even if he *is* found guilty. Then what? He's an old man. These are historical crimes. He'd get maybe eight, ten years. Serve half. Then come out and live the rest of his life in luxury with the cash I *know* he's got stashed away in some tax haven. He's been preparing for this day ever since he abused his first victim.'

'He'd get destroyed in prison,' I tell her. 'Famous *and*

a paedophile? He'd be a living, breathing target. They'd do a lot more damage than I ever could.'

'Would he though? He's a fucking psychopath. He's a puppet master. He knows how to play people. How to make friends and influence people. He's the original fucking influencer. Do you really think he'd have it hard? Or do you think he'd win bored lags over with his tales of showbiz debauchery? And it's not like he was abusing little kids. I bet more than enough of the men he'd be locked up with have been caught out in similar ways. Fifteen doesn't really count, does it? It's jailbait.'

My mind returns for a split second to the website with the countdown ticker on it, leading up to my sixteenth birthday.

'Kitty. I know you want to do this. You wouldn't have come otherwise. You came here to kill. I know you did.'

She's right, of course. I *do* want to kill him. I want to watch his face as he realises he's going to die. I want to watch him fight and struggle and know that it's the end. What he did to all those other women was enough to make me thirsty for his blood, but hearing – and seeing – what he's done to his own daughter, my friend, is even worse.

'And if I don't?'

'Then I'll go to the police with a different story. Just as juicy, maybe even more so. The beautiful Instagram star who has been trawling the web for rapists and sex offenders to feed her blood lust.'

'So, blackmail basically? It's him or me?'

'Look at him,' she says. 'He shouldn't even have got bail. He shouldn't be spending his time in a luxury hideaway. He still thinks he's untouchable.'

'Unlike my daughter,' he scoffs.

It's that comment that does it for me and I think he realises it as soon as it comes out of his mouth.

'Your dad told me a story about you once, Kitty,' James says. He looks me directly in the eyes. 'He told me about a time you begged him to take you to one of the abattoirs. You were about twelve, I think. You were desperate to know what your daddy did all day. He told me that you wanted a go.'

I know the day he's talking about. The truth is obviously different to the version James has heard. But it was the day my dad learned to keep one eye on what was going on behind him. He'd taken me to the Hampshire abattoir after I refused to eat my cooked breakfast. After throwing the plate at the wall and screaming at me to get dressed, he forced me into his car and drove us there. He showed me the animals that had been delivered that morning. Mostly chickens, which were always killed en masse in a gas chamber. There were calves and piglets and lambs too. It was spring. Baby season. He'd dragged me through the slaughterhouse and given me a stun gun.

'Shoot one,' he'd said. 'Let's see what you're really made of, Kitty.'

Any other twelve-year-old girl would have been beside herself with just the thought of murdering an animal, a baby ripped away from its mother before it was ready. Not me. I took the stun gun, walked up to a piglet – I can remember the way it looked at me, curious, it didn't know I was a threat – and I shot it. Right between its eyes. The stun guns were bolt guns back then. I'd shot a metal bullet into a piglet's head and hadn't flinched. I stood there and watched, feeling nothing as it convulsed on the ground, the other pigs around it starting to panic. I didn't feel a thing. No wonder my dad had a pact with James.

He knew I'd fucking kill him if he laid a finger on me.

'Okay.' I turn to Hen. 'How are we doing this, then?'

She smiles. It's ghoulish. 'See? What are friends for?'

Hen tells me her plan and James just sits there. I'm not even sure he thinks I have it in me. Not until I take the electric stun gun (progress) out of my Chloé handbag and shoot him in the head.

69

THE PEMBERTON APARTMENT, BELGRAVIA

While he's out cold, we've got some prep to do, to make this exactly how Hen wants it. Obviously, I have questions. Many, many questions.

'So why the stalking shit?' I ask her as we begin to get things ready, starting with the handcuffs.

'I honestly wanted to have a bit of fun with you. I know it's twisted but I think that's something that comes with my dad raping me for years. I was jealous of you. I wanted my dad to fucking disappear. Everything's always been so easy for you, hasn't it? You've just had it all handed to you. And then *both* your parents fuck off, leaving you in a fancy apartment, with a huge stash of money. I mean, lucky fucking break or what?'

'You have no idea what goes on behind closed doors, Hen. I mean, you of all people should realise that. I've done nothing to you apart from be your friend. Why would you want to scare me?'

'My *friend*?' She practically spits the words into my face. 'You've not been my friend. You're all about yourself, Kitty.

Or Tor. Or Maisie. And now Charlie. Jesus Christ, even my own dad likes you better than me. Do you know what it feels like to constantly be in the shadow of someone? Of course you don't because you never have been.'

She pauses for a breath and a gulp of wine as we heave James from the sofa, along the corridor – I'm grateful for the marble floors, it really makes the whole traction thing much easier – and into the master bedroom. It's been so many years since I've been to this place, I'd actually forgotten how big it is.

'Obviously the whole thing with Adam damaged you. You weren't the same after that, were you? Not as much as him though. I know you were behind that too.'

'What? What are you talking about?'

'I went to see him after you killed that Joel guy. Had a nice little chat with him. It's amazing how much information you can get out of someone who can only blink. Mind you, takes an absolute lifetime. No wonder there was never a second book.'

I stare at her. 'He told you it was me?'

She nods. 'But don't worry. He's not going to tell the police. He seems to think he's getting some kind of Living Karma for cheating on you. I mean, fuck though, someone had better warn Charlie not to get on your wrong side.'

'You're going to need to get serious help after this,' I say, as we heave James's unconscious body onto the bed and handcuff him to it.

Hen laughs. 'A man-hating, *vegan* serial killer is actually lecturing me about needing to get help. Oh, you've always been hilarious, Kits.'

'I'm serious,' I tell her. 'And him. Did he touch Antoinette? Did he rape her too?'

'I don't think so. He was a big believer in that old phrase about three people knowing a secret. You know, how it can only stay a secret if one of them's dead. Or something?'

We peel off his trousers. Well, I do this bit, while Hen vomits into the en suite toilet. She's clearly seen more than enough of her own father with his pants around his ankles. Getting the fishnet tights onto him on my own is a bit of a struggle though.

'Are you sure this is how you want it? We could easily just take him down to one of the abattoirs and sort him out there? It's surprisingly easy.'

'That's because you've had a lot of practice,' she shouts from the bathroom between retches. 'No. This is what I want. Maximum humiliation. It's what he'd hate the most.'

I shrug. 'Your call. You'd really enjoy the chopping up though. It's the best bit.'

By the time Hen's finished vomiting, I'm just about done with James and am standing back to enjoy my handiwork. He's starting to come round from the taser.

'Thanks for the help, by the way,' I say to her.

'No worries. You've done an awesome job.'

I agree with her on this. James looks ridiculous lying there, cuffed to the bed, in a leather thong and fishnets. He's got a stocking stuffed into his mouth and one tied around his neck. To complete the look, I've even added some bright red lipstick – Charlotte Tilbury, shade Tell Laura, if you must know.

He comes round slowly, how I'd imagine a bear waking from hibernation. His eyes dizzily move between Hen and me as he realises the situation he's in. He attempts to say something but the stocking in his mouth stops the words from coming out.

'Want to hear his last words?' I ask.

'There's nothing he could ever say that I'd want to hear. Just get it over with.' She doesn't hang around to watch and heads back into the living area. I hear her pop the cork out of something and pour a long drink.

Before all this started, I had the idea that squeezing the life out of someone would be easy, they'd just go a bit floppy, like falling asleep. But it's really not like that. There's a lot more thrashing around than I ever imagined, for one thing. Once they realise what's happening, they get this wild look in their eyes and try to fight it. It's amazing how even the worst monsters are so desperate to hang on to their lives.

Take James. He's an uber-thrasher. He really hasn't worked out that it's pointless – seeing as how he's firmly cuffed to the bed – and the easiest thing would be for him to let it happen. He's just hurting himself this way. I give the stocking I'm using as a makeshift noose an extra hard tug and watch as his eyes do that bulgy thing, like they're trying to escape from his head. Sometimes they even kind of pop – it's blood vessels or something – and the whites turn completely red.

'How does that feel?' I say. 'Nice and tight? That's how you like it, isn't it?

Hen may not want to hear his final words. But *I* fucking do. I want to hear him whimper and beg for his life. Like

356

I said, this is my last hurrah. I take the stocking out of his mouth.

'Please, the kids.'

'I think you know exactly how they feel about you right now.'

'You're a fucking bitch.'

'I didn't fuck you though, did I?'

Well, that was hardly Hemingway. I shove the stocking back in, bored already, by pinching his nose and forcing him to open his mouth.

The other thing about asphyxiation is that it takes longer than films would have you believe. I've been straddling James Pemberton for a good six or seven minutes now and he's only just dropping into unconsciousness. At least the thrashing has stopped. It's times like this when it would be really handy to be able to order from room service, a nice glass of Chablis would be beyond lovely right now. Maybe I should start bringing a hip flask or something?

I take a last look at James, who finally seems like he's shuffled off his miserable mortal coil and press my chest up against his, letting my ear drop to his lips. Silence. I ease his eyelids down over his eyes and sit back to admire my work. I think this is my favourite part of it all. They look kind of childlike and peaceful, before I get busy chopping them into pieces for the mincer.

'All done,' I say as I walk back through the apartment and join Hen on the sofa. She's poured me a wine – a nice, chilled Montrachet. 'So what happens now?'

'We leave him here. I'll give the police and a paper a tip-off from a burner phone. Then he'll be found. The powerful and commanding James Pemberton, strangled by a stocking. Seeing as he loved fucking so much, it's almost poetic that everyone will think he's died in some kind of sex game gone wrong.'

She chuckles, but it's hollow.

'And what about me?'

She looks at me, disdainful. 'What about you? Why are you always trying to make things about you?'

'I just mean, what are your plans for me, Hen? I'm not trying to steal your glory here. You made the right decision. The world is a better place without some people contaminating it.'

She shrugs again. 'I guess you'll go back to your happy little life with Charlie while I'm left to hold the pieces of my family together.' She pauses for a moment. 'Can I ask you something?'

'I think we're past the stage of having any secrets from each other. Fire away.'

'What really happened to your dad? He's dead, right? You killed him?'

'Yeah,' I say. 'Walked in on him trying to rape my mother and smashed his skull in with an antique vase.'

'Did he go through the mincers?'

I nod. 'You really can't trust processed food these days.'

'True. But what *can* you trust?' She sighs and leans back into the sofa, taking two long gulps of her wine. I also take a slug of mine before placing the glass on the coffee table and reaching for my bag.

'I'm going to need a hell of a lot of fucking therapy to get through this,' she says, tucking her feet under her bottom and closing her eyes.

'Tired?' I ask her.

She laughs that hollow laugh again. 'Funnily enough, yes. It's amazing how exhausting it is having to lie like that. Thank fuck I didn't have to do it in court.'

'What? Lie about what?'

'He didn't really rape and abuse me,' she says, sitting up and smiling at me like we're ten and playing dolls. 'I only said that because I knew it would be the one thing that would get to you. That's probably the only truthful thing he said.' She sits up straighter, opens her eyes wide and smiles at me. 'Maybe you're not the only one who can be all sweet and psycho.'

What. The. Fuck?

'Wait. So you're telling me that you lied about being sexually assaulted by your own dad so I'd kill him? After stalking me for months through my phone and scaring the shit out of me on Instagram? There's no doubt about the psycho part, Hen.'

She shrugs. 'Takes one to know one and all that.' She settles back into the sofa, closing her eyes again, looking peaceful and at ease.

The mad fucking bitch.

'That reminds me actually. That saying you couldn't remember earlier about secrets. It's "three can keep a secret, if two of them are dead". I looked it up on my phone.'

Her eyes open again. Just in time to see me lunge at her with the stun gun, right through her left temple.

'Sorry, Hen,' I say. 'But I'm not taking any chances.'

70

COLLINS' CUTS ABATTOIR, HAMPSHIRE

I have to admit that I get absolutely zero joy out of cutting Hen up and putting her through the mincers. Especially when I realise that I need to put something on her Instagram to convince people she's gone away for a while. I figure this will tie her nicely to her dad's death, what with her DNA being all over that apartment anyway. The trouble is her phone is facial recognition only and I've already thrown her head into the waste disposal where it will eventually end up as dog food or fertiliser.

I doubt there's anything recognisable about it now.

I frown, wondering what her passcode could be. She says that mine was predictable. I take a punt and tap my date of birth into her phone. Amazingly it unlocks.

Fuck.

She really was one crazy bitch.

I scroll through her apps and open Instagram. I post a black square on her feed and write: 'Following the devastating revelations about my father, I've decided to take some time away from the spotlight as myself and my family try to process what has happened. Thank you for your support and we appreciate your respect for our privacy at this difficult time. I will be away from social media for the foreseeable future as I take some time alone to heal.' I smile as I hit post and chuck her phone into the waste disposal to join her.

Well, some bits of her.

One thing I *will* say though is that it was much easier moving and disposing of a female body. I found a suitcase in one of the wardrobes and just folded her right up in that for our trip to the slaughterhouse. Maybe this is why so many men kill women. It's far less hassle than picking on someone who actually stands half a chance in a fight with you.

The sun is beginning to peep over the horizon as I lock up, and begin the drive back to London. Hopefully I'll make it home before Charlie wakes up so I can snuggle next to him and pretend this was all just a horrible dream.

71

Shamed music mogul found dead in Belgravia home

Shamed music mogul James Pemberton has been found dead at one of his London properties, the Metropolitan Police confirmed earlier today.

Pemberton, 58, was on bail after being arrested on suspicion of historical sexual assault, sexual offences with minors and rape.

The accusations date back to the 1980s when Pemberton was launching Ripe Records, the recording company that went on to make him one of the most respected names in the music industry.

Unconfirmed reports on social media say Pemberton's body was found dressed in lace underwear and stockings. Officials believe the death resulted from a sex game gone wrong.

A police spokesperson confirmed the death. 'James Pemberton was found dead by his wife earlier today. Police are investigating the death but aren't looking for anyone else in connection at this time.'

Pemberton had pleaded not guilty to several charges of historical sexual assault earlier this month and was awaiting trial.

Instagram

Claire O'Donohue (@ClairyFairy1999)

Does anyone else think it's a bit weird that not only has that pervert been found dead, but now Hen Pemberton has disappeared? Have you seen her latest post? It's just a black square which – hello? Tone deaf or what – is meant to be for the #BLM movement. Anyway, she's saying she's taking an indefinite leave from social media and is going away to 'heal'. WTF? What about his victims? They're the ones that need to heal. Whoever killed him though is a hero. #MeTooKiller

Replies:

@Tofiona: *Bit harsh, if your dad was outed as a massive paedo and then found dead, I bet you'd probably want to do a disappearing act too. But yeah, hijacking the black square is shitty.*

@LaraLoo191919: *Maybe she killed him LOL!*

@ClairyFairy1999: *Well whatever happened I'm glad that old perv is dead. I hope the cops don't spend too long working out what happened and just get him in the ground as soon as possible. Disgusting old c*nt.*

@LaraLoo191919: *Agree. Rest in Hell. #ReclaimTheNight #ReclaimTheStreets #MeTooKiller*

Epilogue

AQUA SHARD AT THE SHARD, SE1, SIX MONTHS LATER

'I swear every single New Year's Eve I end up saying "well what a fucking year that was, thank fuck it's over". It's not just me, is it?' Tor asks the table as we're doing NYE like adults this year, which basically means eating actual food before we get drunk off our skulls and pass out.

'Definitely not just you,' Maisie says. 'This year has been a particularly horrible anus in many ways.' She's quiet for the splittist of seconds and gazes at Rupert next to her, who is eagerly making his way through his quail and duck egg starter. 'But in others it's been the best ever.'

Poor Roo hasn't quite realised that his girlfriend has basically toasted him and looks up, quite startled when he realises no one is talking. He looks at Maisie. 'Oh God, what? What have I done now?'

She smiles at him. If she were an emoji, her eyes would've turned into hearts at this point. 'Nothing. Nothing at all. I was just saying that I've had worse years.'

'Well, if one of your best friends vanishing off the planet

and her murdered dad being outed as a paedophile is your bag, baby.'

Bless him. He's trying humour.

'Too soon?' he asks me, specifically.

'I'm not sure there's a time limit on these things,' I say. 'But I *think* she was actually talking about you. I'd like to raise a glass too. To friends, old and new. And to our beloved Hen, wherever she may be.'

She's quite likely the contents of a sausage roll, but no one here needs to know that.

Men are funny creatures, you know, the proper ones. The ones who don't feel the need to shout and bully and push and shove their way through life. Rupert – and I still can't imagine him as anything other than a Boy-Blow-Dry-in-Red-Trousers – is one of the good ones. I wasn't sure at first. I had my eye on him. But I've never seen Maisie look so happy. I can't think of a good way to describe the way they look at each other, but it's like their souls have found homes. They just fit. Don't get me wrong, they fight and bicker and whine about each other, but when they're together there's this aura of . . . I don't know. Peace or something. It's when I see them together, or when I catch Charlie looking at me, like he's doing now, that I realise I grew up not knowing what love is. How to give it. How to take it.

Tor is sat to my left and is sipping Champagne. She's brought her mum as her plus one, and, bit by bit, is putting herself back together after the horror she suffered over the summer.

Things between Charlie and me have never been better.

After James was found dead, Charlie panicked – A LOT – about the cashflow into his charity. Obviously, it was a no-brainer for me. All that money sitting in my bank that I was never going to touch. I put every last penny of it into The Refugee Charity and now amazing things are happening. Schools and hospitals and housing are being built. I've paid money out to the girls and women who suffered at James's hands too. The ones who wanted their voices to be heard, but didn't get to in court. I've – anonymously, of course – encouraged them to speak out, tell their stories, tell their truths. Two books have already been published, and I think there are three more on the way. There's at least one Netflix doc in the pipeline, but it's got to get past the Pembertons' lawyers first. Others have written the most beautiful, heartbreaking personal essays and published them everywhere from *The New Yorker* to *Metro*. Killing James hasn't silenced these women. It's given them the power and confidence to speak out about their experiences.

Actually, when I say 'every last penny' that's not quite true. I used a good chunk of it to send Adam to the States. He's taking part in a study to see if there is any way of unlocking locked-in syndrome. It's very early days, but I'm going to do everything I can to make sure he's as looked after as possible.

No catch.

Promise.

And me? Well, I've got everything I've ever wanted. Charlie has filled the huge hole in my heart, which is supposed to be overflowing with a childhood full of love. Neither of us really had that, so we're happy filling each other's holes. Shut up. Don't make something so precious so smutty (although I'm secretly laughing too). Fuck, we've even made plans to go and see my mother in France next year. I mean, who even am I?

And that burning need to destroy every bad thing I see, every bad person, every time someone wrongs someone who doesn't deserve it? I'm learning to sit with those feelings. To feel them. To let myself be angry at the injustice in the world, but remind myself that there are other ways I can help that don't involve abattoirs, stun guns and a selection of butcher's knives. Whatever red beast that had been awoken in me has been gently soothed back to sleep by love. I know right, utter vomit.

After our meal, Charlie and I head to the room we've booked in the hotel for a 'snooze' – aka a couple of hours of sleeping and lazy sex – before we go to the bar to see in the new year. Hoping this one comes empty-handed, with no murderous friends, etc.

'I know I sound like a complete boring twat,' Charlie says in the lift as he pulls one of my tits out of my dress and begins to play with my nipple. 'But I'd really quite like this year to be drama free.'

I'm laughing as we reach our floor and I rearrange my clothes. I'm sure we've just put on a good show for the security camera guys – well, it *is* the season of giving.

We head into our room and Charlie pulls a bottle of Champagne out of the minibar fridge. 'Shall I run a bath for us?' he asks me.

'Sure,' I say, although I'm distracted by a breaking-news story on the TV. 'Hold on though, I just want to watch this.'

The reporter is a pale and nervous-looking woman of

indeterminable age. She's fiddling awkwardly with her microphone and is standing on the embankment, with the Thames behind her. If the camera turned around, it would show my building. There's a lot of action going on behind her. Men in full hazmat, one of those white tents. The whole shebang.

She says into a microphone, 'Once again a body has been recovered from the Thames near the Chelsea Embankment as police continue their search for thirty-four-year-old Bethany Miller, who has been missing since Christmas Eve. The trainee vet was last seen walking home from her Christmas party, which was held at a venue in Soho. It's thought that Miss Miller may have got into a car believing it to be an Uber. A police spokesperson has confirmed this is a murder enquiry.

'Police are urging women in the London area to remain extra vigilant as Miss Miller has been the second woman to be found dead in recent weeks. In November twenty-six-year-old Nala Sidhu's body was discovered in a wooded area of South West London. If possible, the message is not to travel alone, especially at night.'

Charlie's saying something in the bathroom, but I can't make out his words. All I can hear is the gushing of my blood as it starts pumping harder and faster around my body. In the pit of my stomach, I can feel something stirring, opening an eye, stretching out like an animal after a long sleep.

A Letter from Katy Brent

Thank you so much for choosing to read *How to Kill Men and Get Away With It*. I hope you enjoyed it! If you did and would like to be the first to know about my new releases, click here to follow me on Twitter: https://twitter.com/Littlemisskatyb

Funnily enough, the seed of *How to Kill Men* was planted while I was watching an episode of *Made in Chelsea* some years ago, and wondered what would happen if one of the girls just went completely Patrick Bateman on all the cheating men. It sat in my head for a while until the #MeToo movement started to make waves in 2018. It was around that time I started to make some very rudimentary notes about what could happen if women snapped back. I clearly wasn't alone with this train of thought and have seen wonderful writing about women's revenge stories over the last few years. Obviously *Killing Eve, Promising Young Woman, I Will*

Destroy You, Sweetpea and *My Sister The Serial Killer* all spring to mind and I owe them all thanks for helping to pave a path for Kitty's story. Eventually, my notes became *How To Kill Men*. If you're a film noir buff like me, you'll also recognise the name, Kitty Collins.

I truly hope you loved *How to Kill Men and Get Away With It*, and if you did I would be so grateful if you would leave a review. I always love to hear what readers thought, and it helps new readers discover my books too.

Thanks,
Katy xxx

Acknowledgements

I have been mentally writing one of these since I was about nine years old (obviously some of the names have changed along the way) so this is a bit of a seminal moment for me. One I didn't expect to be doing in my dressing gown, eating a cheeseburger because I missed the McD's breakfast slot on UberEats.

Firstly, the biggest thank you to my wonderful editor, Belinda Toor at HQ. Thank you for taking a chance on Kitty and giving her – and me – a home. Your enthusiasm for my writing has pulled me out of many melodramatic fits of despair over the past year or so. 'Thank you' doesn't feel enough. Also to Audrey Linton and your magical eyes which spotted things other edits had not.

Thank you to everyone else at HQ and HarperCollins for your hard work on the cover, the marketing and that pesky, pesky title. We got there. Now, buckle up.

Thanks to my brilliant agent, Euan Thorneycroft at AM Heath for your unwavering belief in my writing.

A huge shout-out to two women – and fellow (fellow!)

authors who have been brilliant mentors and friends to me over this process, Julia Crouch and Stephanie Butland. Your guidance and advice have been invaluable to me. As have the care packages. Special thanks as well to Simon Trewin. I'm going to wear you down, yet!

My wonderful friends who have kept pushing me and encouraging me, even when I behaved like a harpy and swore I would never write another word again. Charlotte, Annaliese, Donna, Becky, Laura, Louise, Gwefs and Craig. I love you all very much. Thank you for putting me back together when I needed it.

My sisters, Vicki, Luci, Emily and Chloe. Thanks for having my back.

My Faber WhatsApp/email groups who also kindly acted as my Beta readers: Beatrice, Josie, Karen, Maysa and Catriona. You're next. I've seen what you're all capable of, remember!

Thanks to Rob Dinsdale and David Lewis for stepping in as my 'male sensitivity readers' – yes, David, this does sound like a very odd medical procedure for penises.

My dad, Paul Brent, I'm so sad you're not here to see this. I did it, Daddy! If there *is* an afterlife then I hope you're at the afterparty, raising a glass and bragging to your mates about your baby girl who has written an actual book. I miss you.

My mum, Carla, for supporting me throughout this. I think we can both agree it was harder than birth and the teen years combined. I love you. And my stepdad, Keith, for putting up with me. I love you too.

And most of all, my children, Seb and Sophia. You're not allowed to read this for many, many years. But you've always been the driving force. Everything I do is for you. Words just aren't enough to express how much I love you both.

Also, a quick shout-out to Louise Thompson, Millie Mackintosh, Olivia Bentley, Sam Thompson, Spencer Matthews and everyone else who has appeared in *Made in Chelsea* for inspiring this novel. Even if unintentionally ☺

Dear Reader,

We hope you enjoyed reading this book. If you did, we'd be so appreciative if you left a review. It really helps us and the author to bring more books like this to you.

Here at HQ Digital we are dedicated to publishing fiction that will keep you turning the pages into the early hours. Don't want to miss a thing? To find out more about our books, promotions, discover exclusive content and enter competitions you can keep in touch in the following ways:

JOIN OUR COMMUNITY:

Sign up to our new email newsletter: http://smarturl.it/SignUpHQ

Read our new blog www.hqstories.co.uk

🐦 https://twitter.com/HQStories

📘 www.facebook.com/HQStories

BUDDING WRITER?

We're also looking for authors to join the HQ Digital family!

Find out more here:

https://www.hqstories.co.uk/want-to-write-for-us/

Thanks for reading, from the HQ Digital team